THE MISSING SPY

A DANIEL KNOX THRILLER BOOK TWO

J.A. HEATON

FLANNEL AND FLASHLIGHT PRESS

1

Number 2 Dzerzhinsky Square, Moscow.
Deep in the KGB archives.
September 3, 1987.

DMITRI PETROV FROZE.

He checked again.

He leafed through the thick file adjacent to the one he had just placed into the file cabinet. A piece of paper stuck out oddly, and he would have to straighten it so that he could shut the file cabinet.

The paper came out of the file with ease. It was misplaced. Dmitri could not help but look at it.

Inaccurate filing was a cardinal sin among the KGB officers in the archives. At the very best, carelessness resulted in wasted time and effort in the future while the KGB searched for lost bits of information. But at its worst, one misplaced piece of paper could mean not only the death of the unfortunate KGB archivist, but it could also result in a security breach that could harm the Soviet Union in incalculable ways.

The protocol was clear about what Dmitri should do. The problem had to be rectified immediately. But for Dmitri, it wasn't so simple. Moments before Dmitri had entered this row of the archives, he saw another KGB archivist, Kozlov, whom he despised.

Kozlov was a lazy womanizer from an influential family who didn't mind letting others know how powerful he was. Though his family connections were strong, his incompetence had kept him from rising higher in the KGB, even though he was already multiple levels above what his skill merited. In Dmitri's opinion, Kozlov was an infantile intelligence officer. Kozlov was certainly the arrogant idiot who had misplaced the piece of paper. Despite what protocol dictated, Dmitri hesitated. Kozlov would not go down without a fight. His family would make sure Dmitri's life was made very difficult if Dmitri got Kozlov into trouble.

Dmitri exhaled deeply. Not for the first time, he was glad that he had been without a family for years. Nobody could threaten his wife, for she had died. Nobody could threaten any children, for they had also died. It was just Dmitri, and he would have to answer for his actions.

The major complication was what the piece of paper contained.

Dmitri was not well versed in global affairs, but he knew that the paper Kozlov had misplaced was a gold mine for the United States and her allies in NATO. This document was a list of Soviet agent codenames and their corresponding real names. Granted, some of these codenames could have been given to people whom the KGB was observing or hoping to use as a source, but Kozlov's superior was known to have the most valuable agents.

Dmitri could not tear his eyes away from the paper as he pondered what to do with it.

He recognized one of the names.

Human lives would be exchanged for the information on this piece of paper, Dmitri thought to himself. *If this piece of paper fell into the wrong hands...*

A dull thud elsewhere in the archives snapped Dmitri out of his state of wonder.

He instinctively hid the paper behind his back and looked about. Nobody was there.

Dmitri forced himself to think. He didn't feel like he could follow protocol. Kozlov would undoubtedly accuse him of something. But there was no way Dmitri could file it correctly. Doing so would require too much research on his part, and then he would have to answer as to why he even had such a document in his possession to begin with.

Though Dmitri hated Kozlov, he hoped this could be a chance to ingratiate himself to the slob. He had to find Kozlov before he left the archives, let him know that he might have forgotten something and that he should go check. Kozlov would certainly fix his error, and he might even thank Dmitri for it in some way.

It can't always hurt to have a snake on your side, Dmitri thought to himself.

Dmitri hurried to the exit of the archives and asked the man at the security gate if Kozlov had left yet.

The guard at the only entrance and exit to the archives gave a bored, "No."

Relieved, Dmitri set out to find Kozlov. The store of paperwork and documentation was vast, but he knew which section Kozlov would typically be in, and he knew that they would most likely be the only two in the archives. Dmitri walked down the long aisle, looking down each row in turn, until he came upon the working tables where the gophers like him could organize and sort files to prepare for their KGB superiors.

Finally.

Kozlov sat at one of the tables with his back to Dmitri.

Dmitri approached slowly, but made sure his footfalls were heavy enough to alert Kozlov to his presence. But Kozlov did not move.

"Comrade Kozlov," Dmitri said, stopping behind Kozlov's chair.

No response.

Dmitri leaned forward and repeated the name. And then gave Kozlov a tap on the shoulder.

Damn, Dmitri thought to himself. *Did he drink so much the night before that he has passed out at work?*

That would explain why he had filed the paper incorrectly, despite its importance. However, Dmitri didn't smell alcohol, just the ever-present musty scent of pulped wood pressed into paper in service of the Motherland's archives.

Dmitri gave Kozlov a firm shake on the shoulder, but the man didn't move.

A new possibility arose in Dmitri's mind. He felt for a pulse on Kozlov's neck. Placed his face near Kozlov's nose and mouth.

No pulse. No breath.

Now Dmitri really thought to himself: *damn. The bastard is dead.*

Given the new circumstances, Dmitri did not have long to ponder. Instead, he acted instinctively.

Dmitri ran to the guard at the front of the archives, not caring how loud or rapid his footfalls were.

"Did you find comrade Kozlov?" the man asked.

"Yes," Dmitri answered between heavy breaths. "But call an ambulance. Kozlov must have had a heart attack. I think he's dead."

The guard got on the phone and began speaking rapidly.

Dmitri pulled at his sweaty collar as he hurried back to Kozlov's body. He passed it and went on to retrieve the misplaced document.

Dmitri thought it through for the first time.

If I continue, there is no turning back.

He took one last glance at the paper as he held it before his eyes and muttered a name he saw written on it. Then he began folding it rapidly, thus intertwining his own fate with that of the document.

After reducing the paper to a tiny rectangle, he slid it into a hidden hem in his jacket's lining. He took a few deep breaths, wiped his sweaty palms against his pant legs, and hurried to Kozlov to await assistance.

Moments later, two secretaries for men higher up in the KGB, both with clearance, entered the archives and helped Dmitri pull Kozlov's body to the exit.

None of them exchanged words. They were too afraid to say anything. But that was typical. They never conversed with each other. Asking for a light for a cigarette was the most conversation these men ever had at work. They all knew that any hint of indiscretion could mean not only their career but also their life.

The men loaded Kozlov's body onto the gurney that was waiting outside the archive's exit. Several men were squeezed into the small entryway, waiting to tend to the body and wheel it away.

During the confusion of moving Kozlov, the guard hadn't searched the KGB officers who moved Kozlov's corpse out of the archives and onto the gurney. After the body was gone and the two secretaries went back upstairs to resume their normal duties, Dmitri slouched down onto the ground, exhausted.

"Dmitri?" the archive's guard said. "I need you to sign out. That is, unless you come back in now."

Oddly, Dmitri felt the impropriety of being outside the archives without having first signed out.

"Of course," Dmitri said. He rose back to his feet, and his rubbery legs carried him the few meters to the entrance. He signed himself out from the KGB archives after checking the time.

"It is shocking to come upon death, isn't it?" the guard asked Dmitri.

Dmitri nodded and said, "One rarely comes across such shocking things in the archives."

Dmitri desperately wanted out of the KGB building. He wanted space. He needed time.

The death of a coworker would be reason enough to take the rest of the day off, go home, and drown my sorrows in vodka, Dmitri reasoned to himself.

Dmitri started his way up to his superior's office to request the rest of the workday off, which he was sure would be granted.

With each step upward, he became increasingly suspicious that this was an elaborate trap.

Had the file been misplaced on purpose to test me? Dmitri wondered. *Or, are they already on to me?*

It had worked out perfectly for Dmitri. Almost too perfect.

But they couldn't have planned Kozlov's heart attack. The truth was that Kozlov had misplaced the file. Nobody would have any reason to think that that one piece of paper was missing. Who knew how long it would be, if ever, until somebody would go searching for that record?

If they were ever to trace the blame, the logs would indicate that Kozlov was the last one to handle that file and replace it. And Kozlov was now dead. If they suspected any funny business, the investigators would come across the same problem. Kozlov was now dead. Dmitri knew it was most likely that this piece of paper's absence would not be detected for years, if ever. And nobody would be able to trace the blame back to him, for Kozlov was the man responsible for it, and he was now dead.

Yes, Dmitri thought to himself. *This is the perfect bit of espionage, and I'm going to deliver a goldmine to the Americans.*

Once he had leave for the day from his superior, he went to deliver the signal to arrange the delivery to his CIA handler.

Agent Bishop, as Dmitri was also known, knew that this piece of paper would make him the most valuable spy to the West, even more valuable than Colonel Penkovsky from decades before.

———

LATER THAT EVENING in the US Embassy in Moscow, the American Patrick Riley went to his office mail slot to check for messages. Although Patrick was in the same city, Moscow, as Agent Bishop, he was in a different world. The US Embassy was the most secure location for the United States within Moscow. It had been the ongoing victim of repeated attempts by the Soviets to break their codes, steal their communications, intercept outgoing messages, and track every living being that entered and exited the embassy. Paranoid to the degree that Americans couldn't understand, the Soviet Union was hell-bent on finding who was helping the Americans, and who in that building knew about it.

From his mail slot, Patrick pulled out a postcard and a flyer.

The flyer had a picture of ballet slippers along with an announcement that Patrick merely glanced at. The back of the postcard had a few scribblings of niceties from a colleague, but the front had a picture of St. Basil's Cathedral in the Red Square. He ignored the flyer completely focusing instead on the image of the cathedral.

Now it was Patrick's turn to think: *Damn.*

But how am I going to make that fit into my schedule? Patrick thought to himself. Despite his job flexibility, if Patrick couldn't make the meeting with the proper counterintelligence protocols, his source would be compromised. And his career would be over. A made spy.

Patrick's cover was that of a cultural and sports attaché and reporter for the US Embassy. The idea was that Patrick would report on all the wonderful cultural and sporting events in the Soviet Union for a mid-sized New York paper, and a Soviet counterpart would do the same in America. It was a meaningless sign of goodwill between the two countries locked in a Cold War. Both sides were willing to admit a reporter who would report on such insignificant things if it made them look better in the eyes of international observers.

And Patrick did indeed report on many sporting and cultural events within the Soviet Union. It kept him moving about the city, and sometimes outside of Moscow. And even though Patrick genuinely enjoyed his job, he had grown lonely doing it. As a single man in his thirties, he had long desired female companionship, ideally a devoted wife.

This James Bond never seems to get the girl, Patrick had often thought to himself.

But now, having been posted in Moscow for the last two years, he knew there was no way he could find such a woman. A romantic liaison with a Muscovite woman would draw the wrong type of attention. A relationship with a fellow US Embassy worker would also not be appropriate. Patrick was more than a CIA officer using his job as a reporter on all things sporting and cultural in the Soviet Union for cover. Unknown to all, except for two people at the US Embassy, Patrick was the handler of Agent Bishop, one of the most consistent sources of intelligence in Moscow for the United States.

The postcard had come from a known CIA officer who had seen Agent Bishop's indicator earlier that day. It was the signal that indicated Agent Bishop needed an urgent brush pass the next morning on the subway. Of course, the CIA man did not know that it meant all that. He only knew that when he received such a signal, it was his job to deliver a postcard with St. Basil's Cathedral on it into a numbered box at the US Embassy. He didn't even know whose box it was.

Patrick had one night to figure out how to make his schedule fit plausibly with meeting Agent Bishop on the Metro the next morning. As horribly inefficient and maddening almost all bureaucracy was in the Soviet Union, especially for Westerners, the subway system was one thing that ran well and on time. There were simply too many people for it to do otherwise. It also meant that Patrick had to board the specific subway car at precisely the right time, to ensure that Agent Bishop could brush by him and place whatever was so urgent in his pocket. It wasn't an easy problem to solve, but Patrick was confident he would find a winning route that evening.

As Patrick sat alone in his apartment that night, poring over the subway map and going through his black book of possible locations, people, and meetups for his job, he recalled the only time he had held a conversation with Agent Bishop. It had been two years earlier, and Agent Bishop had already been providing excellent intelligence two years prior to that.

A small chess tournament in Sweden served as a goodwill event between the two superpowers. Naturally, as the cultural reporter for a New York paper, Patrick had been included in the spectacle. Agent Bishop, harmless paper shuffler and pencil pusher, had been granted the privilege of going with his superior on this trip. He had indulged in buying many fine Western goods for his comrades while in Sweden. But he was also known as a sharp chess player amongst his colleagues.

Agent Bishop and Patrick had faced off in their chess game, which didn't last long. Patrick knew how the game was played, but he did not understand its intricacies or traps. It wasn't long before Patrick made a few regretful moves and found himself down two pieces.

"At least I still have my white-square bishop," Patrick had said. "I always find that I regret losing my white-square bishop."

"It doesn't matter which bishop it is," Agent Bishop said. "If you have only one, I just place my king on the opposite color, and there is no threat."

"But the knight can take forever to get across the board if needed late in the game," Patrick argued back.

"Based on the results of our current game," Agent Bishop replied, "I think that my opinion on all matters related to chess carries more weight."

"Sure," Patrick conceded. "But if you make a tiny mistake, it could cost you the game, even though you are winning by two pieces."

"But it's more likely that I will crush you with my advantage," Agent Bishop had said.

Two moves later, Patrick pushed his king onto its side, resigning the game.

The conversation had taken place in Russian. Patrick intentionally did not speak Russian well with Agent Bishop. The observers mustn't think Patrick was a potential spy. Had it been a mistake to put the two of them in contact with each other at the chess tournament? Patrick thought it was okay. Having a personal connection with his agent, he thought, outweighed any risks. Besides, if he and Agent Bishop were ever caught together, they would have a plausible reason as to why they would be meeting. They had met before.

It was after that chess game that Agent Bishop received his name. It had been decided that his codename needed to be changed because it had been in use for a couple of years. Thinking that the codename, if discovered, would divert the KGB to somebody in the Church (whom the KGB always suspected), Patrick thought Agent Bishop fit. It was a private joke between the two of them that Agent Bishop preferred the knight in the endgame of chess.

Like the game of chess, a tiny detail overlooked could lead to checkmate, and that's what Patrick was making sure of as he pored over the subway map. He preferred Line 1; its stations were the most beautiful, something he couldn't overvalue in the otherwise drab city. But that couldn't be a priority now. He followed one possible route. Would it allow him to lose tails and still be plausible for his work? More importantly, would he be able to meet Bishop at the precise time?

If not, Patrick wondered if it would cost Agent Bishop his life.

He estimated he would miss Bishop by three minutes, at best.

He tested another route. But it included a line he had never traveled before. Anybody watching would follow him intently if he took a subway he had never used before. He discarded that option and decided he would soon use all the subway lines regularly.

Patrick rubbed his eyes to refocus on the subway map. He needed a good route for the meetup; Agent Bishop's life could depend on it. He poured himself a drink, realizing that it was going to be challenging to plan the perfect path for his brush pass with Agent Bishop. Beginning to fear it was impossible, he started weighing the possibilities of putting Agent Bishop at risk. Would he not meet with him? Or, would he take a calculated risk and meet with him via a potentially unsafe route?

Without a wife or girlfriend to comfort him, Patrick knew he needed a break. He gulped down his drink and studied the flyer he had received along with the postcard, hoping for inspiration.

———

IT WAS LATE when Patrick found a plausible subway route that he could take the following morning. The ballet flyer had proven crucial. The route, after one transfer, a brush pass with Bishop, and then another transfer, would land him near a ballet company where he could plausibly do research for an article about ballet. Having solved the problem, Patrick wondered what would happen if he were followed. Patrick had not felt followed in quite a while.

During Patrick's first year in Moscow, the KGB followed him every day, sometimes obviously. However, Patrick had played the role of a bumbling sports reporter perfectly. He wasn't too proud to show his ignorance of more cultural matters like the ballet. The KGB would have reasonably concluded that Patrick really was a clueless idiot. And other CIA personnel, even Billy, Edwards, and Fitzpatrick whom he knew best, would report the same to the KGB if they were compromised.

What Patrick found the most difficult was not revealing how well he spoke Russian. He, in fact, spoke Russian excellently. He spoke so skillfully that, if needed, he and Agent Bishop could exchange coded phrases quickly and quietly. That was not possible for even an intermediate skilled Russian speaker. He often had to bite his tongue around other Americans whose accent and grammatical blunders hurt his ears. And his ego. But he could live with that as long as he handled America's best asset. And when he spoke haltingly and poorly, it only further convinced the KGB that he was an incompetent American boob.

After not sleeping well—Patrick was tormented trying to figure out Agent Bishop's reason for calling the urgent meeting—Patrick followed his normal routine. Eggs. Lousy coffee, though it was the best he could get even with Embassy connections. Out the door and on the way to the subway, a few glances at the clock to make sure he would get on the correct train. He had one transfer, then the brush pass, then another transfer, and then the ballet.

Minutes later, Patrick entered the subway car that would take him three stops. Then he would get off and transfer.

The paranoia of Moscow must be rubbing off on me, Patrick thought to himself. *Agent Bishop might be in danger for his life, but it's also possible he has something incredibly valuable to pass off to me. Something that could break this Cold War. Something that could save American lives.*

Patrick decided he would try to be more optimistic. This optimism made Patrick glance around the crowded Moscow subway that morning. As was typical, everybody kept to themselves, eyes glued to the floor. Although everybody felt as though they were living in a worker's paradise, none of them wanted to express too much happiness about it to anybody. Nobody wanted to draw attention to themselves.

Patrick counted off the stops and then hurried out with the crowd and worked his way to the adjoining station.

The clock looming over the metro platform informed him that he was a few minutes early and had to wait.

Better than a few minutes late, Patrick thought to himself with relief.

Patrick controlled his breathing as the subway arrived, and he forced himself to calmly board the necessary subway car.

The brush pass would come next.

As with the previous subway, nobody made eye contact, talked, or smiled. Holding onto a pole while standing, Patrick forced himself to do the same. Looking down at the floor, he recalled everybody surrounding him. The seats were full, and those standing were packed in tightly.

Perfect for a brush pass, Patrick thought to himself. *No Agent Bishop yet, though.*

Patrick counted the stops as others came and went. He only had three more stops, and still no Agent Bishop.

Unless he was so good not even I noticed, Patrick thought to himself. But he didn't dare check his pocket. Patrick calmed his nerves by reminding himself that Agent Bishop might not make it to the brush pass. But that only tempted more anxiety: was Agent Bishop's time up?

The subway was reaching the final stop at which Patrick would have to get off.

Patrick couldn't help but glance up. A man holding a folded *Pravda* quickly looked away.

Patrick looked back down.

Am I just being paranoid? Patrick wondered.

Patrick's instincts kicked in. If that man were KGB, watching him, any contact with Agent Bishop could be disastrous.

The last stop was coming. If Agent Bishop were on the subway and ready for the brush pass, he would have to do it soon.

Patrick forced his eyes to the floor, refusing to glance about to see if he could spot Agent Bishop.

Patrick coughed a few times, hoping it would alert Agent Bishop if he were nearby.

There it was again. The man reading the newspaper looked at him.

Now Patrick felt confident that this man was KGB. But was the KGB observer for Patrick? Or was he for Agent Bishop?

Something got ahold of Patrick, who was tired and frustrated playing the game passively, even though he was in the belly of the beast. Patrick took a few steps over to the man reading the *Pravda* and looked him in the eyes.

Intentionally speaking in halting Russian, he smiled broadly and said, "Did you find anything interesting? In the newspaper?"

The man stammered and replied, "Everything is normal."

Now Patrick was more confident he was needling a KGB observer.

Patrick extended his hand and said, "Hello I'm Patrick, I'm an American. I do newspaper stories on sports and culture. As a good citizen of Moscow, what do you love about sports and culture in Moscow?"

"A ballet is good, I hear," the man answered confidently.

Patrick held the man's eyes for a few moments, sensing that everybody around them was trying not to look, having heard an American speak with a fellow Muscovite. The subway came to a stop, and Patrick went to get off.

"I was just on my way to do a story on the ballet. Funny, that," Patrick said with a slight smile. Patrick got off the subway and emerged a few minutes later back onto the streets of Moscow. He felt the exterior of his pocket.

It was empty.

He was relieved Agent Bishop hadn't made it, but he was uncertain if that was good or bad news.

Patrick would have to go to the backup dead-drop point for Agent Bishop. He could plan for that in the afternoon, but his thoughts were elsewhere as he sought to interview anybody connected to this ballet studio.

Patrick knew he would probably get in trouble for being so aggressive with the man following him on the subway. But at this point, Patrick didn't care. He sensed his time in Moscow was almost over, and he enjoyed for the first time playing with a KGB man. He looked forward to having a laugh over the whole affair with Billy the next time they met at a pub. Billy always enjoyed a good laugh over a drink, especially if it was about the inanities and tedium regarding working behind the Iron Curtain. He decided to submit his report via Edwards who would, no doubt, sympathize with his frustration. And then Edwards would pass it on to Fitz-patrick who would, hopefully, gloss over the report. Perhaps he would avoid censure.

Either way, Patrick wasn't going to get it as severely from his superiors as the KGB observer was going to get it from his. He just hoped Agent Bishop was still safe and that the world was not on the edge of WWIII.

2

Washington D.C.
September 7, 2002.

DANIEL STOOD BACK at a distance from the funeral. He held his hands in his pockets and looked up to the overcast sky. He hoped it wouldn't rain before the funeral ended. After several minutes, the huddled masses of people dressed in black slowly dispersed from the graveside. Daniel tried to spot the woman he was looking for. Finally, only three people remained.

The two older people must be the dead man's parents, Daniel thought to himself, *and the last person must be her*. Daniel took a few steps closer. It was Tina, the woman he needed to talk to.

As Tina walked away from the grave site with her head down, Daniel carefully approached and said, "My condolences, Tina."

The young FBI agent with brown hair nearly as dark as her

black coat looked up at Daniel. He sensed she struggled to remember where she knew him from.

"Daniel?" she said. "You're the guy who got whisked away by the government from your own party? Last January, right?"

"That's me," Daniel affirmed, referring to when he had first met Tina at a party months ago before his job unexpectedly took him away to Central Asia.

"I didn't recognize you at first," Tina said. "You seem a lot more... *Different.*"

Daniel hoped she was referring to his stronger physique, now that he had been following Rex's strict training regimen. But Daniel wasn't talking with her for personal reasons.

"I heard about what happened to your partner," Daniel said. "I'm really sorry about that."

"Thanks," Tina said. "If you don't mind, I need to—"

"Can I take you for breakfast?" Daniel asked. "I know a great place nearby, whether you prefer bacon, pancakes, or something else."

"I really need some time and space," Tina said as she continued walking past Daniel. "It's hard enough, but when it's somebody I cared for more than just a work partner—"

"Tina, the breakfast is professional," Daniel said. He wondered if she had been romantically involved with her partner.

"I still need a little extra time and space," Tina answered. "I'm taking at least two months leave. You always know it's possible that somebody's going to die, but I guess I never thought it could be him. And so fast."

"From what the news is saying," Daniel said, "he died doing the right thing."

"We unexpectedly came upon suspects," Tina said clinically. "Before we recognized the threat, one of them fired at my partner.

But before that, I had felt a tingle, that something wasn't right. Every bone in my body told me to draw my firearm and put the man on the ground. But going by the book didn't allow me to shoot because of a tingle. Protocol killed my partner. If I'd gone with my gut, he would still be alive. I wish he were just another agent to me, but he's not."

"Another possibility is that you could've killed an innocent man."

"No, that's not possible," Tina disagreed. "I've gone over this in my head a million times, and trust me, I don't want to talk about it more."

"Okay," Daniel said as he walked beside Tina, farther away from the gravesite. "But I don't think you want to pass this breakfast up. Like I said, it's professional, and after what happened to your partner, I think you're going to like it."

Tina gave Daniel a sideways glance.

"I can't explain here," Daniel said. "Trust me on this one."

Tina conceded, and Daniel drove her to Officer Carter's favorite breakfast restaurant about fifteen minutes away. Benny's Pancake House was a breakfast joint that was mostly frequented by blue-collar workers. Officer Carters had a soft spot for it in her heart; she always had a back room reserved for such meetings.

When they walked into the back room and Tina saw Officer Carter, Tina gave Daniel a suspicious look. Officer Carter sat at the table with a cup of coffee, dressed in a white pantsuit. Tina probably recognized another tough-as-nails-woman when she saw one, but she couldn't figure out how she was connected to Daniel.

"Have a seat, Tina," Officer Carter said. "I know you just lost your partner, which is tough. But hear me out. Hear Daniel out."

Tina sat down, and a waiter came in and delivered a plate of fresh bacon. Daniel sat down next to Officer Carter, who indicated to the waiter to close the door and to not bother them. After the door shut, the din of the breakfast restaurant was nearly gone, and the three of them were alone.

"Help yourself," officer Carter said, pointing to the bacon.

"No appetite, thanks," Tina said.

"Let me be blunt," Daniel said. "Officer Carter and I have looked at your training profile and what you've done since you've been on the job. You have incredible instincts, and you have street smarts. That is exactly what we are looking for."

"What do you mean?" Tina asked. "I already have a job with the FBI. I already get to use those."

"I'm heading up a new team that is going to be focused on global counter-terrorism," Officer Carter explained as she reached for a piece of bacon. "Officially, it's called the MDF. A Multi-Disci-plinary-Force. The team includes language and cultural experts like Daniel, computer experts like Jenny, whom you know, and special operations soldiers from all branches of the military, should we need to bring force to bear. But we need somebody like you who is familiar with using force, but also has more investiga-tive skills, plus, as a woman, though it's not politically correct to say it—"

"My good looks," Tina said bluntly. "I've read enough spy novels. I'm not whoring myself out. I've earned my spot."

Daniel looked away, embarrassed. Anybody could recognize that Tina was attractive, and he was thankful that she was willing to bring that fact out into the open.

And this is why Officer Carter is here for the pitch, Daniel thought to himself.

"And let me be equally candid with you," Officer Carter said, and took a sip of coffee. "We must use every advantage we have in the War on Terror. That might include your looks. But you have my word that, at most, we will use your good looks to lure them in, but then you castrate the bastard before it gets any further than that."

Tina raised an eyebrow before saying, "I don't know. It's a big change. I need some time. I feel like I've hardly gotten started with the FBI, and I've already lost my partner. I just need some time."

"We don't have time," Daniel said. "The terrorists will strike again. We don't know where, we don't know when, but the clock is ticking until the next attack. The anniversary of 9/11 is four days away. You can bet the terrorists have a plan. It's going to happen again. We don't have a lot of time, so take a day at most. If you decide not to join us, just remember that this conversation never happened, and we wish you the best. But you and I both know that your partner died because the system failed him. You two did everything by the book, what was right. And he ended up on the wrong end of that. We're dealing with global terrorism, and the gloves have come off. We have a lot more latitude as to how we take out the bad guys."

Tina stared at both Daniel and Officer Carter while she thought.

"I like the sound of that," Tina finally said as she reached for a piece of bacon. "But I've got one more question. Is the name MDF intended to make congressional bean counters think that the MDF budget is for medium-density-fiberboard? If so, count me in."

"She's politically savvy too, not just street-smart," Officer Carter observed.

Daniel looked forward to having Tina on the MDF team.

———

Monday morning, two days later.

"I DON'T like the feel of this," Rex said over the radio.

"Me neither," Daniel responded. "That's why we send guys like you."

"Yeah, right," Rex replied simply.

Daniel stood behind Jenny at her computer in her office in Washington D.C. Muhammad, Daniel's most recent Arabic-speaking recruit, sat at a computer next to her. An empty seat was next to him. It had been for Max, Daniel's Russian-speaking recruit, but he couldn't make it. Tina, still awaiting full clearance, was observing, but not participating.

Daniel had explained to the MDF team that Rex and his men were approaching a small cabin that was off the grid, deep in the Virginia woods. It belonged to a suspected bomb maker. With the first anniversary of 9/11 approaching, everybody was on high alert.

As Daniel and the others waited for another update from Rex, a man with slicked-back dark hair entered and lingered in the background. Daniel didn't have time to question him. The credentials on his badge were sufficient.

"When is that drone going to be overhead?" Rex asked over the radio.

"Bad news," Daniel responded. "It won't be. Despite the high level of threat, we don't have the authority to use a drone to spy on a US citizen."

Daniel rightly guessed Rex was cursing the system that gave the MDF team clearance to raid the cabin but withheld an overhead drone.

Daniel glanced towards the smartly suited man standing in

the corner. Whoever he was, he was from higher up in the CIA, and Daniel hoped he noted his care while operating on American soil. His black hair had gray streaks, but he exuded confidence befitting a man who had served in the CIA from the time Reagan was in office, if not earlier. His slicked-back hairstyle certainly fit the stereotype of a high-ranking government official.

"A US citizen?" Rex finally responded over the radio. "But I guess it's okay to send my buddies into God-knows-what so we can get our asses blown off? The judge, or whoever needs to authorize a drone, should know that I can't get an infrared reading on the cabin. I can't see how many people, if any, are in there. They knew what they were doing. They've insulated that little cabin with some serious stuff."

Muhammad fidgeted with his sweaty hands as he intermittently adjusted his earpiece and microphone. Daniel gave Muhammad a tap on the shoulder. Daniel felt that he had a lot of promise, and he knew he was highly motivated. His family had fled from Saddam Hussein's regime.

"There is a door on the front, a door on the back, and a window next to each door," Rex reported over the radio.

"You need to go in, Rex," Daniel ordered over the radio. "You have the most experience, and we may need your eyes in there to make a split-second decision."

"I wouldn't have it any other way," Rex said.

"Your men in position?" Daniel asked.

"In a few seconds. I'm doing one last visual sweep, and then I'll work my way to the front door undercover."

Daniel paced about a few steps as he waited for Rex and his men to finally get into position. Muhammad looked back at Daniel and wiped his hands on his pants.

Tina clenched and released her fist. Daniel sensed she wanted to be the one kicking down the door.

Jenny sat up straight, nervous that Rex was in the thick of the action.

"I'm in position," Rex said. "I'm placing explosives on the door just in case they decided to lock it and didn't want the big bad wolf to come in."

Daniel appreciated Rex's levity.

"Hold on," Jenny interrupted. "I've got activity on their cell phone."

Muhammad shut his eyes and listened to the Arabic conversation on the tapped phones.

After a few seconds, Daniel asked, "What are they saying?" To Rex, he said, "Wait. They're talking on the phones right now."

Muhammad began to translate on the fly as he listened to the conversation in Arabic. To Daniel, the words came rapid fire, nearly incomprehensible. But he could pick up the gist of what they were saying. They were greeting each other. They were confirming that everything was okay. Vague statements that were probably coded in some manner.

"Do you know where they're from?" Daniel asked.

"One of them is Egyptian," Muhammad said quickly. "I hear other people talking in the background. There must be at least three or four people in the cabin." Daniel passed the information by radio on to Rex.

"While they're talking on the phone is the perfect time for me to make my entrance," Rex said.

"You have clearance," Daniel confirmed.

"Breach in three, two—"

"Wait!" Muhammad said.

"Hold! Hold!" Daniel said over the radio to Rex. "What is it, Muhammad?"

"One of the other men started talking on the phone," Muhammad said. "At first, I thought he was Palestinian, but something seems a little bit off. I wouldn't be surprised if he's Israeli."

"What the hell?" Daniel said.

"I don't want to sit here forever," Rex said impatiently.

"Hold," Daniel repeated.

"They've hung up," Jenny said.

"I don't understand," Muhammad said, looking at Daniel. "Why is there an Israeli working with these terrorists?"

"It doesn't make sense," Daniel said. "Screw this. Rex, are you still in position?"

"Make up your mind, dork," Rex said over the radio.

"I don't care if there's an Israeli in there," Daniel said. "We're on American soil."

"Okay, getting ready to breach in three, two, and one..."

A blast sent white noise over the radio, and then they listened for Rex to enter the cabin.

But everything was quiet.

"Perfect," Daniel said happily.

"What the hell?" Tina asked.

"Yeah, what happened?" Muhammad said. "Is Rex okay? Did a bomb go off? Why are you happy?"

"I'm sorry, Muhammad," Daniel said, giving him a slap on the back. "That was a training exercise. Rex is somewhere else in the building, pretending to talk over the radio with us."

"Was that some kind of a test?" Muhammad asked.

"Exactly," Daniel said. "I had to know during a mission how sharp your linguistic skills were. How deep your knowledge of the languages is, and how well you could tell where people were from

on the fly. Those were all staged recordings and old conversations," Daniel said. "And you are exactly right. One of them was an
Israeli speaking in Arabic. What we can't afford is to blow up a
Mossad operation somewhere else in the world because we are
overzealous. But you caught it."

"So, if that had been real..." Tina asked.

"I don't think the *Mossad* would be operating like that on our
soil," Daniel said.

Muhammad abruptly got up out of his seat, excused himself
and made his way out the door. "I think I'm going to be sick," he
announced loudly as he headed towards the restroom.

"He is not as tough as you," Daniel said to Tina, "but he has
the exact skills we're looking for. I'm going to request that his top-
level security clearance gets fast-tracked so he can join the team."

Daniel couldn't help but notice the observer in the corner grin
with appreciation as he came towards Daniel to introduce himself.

———

"YOU NEED to come with me, Dr. Knox," the man with slicked-back
hair said to Daniel and his team.

"Not again," Tina grumbled.

"You need to come with me to Officer Carter at the main building," the man said.

"Why didn't Carter just call me?" Daniel asked. Since Officer
Carter's office had moved to the main CIA building, she had never
sent a messenger to retrieve him.

"Because I'm the one who called the meeting," the man said.
He took a few steps towards Daniel and the rest of his team and
extended his hand. "Edwards. I knew your father, and when I
saw somebody with the same last name forming a new countert-

errorism team with ties to the CIA, I had to come to see it myself."

Daniel warily shook Edwards' hand and said, "If you know about my team, then you must be pretty important. What did you say your name was again?"

"Edwards," the man repeated. "And I'm not too surprised you haven't heard of me. Unlike some guys, I haven't spent my whole career trying to boost my ego to advance myself. To those who pay attention to results, they know that while I was in my prime, I was one of the best. I was chasing down KGB spies behind the Iron Curtain when you were busy chasing down Decepticons and playing with Transformers."

Edwards released a winsome grin.

Daniel rode with Edwards over to the CIA headquarters in Langley in silence.

After they arrived, Edwards checked him through security, and neither of them could help but look at the Memorial Wall as they continued to the elevators.

"I don't expect to find myself up on that wall any day," Edwards said. "At the least, you have to die on the job to get your star on the wall. I'll probably die wearing my slippers and watching a hockey game. Or, perhaps I'll accidentally shoot myself at the target range. I still like to show those young whippersnappers that the old guys can handle a gun like a pro."

Daniel lingered before the Memorial Wall a moment longer than Edwards. Each star represented a man or woman who lost their life while serving the CIA. Some of them were unnamed, the recipients having died in secret operations that had to remain classified.

Minutes later, they both entered Officer Carter's office, which Daniel thought was not near as spacious or large as her old one, but he figured it must have seemed more prestigious being in the main building.

After a nod of greeting between Officer Carter and Daniel, Edwards started the meeting.

"I'm hand selecting Daniel to help me with a special operation."

"I'm listening," Officer Carter said.

"There will be a three-day conference for international security overseas, a week from tomorrow," Edwards began. "I'm busy hunting somebody down. We have a traitor in our midst."

Both Officer Carter and Daniel sat up straight at the mention of a mole.

"I have prime suspects," Edwards continued. "I've narrowed the mole down to three men, and they will all be at the conference. It will be the first time they are all together, and it may never happen again. It is the perfect time to uncover the mole."

"Why me?" Daniel asked again.

"The international conference for security is being held in Tashkent, Uzbekistan," Edwards said. "It starts next Tuesday, and it will only last three days, so we have a tight window in which to work. And this is not something I orchestrated, either. The mole won't be suspicious of being lured into a trap. And because the conference is taking place in a country that is allied with us and supporting us in the War on Terror, it's a good place for us to catch the mole."

Daniel recalled that Nigora, the woman he once loved but who was now suspected of being involved with the Russian mafia, had warned him to never interfere with her business in Tashkent. That thought left his mind as quickly as it entered.

"And because it's an old Soviet backwater, nobody cares what happens there," Daniel added, "and we don't have to play by the same rules as if we were in the United States. Am I right?"

"See, you're not such an amateur, after all," Edwards said kindly.

"This would be an excellent chance for you to strengthen your intel skills in the field, Daniel," Officer Carter said. "Edwards has vast experience in this area, and he is the perfect man for you to learn from."

"With all due respect," Daniel said, "the War on Terror is different. I'm certain that Mr. Edwards was the best at what he did during the Cold War, but just like it was disastrous to use World War II tactics in Vietnam, I don't want to use Cold War tactics now."

"I see." Edwards sat back, and instead of giving Daniel the scolding or lecture from an elder, he said, "Mole hunting is some of the most difficult work in the intelligence world. And it might not get the fast results that newer and more technological efforts can achieve."

"Don't turn down an opportunity to learn from a legend," Officer Carter said. "I have half a mind to order you to take this mission."

"I don't want him unless he is completely on board," Edwards interrupted. "This is dangerous business, and unless his heart and mind are completely in it, it could end up disastrously for all of us."

"I would have a hard time buying into this mission," Daniel said, "not because I don't think I have much I can learn about intelligence from a professional like you, Mr. Edwards, but more because I believe my team's focus should remain solidly on catching terrorists. As hard as it is for you to believe, a spy who has been working for the Soviets and now the Russians is simply not as dangerous as the terrorists I'm trying to catch. What's the worst that could happen if this mole betrayed secrets to Russia, which is just a crumpled heap of a collapsed and corrupt Soviet empire?"

"It's understandable that you think I'm an old man fighting old wars," Edwards said patiently. "But you should be open to the possibility, as well, that perhaps your analysis of history is short-sighted and that you may be underestimating an enemy. It's no accident that I've been winning this game for a long time. You had better be certain you're playing the right game. Because right now, you're so amateurish, you don't even know what you don't know. I don't make offers like this to younger officers often, so carefully consider my offer."

"I urge you to join Edwards," Officer Carter added.

"Now is not a good time, even if I really wanted to join you," Daniel said. "I'm building a team, and it's not complete yet."

"This is not what I expected," Edwards said, reverting to his pleasant demeanor. He took a deep breath and leaned back in his chair before continuing. "I would have expected differently from the son of the Knox that I knew. This mole is known as the Wolf, and we've been hunting him for years. He's caused the deaths of multiple US assets. He made Reagan and every single president since him crap their pants, and he will make Russia a real threat to the security of the United States much sooner than many would like to think. So maybe I am just an old man stuck in my old ways, and I need to change with the times instead of hunting down my own whale. But if nothing else, I know the Wolf is responsible for many American deaths, and for that, I'm gonna make sure we catch the Wolf."

Daniel remained steadfast in his decision. He needed to finish building his team, and they needed to focus on catching terrorists, not hunting ghosts from the Cold War.

"Okay then," Edwards said. "I tried, but like I said, I'm not going to force you to join me. Having said that, I do have a small favor. I suppose you know Max?"

"The analyst who knows Russian, Uzbek, and spends too much time at the Russian bathhouse?" Daniel said. "What about him? I'm trying to get him to join my MDF team."

"That's the one. Be careful. Keep an eye on him."

"Are you saying that the Wolf might have a connection with Max?" Daniel asked.

"I didn't officially say anything of the kind," Edwards said with a smile. He rose from his chair and extended a hand for a handshake from Daniel. Daniel accepted, and Edwards left.

DANIEL ALREADY KNEW the results were embarrassing. He put the gun down that Rex was making him take target practice with and pulled the target towards him. All his shots were off the mark. He was glad nobody on the team was there to watch, especially Tina. Taking a few deep breaths and trying to relax, Daniel put up another target. This time, he left it closer than the previous one.

The gun felt unnatural in his hands, but Rex wanted him to become accustomed to a variety of firearms. Daniel understood the reasoning, but he seemed incapable of making progress. Daniel fired off several shots in quick succession. Before he continued, he noticed that somebody else entered the firing range and stood behind him.

It was precisely what he feared. Tina was standing behind him. She watched him finish the magazine, and they both knew the results were not good.

"I hope my life is never on the line when you're shooting,"

Tina said. Daniel knew she was joking, but it still hurt. After a quick look back to Tina as if to say, "That was just unlucky," Daniel put up another target and placed it at the full distance.

Daniel took a few more deep breaths and tried to refocus his thoughts. Another round of inaccurate shooting in front of Tina would be shameful. Instead of firing, he put the gun down, turned, and explained to Tina, "Rex is making me practice with guns I'm not used to. This one is new to me."

"Beginner," Tina mumbled without empathizing with his excuse. She moved into the spot next to Daniel and grabbed the gun he had put down. Daniel stood back to watch, and what he saw made his heart stop.

After her first shot, Tina turned her head and said, "You shouldn't be checking me out at work."

"I... I was just noticing your..."

Damn, I can't say form, Daniel thought to himself.

She finished the magazine and pulled out another gun. It was a Glock, just like the one he preferred. Unfortunately for Daniel, he continued to dig himself deeper into a hole.

"What were you noticing?" she asked, just before firing several more rounds.

"Your gun. It's just perfectly balanced. It's well-made, it's beautiful to look at, and yet it's extremely effective."

Tina took another shot. They both knew it was a perfect one.

"You like my gun?" Tina asked. "You jealous?"

Another shot that hit the target perfectly.

"I'll give it a try," Daniel said. Tina set the gun down and took a few steps back. Daniel took her place.

Daniel picked up the Glock, and it felt a little bit differently from what he expected. It was warm from Tina's grip, and he could tell from its weight that it was neither full nor empty. It was somewhere in between. But it was just as he had said. The gun felt perfect. It was the same type of Glock his father had made him practice with.

Despite his nerves, Daniel quickly raised the gun and, without thinking, squeezed off a shot. It was just as perfect as Tina's previous ones.

"Maybe I was wrong," Tina said. "It seems that you like my gun."

"I love it," Daniel said. He regretted it as soon as he said it.

He couldn't look at her. They stood in silence.

Daniel wanted to say more, but he figured that Tina was still in mourning for her partner's death. He took one more shot.

Daniel exhaled and put the gun down. He took one deep breath and braced himself for what he was going to say to Tina.

Daniel turned around and said to her, "I know we just became coworkers, but..."

Daniel found that he couldn't talk anymore.

Tina stood and waited. Daniel feared she wasn't going to bail him out.

"You can borrow my gun if you want it," Tina said.

"No, it's not about that at all," Daniel said.

"Then...?"

"Can I take you out for dinner sometime?" Daniel said quickly. His throat nearly constricted, and he was hardly able to get the whole sentence out. As soon as he said it, he imagined how happy his mother would be, and how Jenny would be excited because she had first tried to hook Daniel and Tina up.

"Yeah," Tina said. "I'll let you know when Carter gives me a free moment."

Daniel was unsure if that was a good sign or not, but he was thankful she hadn't entirely shot him down.

"Speaking of Officer Carter, I have a meeting with her tomorrow I need to be ready for," Daniel said quickly as he rushed away. "I'll be in touch about a time, maybe Saturday night."

Daniel hurried out.

"What about *where*?" Tina asked.

Daniel didn't hear the question as he left because he was amazed that the disastrous gun discussion had somehow turned into a date with Tina.

And she's my coworker now, Daniel thought.

3

Moscow.
September 4, 1987.

THE POUNDING on the door woke Dmitri early. This was the morning Dmitri was to pass his goldmine of information to the American.

Confused, he checked his clock. It read 5:59am. His alarm was due to wake him up in one more minute.

Who the hell could be pounding on my door at this time of the morning?

Dmitri froze as he came to his senses. He knew exactly who could be pounding on his door at any time they damn well pleased. But normally, they would come at night. Normally, they would enter unannounced.

That was little comfort to Dmitri as he turned the locks and braced himself to face the chill that would creep under his bathrobe when he opened the door.

Dmitri had always hoped that when they came to take him away to never be seen again, he would be dressed decently and go with dignity. He feared he was about to be denied this wish.

When he opened the door, he was relieved to see a low-level KGB gopher, perhaps the one from night duty. Dmitri looked about outside, but nobody else was with him.

"Your presence is urgently requested," the man explained. "Come as you are. Do not bring anything. Everything you need will be provided. You will understand when you arrive."

Dmitri glanced down at his threadbare slippers and his worn bathrobe, and the man nodded as if to say, "Do put something on more than that."

Dmitri put on pants, shirt, socks, and finally his shoes. As he dressed quickly, he calculated in his mind. He put his coat on. The paper was still hidden in a hem.

He hesitated to take it with him, but he knew his apartment would be searched, and he couldn't hide it now without raising suspicion from the man waiting in his doorway.

With one last glance around his apartment, Dmitri wondered if it would be the last time he saw it. He looked at his old family photos for a moment.

What would my father think of me? Dmitri asked himself.

Dmitri followed the driver down to his car. He considered attacking the driver and then fleeing to the US Embassy. But there were no other KGB in sight. The driver seemed as if he was only doing his job, and that there was no reason to be afraid.

Dmitri took a deep breath before he got into the back seat of the vehicle. Dmitri hoped that he had not missed his last chance to escape to the US Embassy. When it came down to it, Dmitri knew the young driver was merely doing his job. He couldn't bring himself to attack the young man on the slim chance that he might be able to escape.

"This is unusual," Dmitri observed to the driver as they pulled away. "Do you know what this is about?"

The driver gave him a quick glance in the rearview mirror and shrugged his shoulders.

The car zoomed down the center lane towards the KGB head-quarters. When they arrived, a man let Dmitri out and led him higher up into the KGB building.

Not to the basement, Dmitri thought to himself.

Untold numbers of Russians had met their gruesome fate in the basement of this building. Some were intentional, some were torture gone too far, some were KGB colleagues, but many were simple Soviet citizens. Dmitri didn't dare guess how few of them were genuinely guilty of doing anything wrong.

Dmitri again noted that no guards were there to force him along, and the further away he got from the basement, the more he felt that he would survive. But he was going up so high to a KGB office, Dmitri wondered who had summoned him.

When they stopped climbing, the guide led him through a double wooden door. The guide nodded to a secretary at a desk, and then pushed open another double wooden door. They entered a large office whose walls were lined with portraits of Soviet heroes. Behind a massive wooden desk sat an elderly mound of Russian flesh wearing glasses, smoking, and drinking more vodka before 7 AM than the average Soviet drank before noon.

Dmitri managed a slight bow, unable to speak. He felt naked without his proper uniform. He could not calculate how many layers and steps of the hierarchy this man was above him.

"I am sorry for the unusual timing," the elderly man said without hardly looking up from his desk to Dmitri. He was writing furiously with a pen. "Kozlov's death yesterday was unfortunate."

Dmitri tensed slightly, wondering if he was under suspicion.

Did they suspect foul play in Kozlov's death?

Dmitri was relieved when the old man continued, "Kozlov was due to depart for a new post. I, for one, am thankful that he died. He was an over-privileged and incompetent pig. It's only because of his family connections he rose as high as he did, and his family connections are a constant source of headache for me." The man grunted and took a slow pull on his cigarette before coughing and then continuing. "However, he was about to depart for an important post, which he is now unable to fill. You must take his new post. You will receive your orders when you arrive. It is in the far reaches of the Soviet Union. But don't let the distance from Moscow fool you. The KGB is most needed there. I don't trust the military, and I certainly don't trust the politicians. Your train leaves immediately. Everything will be provided, and your personal effects will be sent on from your own apartment."

"Thank you," Dmitri murmured, unable to speak without great difficulty. Relief swept over him as he thought of the paper folded in his coat hem instead of waiting at his apartment for discovery. "I will fulfill my post honorably."

"Once you arrive and receive your orders," the old man said with a raised voice as the guards led Dmitri away, "it will make sense to you."

Now two guards hurried Dmitri down the stairs. These two men were more urgent and seemed like the type who would lead victims to the basement.

What if the old man was just toying with me, Dmitri thought to himself. He resisted the urge to touch his fingers to the paper tucked inside his hem, fear gripping him.

But it was too late for Dmitri to resist. He could perhaps kick one of the men in the groin, but he would never get away from both of them.

When they reached the ground floor, Dmitri stopped to double over and claimed that he was not feeling well.

"We don't have time for this," one of the men said gruffly. The two bent over, and each of them grabbed Dmitri by the shoulder and elbow. They began dragging Dmitri, and fear took over. Dmitri was about to yell, but they opened the door and took him outside, towards another waiting car.

They aren't taking me to the basement? Dmitri wondered.

His legs were still rubber, and as his head spun, the escorts drove him to a train that they nearly tossed him onto as it was beginning to pull away.

Dmitri sat and looked about. There was a guard at each end of the compartment, but Dmitri knew he had no choice now. Dmitri thought he would have to jump off the train at some point. Dmitri was sure that this train was taking him to Siberia, and a life of misery. But not everything made sense. His wrongdoing deserved execution, not a labor camp.

Why are they sending me to Siberia? Dmitri wondered.

As the train headed east, Dmitri tried to speak with the guards to discover where they were going. The guards were not forthcoming, so he made the most of the comfortable train, tea, and bread. He feared that those, too, were part of a cruel joke by the KGB that would finally be revealed when they dumped him at a gulag.

———

In Moscow, the KGB prepared Dmitri's apartment for its next occupant. Dmitri would never return. They had to search it before the next KGB bureaucrat replaced Dmitri.

Although Agent Bishop had been a productive asset, he never had a radio. And so the search team never found a radio. They did not uncover paper for invisible writing or cameras. Even after tearing up the floorboards, they found nothing to indicate that Dmitri was a spy.

The search team put Dmitri's family photos, those of his parents, in a box. Most of his books had not been read for years, other than an old copy of Marx and Engels' work. Unknown to the search team, this book had served as the key for the rare coded written messages that Agent Bishop had sent to Patrick Riley. But to the search team, this was a typical book for a loyal communist to have in his apartment.

Although the search team's job was easier when they found nothing incriminating, the leader of the search team had always relished the excitement of discovering something suspicious. But in Dmitri's case, Agent Bishop was such a professional spy, his apartment was without blemish.

Almost too *clean*, the leader of the search team thought to himself.

But the one disastrous bit of incriminating evidence was with Agent Bishop himself, neatly tucked away in his coat's hem.

The search team left with Dmitri's family photos and reported that the apartment was ready for its next occupant.

———

Two days later, the train bearing Dmitri eastward suddenly began heading south. Dmitri wondered if the tracks would veer off to the east again, but he was soon convinced that he was not going to Siberia. He was going somewhere far to the southeast of the Soviet Union. He would later discover that he was going to the Uzbek Soviet Socialist Republic in Central Asia.

————

DMITRI PETROV HAD BEEN BORN on the outskirts of Moscow. The year had been 1933, and so he was young when the Nazis invaded. He remembered waiting in Moscow, confident that the Nazis would lose, although the Nazis had always seemed victorious in the past. And yet the winter turned back the Nazis, and so Dmitri and his father both survived the war.

His mother, however, did not. Physically, she was not stout. Some might say she was frail. Looking back at old photos, Dmitri understood what he did not and could not have understood back then. His mother was slender and beautiful. His father was portly and ugly. His father had the wits about him to be on the right political side, and so his father joined the KGB when it was called the NKVD.

Dmitri's mother, however, was from a much lower station, and yet beautiful. Her looks allowed her to marry a man who had a position in the KGB that would afford her some safety, for she secretly practiced her Russian Orthodox religion. Though technically allowed, it was frowned upon. Dmitri remembered her saying prayers, referring to scriptures, and even occasionally humming a song. His father ignored all that religious stuff. He had clearly married her for her looks. And so, when she died during the siege of Moscow, although it was heartbreaking for Dmitri, her death was only one of millions. His mother's religion had not saved her, and his godless father had survived.

Unfortunately for Dmitri, he inherited his mother's physical frailty, but he also inherited his father's bad looks. To his advantage, however, he inherited his mother's intellect who, although her husband was no dummy, was sharper than her husband ever would have admitted. Some might say that Dmitri inherited her religious conscience, or perhaps her religious observances somehow took hold in Dmitri's heart.

Dmitri, seeking safety, had followed his father's footsteps into the KGB. His father was willing to do that for him: provide a safe place. But as he had his mother's frailty, he would never be a good soldier, and his lack of physical prowess convinced others he would never survive in the field. The West would chew him up and spit him out, he was so weak.

He recalled his father returning from Hungary in 1956 and recounting for him how the Soviet tanks had put down an uprising. His father felt that he was telling his son secrets about the strength and might of the Soviet Union. For Dmitri, however, his father was sowing seeds of doubt. To Dmitri, squashing the Hungarian uprising was an abuse of power. But Dmitri continued his duties in the KGB as usual. Somebody who merely shuffled papers and dealt with files was not involved in the dirty work.

In 1957, Dmitri married. Ironically, the woman married him for the same reasons that Dmitri's mother married his father. For again, Dmitri was not good-looking, and he was not wealthy or powerful, but being in the KGB did afford some advantages and a small amount of safety. And so, it was that a beautiful young woman was willing to marry him. To her delight, she would learn that Dmitri did indeed have a soft disposition and a kind attitude about him, along with intelligence that his exterior did not betray.

But their marriage together was short. She died while giving birth to their first, and only child, in 1960. By then, Dmitri's father had also died from liver problems, no doubt from massive excesses of vodka, and so when his wife left him, his son was all that he had. A single man trying to raise a son was unusual and unheard of, but the state provided. The KGB took care of it. But it also meant that Dmitri's son would necessarily go to the military.

And so, it was that Dmitri's sole child and love of his life was sent to war in Afghanistan. He was killed there in 1980. Dmitri was handling intelligence briefs about what was happening in Afghanistan, and Dmitri's mind was made up. The Soviet Union was just as, if not more, horrible and corrupt than the czars that preceded it. On occasion, he would check older files deep in the history of the Soviet Union and read about the exploits of the secret police meant to protect its people. He encountered far too many euphemisms that indicated the extermination of thousands of their own citizens.

And so it was that in 1983, Dmitri began spying for the United States of America. Eventually, he would take on the codename of Agent Bishop, and Patrick Riley would be his handler in Moscow.

But abruptly, Dmitri was summoned to the far reaches of the Soviet Union in service of the Motherland. He was sent there on a KGB mission to replace the inconveniently deceased Kozlov.

There, in the Uzbek Soviet Socialist Republic, he made a new start. He had no way of contacting Patrick Riley, or anybody connected to the United States. After a few years, Agent Bishop's past faded away. He had done what he could, but now he was in a corner of the world where he could not do anything. He met another woman and married her, and he had a happy life. It was so happy, in fact, that when the Soviet Union finally disintegrated, he stayed with his new wife. He had learned to love his new home, faults and all.

Besides, he was occasionally reminded that he had indeed

committed treason against the Soviet Union. And even though the Soviet Union no longer existed, he knew that it was old KGB thugs who now ran Mother Russia. And the old Agent Bishop's efforts had previously resulted in the untimely deaths of many Soviet assets. Many of these had been friends of the men now in power. Agent Bishop knew that while Westerners have short memories, Russians have long ones. They hold grudges, and they don't let them go. For years after the fall of the Soviet Union, Agent Bishop lived as Dmitri Petrov, the happily married man in the far reaches of the former Soviet Union.

Then one day, in September 2002, he saw on the newscast a story about the United States that was now making use of an air base in Uzbekistan to fight against the radical Muslim terrorists in Afghanistan. There was video footage of the American Ambassador, Fitzpatrick, and his staff in Tashkent, Uzbekistan. What Dmitri saw in the background made him drop his tea, and it spilled all over the floor.

Without any explanation to his wife, he caught a taxi within an hour to Tashkent. He needed to visit an old friend the next day, September 11, 2002.

4

Washington DC.
September 11, 2002.

DANIEL SWIPED his security pass and limped into the room filled with cubicles.

"You okay?" a woman from three cubicles down asked with some concern.

"Just sore," Daniel answered.

Since the formation of the MDF team months prior, Daniel had been going through a brutal training regimen from 6 AM until noon. In the afternoon, he worked on his linguistic and translation work for the CIA. Daniel loved the translation work and analyzing reports, mind-numbing as it could be at times. But at least it didn't hurt his body like the physical training.

Rex, the SpecOps man and weapons leader of the MDF team,

was getting Daniel what he called "field fit." That basically meant that Daniel, as a part-time job in the morning, had to go through Rex's physical program to make sure he was proficient with weapons and in hand-to-hand combat. Initially, Daniel thought the physical training would give his mind a rest from his analysis, but after one day with Rex, he discovered that the physical regimen was mentally demanding as well.

Daniel plopped himself down into his cubicle and checked the stack of translations that awaited him. His glutes were sore. One hand still shook from all the recoil it had endured from his target practice with the pistol. At least he could respectably handle a handgun. A Glock, anyway.

"Not bad for an egghead," Rex had said when he first took stock of Daniel's shooting ability. Thanks to the training he received from his father, Daniel was better than the average American at handling a firearm, but compared to a Green Beret, Daniel had a long way to go. Rex was not too shy to let him know about that.

"Tough day at the gym?" Jenny said outside Daniel's cubicle. Jenny was always a bright spot in Daniel's day. A computer geek to the core, with a bubbly personality who sometimes could not filter what was going on in her mind, Jenny always maintained an optimistic attitude. They had known each other since college, and through the dot-com boom days. Daniel had gotten her the job in the CIA, and he'd brought her on to the new MDF team as the computer and forensics expert.

"You could say that," Daniel said. "New glasses?" He didn't remember Jenny wearing any glasses other than her dark-rimmed ones, but the ones she had on now were different.

"Don't laugh. They're from high school. I lost my real ones at Rex's place."

Jenny pursed her lips as if to say *oops*, but it was too late.

Before Daniel could tease her, Jenny said, "Rex claims that his training will give you a body that women will die for."

"Did Rex tell you that last night?" Daniel asked.

"I don't remember," Jenny said innocently. "He just said it sometime."

Daniel gave Jenny another glance. They both knew that she and Rex had a thing, but it wasn't something to talk about in the land of cubicles.

"Daniel!" Officer Carter called out from a nearby conference room. "Get in here."

Daniel gave Jenny the *why-didn't-you-tell-me-she-was-here?* look. Jenny went back to the algorithm crunching on her computer, chewing away at some arcane linguistic analysis of chatter between the countless dialects of global terrorists. Daniel carried himself to the conference room, guessing Officer Carter was not happy with him. His suspicions proved correct when he plopped down into a chair opposite her.

"You still don't have the language specialists that we need for the MDF team," Officer Carter said. "I expected you to have at least one on the team by now, especially if they will need field training like you."

"It's not so easy," Daniel explained. "Once we do find people who speak all the languages that we need, it's tough to get them cleared to do anything. I've interviewed and talked with nearly every Arabic speaker at every college and university within three hours of Washington D.C., and I've flown to many more universities to interview their linguists. But the fact is, none of them strike me as the perfect fit. And that's what we need. We need a perfect fit. Also, I've discovered that even if somebody knows a language or dialect one million times better than any of us, they're often children of immigrants, and so they can understand basic communication, but when it comes to the deep intricacies of the language, they would be useless in the field."

"Spare me your linguistic babble," Officer Carter said. "Because you turned down a golden opportunity to be mentored by Edwards, I figured you must be swamped with recruiting and training. It looks to me like you're working out some and piddling away at translations."

Daniel knew that Officer Carter always had his back, but he sensed something was up when she started pushing him like this. And she knew exactly what Daniel was thinking.

"Yes, your piddling translations prevented the Taliban from acquiring a nuclear weapon," Officer Carter continued, referring to his first field mission in January. "But I wonder if you didn't get lucky. If you are going to be an intelligence professional, you need to work at all aspects of the craft around the clock. You can't train in the morning, translate in the afternoon, clock out, and then go flirt with Tina."

Daniel felt his face turn red, but Officer Carter wasn't done yet.

"The terrorists work on attacking us tirelessly, and that's how you need to be working against them. Otherwise, you're just a government employee at worst, or an amateur spy at best."

Daniel held Officer Carter's gaze, refusing to look away.

"I wonder if you will be able to keep up," Officer Carter said. Daniel remembered that Officer Carter was probably over fifty.

"I've decided to focus on recruiting for Arabic for now," Daniel explained, hoping the lecture was over. "The best lead that I have coming down the pipeline is a relatively young Iraqi man who fled Saddam's regime. It's interesting. He is a Sunni Muslim, like Saddam himself, but that also makes him the minority in the country. He fled Iraq for his life, so I'm wondering how he got on

Saddam's bad side. He's fast-tracked for security clearance, but they can't afford to take any shortcuts. He's the best hope for now."

"What about Russian? How are things with Max?"

"I'd put that aside," Daniel explained. "Do you want me to pursue him again because of what Edwards said?"

She didn't answer the question directly but said, "Get Max on the team, and I'll keep an eye on him."

Daniel nodded his head but decided not to ask more.

The woman from three cubicles down knocked on the door and stuck her head in.

"Check out the news," she said. "It's on in Daniel's part of the world."

Like most Americans, they all feared a terrorist attack on the anniversary of 9/11.

Officer Carter turned on the TV in the conference room and went to an online news source for Daniel's part of the world: Central Asia.

An Arabic news site was reporting a bomb blast in Uzbekistan. More accurately, it was in the capital city of Tashkent, Uzbekistan.

"Our old friends are up to nasty business again," Officer Carter said. "Will you go with Edwards now? This should be an easy first mission for you guys."

"I'll take the team and go with Edwards," Daniel said, "but only because of this new development in the War on Terror. And I'm sure I'll learn a few things from Edwards along the way."

As Daniel left the office, he remembered the pile of unfinished translations sitting on his desk. He would send it down the line to another translator. They were all swamped, but he now had something more important to do. He and Rex would get on a plane to Central Asia in the next few days.

But Daniel wasn't looking forward to it. As far as Daniel was concerned, death and bloodshed marred his once positive memories of the region. Not to mention the one person he knew in Tashkent who had warned him to never return.

————

THE NEXT MORNING, Daniel caught a taxi to the CIA headquarters in Langley. He planned to recruit Max to the MDF team so he could leave with him and Rex for Tashkent.

After Daniel swiped in with his pass, he headed up the elevator to Max's floor. The blinds on his office were drawn, and Daniel gave his door a knock. Max's door was usually open. There was no answer, so Daniel knocked again.

Daniel reached for the door handle, but then he had second thoughts. Max was the kind of guy who might have an office romance while on the clock. Daniel did not want to walk in on that. He knocked on the door louder and said, "It's me, Daniel."

Daniel tried the door handle, but the office was solidly locked.

Daniel found the closest office nearby that was open and asked if they knew where Max was. One man merely shrugged, but a courier delivering a package to the next office said he heard that Max had called in sick. Daniel figured this guy would probably know. He could see the younger guys taking a liking to Max.

Daniel got an idea. He went back to the man's office and asked if he could borrow the phone. He begrudgingly gave permission, and Daniel soon had Jenny on the line.

"So fun, right?" Jenny said with her normal perky attitude. "I can't believe we're still working together. And I'll be using my computer ninja skills while you and Rex are—"

Daniel interrupted Jenny. "This isn't a social call."

"That's too bad. I don't get enough of those," Jenny said.

"I'm serious now," Daniel said. "Check the CIA records and search for Max's security pass.

"Why are you sticking your nose into Max's business?" Jenny asked as Daniel heard her typing.

"Just a hunch," Daniel said. "I need to know if he came into work today."

A few seconds later, Jenny answered, "He swiped in really early this morning, like at 5:07 AM, and then he swiped out and left the building thirteen minutes later."

"It doesn't seem like he's sick," Daniel concluded. "If somebody were sick and couldn't come to work, they wouldn't come in that early in the morning to get something to work on at home. Can you trace his company phone?"

"That'll take a few minutes," Jenny said. "Hold on."

"I'm going to get Officer Carter on the line," Daniel said.

Moments later, Officer Carter joined the call, and Daniel explained the situation.

"That is suspicious," she agreed. "I will notify the proper people. It's out of your hands now."

"Okay," Daniel said. "This is messed up."

"I got it," Jenny interjected excitedly. "The location of Max's cell phone. It's right where Daniel is. Well, almost. It seems like it's sitting on his desk."

"He left, and he wasn't planning on coming back," Daniel thought out loud.

"I've got to check some things out, boss," Daniel said into the receiver before hanging up.

Daniel rushed out of the room and repeatedly pressed the down button on the elevator. When he finally swiped out of the CIA headquarters, he ran to Max's favorite spots. He went by several coffee vendors and bakeries without spotting Max.

He decided to go to the final stop after they all turned up empty.

After a short taxi ride, Daniel got off in front of one of Max's favorite establishments. The Russian bathhouse.

Daniel rushed into the lobby and asked the receptionist if Max was there. She appeared as if she had been working there since Khrushchev was in power.

She paused several seconds before answering and said, "Our whole facility is reserved for a private party all day, sir. Our normal business hours will resume tomorrow."

Daniel cursed under his breath, and he turned to run into the sauna facilities.

"You can't go in there!" the woman yelled after Daniel as he barged in.

"Max!" Daniel yelled. Daniel looked about the marbled room that was filled with steam, but nobody responded. Relieved, he saw that it was not filled with overweight old men disturbed by his presence. Instead, he discovered that the sauna was empty.

Daniel rushed into the next room filled with steam, and there he found what he feared. He spotted a man about the size of Max, slumped back with nothing but a towel around him.

Daniel hurried in to see if the man was alive. Once closer, he confirmed it was Max and felt for a pulse. He was about to go call for an ambulance when he realized he had been sloppy. There were other adjacent sauna rooms, and he hadn't cleared them first. He wasn't alone with Max in the sauna.

———

DANIEL SPUN AWAY INSTINCTIVELY, narrowly evading the garrote the attacker attempted to twist around his neck.

The attacker had another weapon, though. A baton cut through the steam and smash down on the marble, narrowly missing Daniel who continued to roll away.

As Daniel lunged at the attacker to engage him in close quarters, he cursed himself for his carelessness. Officer Carter would chide him for his sloppy tradecraft. Daniel had rushed in without bothering to check for a trap.

Or, had Daniel nearly made it in time to save Max?

Daniel put his grappling training with Rex to good use and brought the attacker down onto the hard floor. The attacker, dressed in black, a ski mask covering his face, was stunned momentarily. Daniel bridged his legs over the upper body and grasped one arm for an armbar. In a competitive match, the man would undoubtedly pass out. In a fight for life or death, Daniel knew he might have to break the arm.

But as Daniel braced himself to lean back to apply the maximum pressure on the arm, something made Daniel hesitate.

Though the attacker was powerful, he lacked the broad shoulders Daniel was accustomed to grappling with.

It's a woman, Daniel thought to himself.

The surprise gave the attacker the opportunity she needed.

She countered the armbar and slipped away. Daniel managed to grab her and yanked at her mask.

She pulled off her mask and sprang to her feet. Her blond hair fell to her shoulders, and she fled from the room.

"Who are you?" Daniel called out as he rose to chase her.

Daniel proceeded through the steam as quickly as he dared.

After hearing a crash, he came upon a heap of hot stones next to a searing hot electric prong. Steam poured forth as the toppled water pail spilled its contents onto the heating element.

Daniel stepped over it, but he slipped slightly and oddly bent his knee. Though he avoided serious injury, it allowed more distance between him and the woman.

When Daniel entered the back rooms, he paused and looked about. Steam no longer obscured his sight, but the laundry rooms and staff locker rooms formed a maze.

Daniel took a few quiet steps towards what he guessed was the shortest way to an exit.

The click of a shutting door lured Daniel through the maze until he reached the rear exit of the Russian bathhouse. Daniel pushed the door open and threw himself into the alley and looked both ways.

He caught a glimpse of the blond hair and black shoes turning into another alley about thirty yards away.

Daniel took a step to go after her, but his tweaked knee protested.

If I can't get her, I need Max alive to find out what happened, Daniel thought to himself.

Daniel stumbled back into the sauna, his knee hurting more with each step. When he found Max, he was breathing, but barely. Unable to calculate the possibilities of what Max had planned or expected in the sauna, he hurried back to the receptionist to call for an ambulance.

After making the call, Daniel turned to the angry receptionist and said, "I think you're going to need to close the sauna for the day."

As Daniel waited, he felt convinced that Max was a traitor. Perhaps Max had been expecting to meet with his handler, but the woman had been sent to tie up loose ends.

5

"I HEARD FROM YOUR FATHER," DANIEL'S MOTHER SAID LATER THAT night over dinner. She had made his favorite. Fettuccine Alfredo.

"That's unusual," Daniel said. "Let me guess: he couldn't tell you where he was, what he was doing, or when he would see you next. Which would be about never."

After being attacked in the sauna earlier that day, hearing about his father was the last thing Daniel wanted. Officer Carter had sent Daniel home from the sauna to get ready for his late flight to Uzbekistan with Rex. After she questioned him for most of the afternoon, she assured him she would handle the follow-up and that he had to focus on tracking the terrorists in Uzbekistan.

"It's not as though you're forthcoming about what you do," Daniel's mother chided.

"Come on. You know why that is. I can't talk about my work. Besides, I'm here, aren't I? You can't say I'm like Dad."

"No, I guess not," his mother conceded. "But aren't you leaving tonight? Have you seen Tina recently? You've talked a lot about her."

"I have?" Daniel asked defensively. "It's work stuff. She's joining the team. She's got some great skills."

"Skills?" his mother asked suggestively.

"Come on," Daniel said again. "Mom, you're incorrigible. We're just acquaintances, and hopefully coworkers. Dating a coworker can be a bit odd."

"It's working for Jenny and Rex."

"Who says they're dating?" Daniel asked.

"Just because I'm not in the intelligence business like you and your father doesn't mean I'm blind and dumb. I see how those two interact, even if they aren't dating, or going steady, or whatever you kids call it these days."

"Okay, so they like each other. That doesn't mean everybody on our team needs to date each other."

"As long as it's not Officer Carter," his mother said. They both laughed at that.

"You don't want me dating a woman your age?" Daniel said jokingly.

"What I want is a woman who can give me grandchildren, not an old lady like me. Of course, I would support anybody you decide to love."

"As long as they give you grandchildren," Daniel corrected her. She didn't argue with that.

"All joking aside, I've already lost your father. He's still alive, but I just wish I had family nearby that I could see and hug."

"Thanks for dinner, Mom," Daniel said as he got up from the table.

"I know you can't tell me what you will be doing overseas, but can you at least tell me you should be okay?"

"Yeah, I should," Daniel said.

"Don't be so carefree about it. Will you continue flying off like this mysteriously, and then look back years from now and regret not settling down? And hardly ever see your mother?"

"Mom," Daniel began to counter. But Daniel wondered if family life was compatible with his work on the MDF team. Officer Carter never married and didn't have children. Daniel's father had, and Daniel hated him because of his career.

"Do you absolutely have to go tonight? Why doesn't Rex go without you?"

"Yes, I have to go tonight."

His mother gave a pleading look. Pepper, the dog laying quietly in the corner, emitted a soft whine as he yawned.

"I'll give it some thought," Daniel promised. "And if it makes you feel better, Tina and I do have a date planned..."

"But now you have to cancel it because you're leaving tonight, don't you?"

Daniel couldn't argue with that.

"After this trip, I'll think this all through seriously," Daniel said. "But now I have to go pack. Pepper will keep you company."

Daniel's mother began cleaning the kitchen, and Daniel went upstairs to his room. His clothes fit easily into one bag, and he saved the gun for last. After unlocking his father's gun safe, he removed the well cared for Glock. Its weight and balance felt perfect in his hand. It was his father's favorite. Daniel packed it for the trip.

Daniel pulled out a file on Edwards and began studying the man who would be his new mentor in Uzbekistan. To his disappointment, most of the text was blacked out, even for somebody with Daniel's clearance.

About an hour later, Daniel's mother called up to let him know Rex was there to go with him to Dulles airport.

Daniel came down with his bag in time to hear Rex reassure his mother with bravado, "Don't worry, Mrs. K., Daniel will take out the terrorists and become a spymaster himself."

"That's what I'm afraid of," she said.

Rex headed back to the waiting taxi as Daniel kissed his mom goodbye.

Minutes later, while the streetlights rushed by as they rode in the taxi, Rex said to Daniel, "Officer Carter told me about your adventure in the sauna. She warned me we need to be careful over there."

Daniel waited for Rex's rebuke for falling into a trap and then allowing the assailant to escape.

Instead, Rex observed, "I agree with Officer Carter's assessment. Just when you are approached to join an investigation into a traitor, a suspect is attacked, and a bomb goes off in a city related to the investigation. Coincidence? Not in our business."

———

TASHKENT, Uzbekistan: a city unknown to most Westerners, it had been the Central Asian capital of the Russian Empire since the 1800s. Once the Bolshevik Revolution took hold, it was only a matter of time before communism spread to the land of the Uzbeks. The peoples of Central Asia were accustomed to being the crossroads of the East and West as the infamous Silk Road wound its way through the mountainous desert, and they were accustomed to all that this entailed. They had grown used to being conquered by foreigners. This had gone on for centuries.

Alexander the Great was the first such conqueror; his empire stretched all the way into Central Asia, and myths and legends still bear his name. But the Mongols and Islam also made headway into these lands. Most of them were smart enough to know which way the wind was blowing politically. None of them had any reason to think a principled stance for freedom, liberty, or independence would lead to anything other than poverty and oppression, and so the population was content, with rare exceptions, to celebrate the arrival of communism. Some resisted, but they were quickly dealt with. If there was any doubt about the benefits of being part of the USSR, those were demolished in 1966.

On the morning of April 25, 1966, a massive earthquake struck Tashkent. By some accounts, ninety percent of buildings were destroyed. The number of deaths is uncertain, but nearly the whole city became homeless overnight. Not willing to allow a disaster to go to waste, the Soviets quickly oversaw the rebuilding of the city. Working with a clean slate, the new architecture was Soviet, and the workers came from many other Soviet republics. This was government job creation at its best. Today, the average Tashkent resident knows that the sugar was sweeter under Communism, and they also remember that the Communists rebuilt their capital city for them.

And the Land of the Uzbeks reciprocated for the good of the USSR. They provided the front-line soldiers during the Cold War in Europe in case WWIII broke out, and the Soviet tanks began rolling West from Eastern Europe. Many such soldiers on the front lines would certainly die, especially if nuclear weapons were used, and so it was best to keep the Russians in reserve as the Central Asians became the necessary cannon fodder. All for the greater good.

Of course, none of them encountered such a fate, but Central Asia continued to serve its purpose for the mighty USSR. The space program launched out of present-day Kazakhstan, far from the prying eyes of the West. Factories and power plants were nestled away. The work kept the populace docile—there was always work, the men would say—even if it were backbreaking and dangerous. But they were also isolated targets, out of the way of strategic bombers, whether they be Nazi or NATO.

The USSR also flexed its technical muscle and showed off its economic prowess when it came up with an audacious goal. They wanted the Central Asian Soviet Republics to produce all the cotton necessary for the USSR. The USSR was dependent on non-Soviet nations for cotton, and they wisely endeavored to wean themselves off any foreign dependencies. Of course, their technological genius could overcome the fact that the land was mostly a dusty desert. The resultant irrigation system did produce cotton, but it also wasted about 70% of the water flowing through it, and it produced the greatest ecological man-made disaster. The Aral Sea shrunk from a resort-like sea to a salt-poisoned mud puddle. Central Asia was not only a good hiding place for industry and the space program, but it was also a suitable place to conceal disasters. Nobody else in the world knew or cared much about Central Asia.

Lastly, Uzbekistan was the staging ground for the Soviet-Afghan War. Always eager to expand, and hesitant to have non-communist neighbors, the Soviets began pressing the issue in 1979 by invading Afghanistan. Although they controlled the cities before long, many of the villages and countryside were not in favor of the new invaders.

Eager to give the USSR a black eye at any chance, the United States supported the guerilla fighters in Afghanistan who opposed the Communists. Many warlords vied for position, but they were all eventually seeking one thing: weapons. Stinger missiles could be used to shoot down the hated Soviet helicopters that terrorized the countryside. When the Soviet-Afghan war ended, the end of the USSR was not far behind.

Consequently, Afghanistan was an unstable mess. The warring factions were impotent when radical Islam exerted its control. Radical Islam also pressed for power in the new country of Tajikistan, embroiling that country in a civil war for years until the Soviet-style president finally regained control. But in Uzbekistan, the Communist leader holdover, Islam Karimov, immediately squashed any opposition, whether it was radical Islam or otherwise. For this, his people loved him. There was no civil war in Uzbekistan as there was in Tajikistan. Anybody who had opposed the president and his heavy-handed policies was done away with. Consequently, despite the injustice and bloodshed, everybody approved of President Karimov.

On an average day, well over 99% of Uzbekistan continued life as usual without fear of crime or war. The government had rebuilt their city, the Communists had given them all the work and food necessary, and so other human rights were not worth complaining about.

When the United States decided to retake Afghanistan from the Taliban in late 2001, Uzbekistan was an eager host. While thankful for the big-brother-like presence of Russia, President Karimov had to assert his power by showing his independence from Moscow. Hosting the Americans in old Soviet bases as they launched a war into Afghanistan was the perfect opportunity. Besides, if the Americans were able to clean out the Taliban, it would mean Karimov would not have to face insurgents from the South.

Daniel knew the language, history, and culture of Uzbekistan better than any other American. But he was still uncertain about one thing. It was clear that President Karimov was in charge. His secret police made sure of it. It was clear he was happy to welcome the Americans to enhance his own prestige and to keep the Taliban out. But Daniel was still uncertain about the one power that had a shifting relationship with President Karimov and his secret police: the Russian Mafia.

6

Tashkent, Uzbekistan.
About thirty-six hours later.
Saturday, September 14, 2002. 6 PM.

About thirty-six hours after they left America, Daniel and Rex landed in Uzbekistan. Jahongir Barakatulla, a police detective, was waiting for them on the runway. Jahongir was leading the bombing investigation. His shoes were black and polished to a mirror-like perfection, which contrasted with his dark-green uniform tinged with teal.

Daniel and Rex shook his hand. Daniel greeted him in Uzbek, noting his shiny and thick black hair above his long nose. Jahongir responded in English.

"I studied at Oxford," the detective said with a slight English lilt. "English will be just fine. I'll take you to the bomb site." Two other members of the police, or *militzya*, followed Jahongir.

When they arrived twenty minutes later in black Land Cruisers, Daniel was surprised. He nearly had to ask where exactly the bomb had detonated.

To Daniel's eye, it was a wealthy neighborhood. The walls and gates that formed the front of every house were ornate, heavy, and well maintained. But that was across the street from the blast site. The blast itself had been in front of a first-floor shop with apartments above. They seemed nice by the standards in Uzbekistan.

"Any Western embassies or other Western targets in the area?" Daniel asked Jahongir.

"There are a few European embassies within walking distance," he answered, "but it is hard to see how this bomb could be connected to them. It would have been easy to detonate the bomb much closer to any number of Western targets."

"Detonating a bomb here doesn't exactly send a message and spread terror, does it?" Rex said.

"Is there a security camera that caught anything?" Daniel asked. "Perhaps from a house across the street?"

"No," the detective responded. "None of them have a security camera trained on this area. The shop is too simple to warrant any security other than locking the metal gate at night."

"Has forensics discovered anything about the nature of the bomb?" Rex asked.

"Nothing was to be learned," the detective said. "Here, we don't bother looking for needles in a haystack, as you would say. Instead, we knock on doors and get people to talk. That's much more effective."

Daniel noticed the other two accompanying police standing

uneasily. For the first time, he saw that one of them had a sprinkling of gray hair.

"And you can always catch some unrelated troublemakers in the process," Daniel said. "You wouldn't want actual evidence to exonerate suspects." Daniel was testing how far he could push Jahongir. The two other police didn't adjust their posture, and Daniel ascertained they couldn't understand English.

"You can't argue with results," Jahongir said, pushing back. "Washington D.C. suffered more murders last weekend than our whole country in the last five years." Jahongir had caught Daniel's verbal jab, and so Jahongir did know English exceptionally well.

"Point taken," Daniel conceded.

Daniel guessed why the crime scene had been cleaned up so quickly. Government officials were keen on making the average citizen forget that such a bombing could take place in their beloved city. Cleaning it up and pretending as if it had never happened in the first place was crucial for outward appearances. They preferred the Soviet style of governing: if the government says there are no terrorists, there are no terrorists. Just as if the government says there is no poverty, then there is no poverty.

"How many dead?" Rex asked.

"Five," the detective said.

"Seems like this was a poor effort at terrorism," Daniel observed. "They didn't touch anything of value to the West, and I hate to say it, but they only killed five people. It doesn't make a whole lot of sense."

Daniel had more to say to Rex, but he didn't want Jahongir to hear.

"Follow me, and let's look at a few things," Daniel said as he went to look at the shop destroyed by the bomb.

"This is a small-fry job," Rex said to Daniel quietly as they huddled together, pretending to look at something so that Jahongir could not hear them. "This is not the type of thing the MDF team is supposed to be involved in."

"We need to start small," Daniel reminded Rex. "Besides, I need to know this guy in case I need his help in the future."

"Jahongir? What for?" Rex said.

"He's secret police," Daniel whispered, pretending to point at a detail on the building. "Soviet-style KGB-like. He's too young to hold his rank in the *militzya*, and those two others, though older, defer to him completely. He studied at Oxford, so he's privileged."

"You sure?" Rex asked.

"Any other questions I can answer?" Jahongir said while stepping closer to Daniel and Rex.

"What can you tell us about the people who died?" Daniel said.

"The shopkeeper was killed, a woman and her child were killed in the apartment above, a man at his car on the curb was killed, and so was another man walking by on the sidewalk."

"Autopsies?" Rex asked. "Can we see the bodies?"

"Are you doctors?" the detective asked suspiciously.

"He is," Rex said, pointing his thumb sideways at Daniel. Of course, Daniel was not a medical doctor, but Rex was half joking.

"Four of the five victims are Uzbek and Muslim," the detective explained. "According to custom, they have been buried within twenty-four hours. But I can tell you, it was the bomb that killed them. The fifth man, an Uzbek citizen of Russian ethnicity, is in the morgue. Dmitri Petrov. Seventy years old. We're still trying to get ahold of his family and find out where he should be buried. He wasn't from Tashkent like the other victims were."

"Thanks for your help, Jahongir," Daniel said. "Not that you need my opinion, but it looks like you're doing a great job here for your country and president."

"Let's let the doctor see that one body then," Rex suggested.

Jahongir shrugged, but a flash in his eyes made Daniel sense he had not anticipated this. They got back into the Land Cruisers for a ride to the morgue.

———

THEY RODE in silence for about thirty minutes. Daniel attempted to keep his wits about him, exhausted as he was by the travel. They parked outside a four-story, rectangular cement building that could have been anywhere in the former Soviet Union.

"Would the doctor like to perform an autopsy?" Jahongir asked as they entered the cool building. "Aren't you young to be a doctor?"

"I'm thirty-one," Daniel replied. "And I might ask the same about you."

Jahongir ignored Daniel's remark and ordered the staff to pull the bomb victim's body out of refrigeration.

Once the traumatized and burnt corpse was before them, Daniel pretended the gore didn't shock him. He made a show of thinking about what he saw while Rex, more accustomed to death, poked about the body.

"I'm sure your doctors will do just fine when they get around to doing an autopsy," Daniel announced after about a minute.

"There is not going to be an autopsy," the detective replied. "We can't afford to pay doctors to cut open bodies that were obviously killed by a bomb."

"Thank you again, Detective," Daniel said. "I think Rex and I will get some rest, then we can meet again tomorrow to figure out what to do next."

As Daniel and Rex rode away in their black Land Cruiser towards their hotel, Rex leaned over to whisper to Daniel.

"That Russian guy killed by the bomb blast," Rex said. "I don't think the bomb killed him. He was stabbed by a knife. If I were to kill somebody, the stabs were exactly where I would've done it. The burnt flesh made it harder to see, but to me, it was clear as day."

"We'll need to think that over," Daniel said as they got out at their hotel. "You think Jahongir knows? If so, what could Jahongir be hiding? But I'm so tired, I need some rest first."

"We've got a poorly executed terrorist bombing and a cagey secret police cover-up of a knifing murder," Rex announced before agreeing they needed rest. "God, I hope we wrap this up soon so that we can get back to catching real bad guys."

As Daniel thought about it in his room while trying to go to sleep, he remembered that he was supposed to meet Tina for dinner. It was Saturday. He hoped she would understand as he finally drifted off to sleep alone in his hotel room.

But the ringing phone woke him moments later.

"I just learned that Dmitri Petrov's widow will be coming up from Shahrisabz after a few days of mourning," Jahongir said over the phone after the customary exchange of greetings. "You could question her then if you would like."

Daniel hung up with a grunt.

———

EARLY THE NEXT MORNING, Daniel and Rex drove southwest through Uzbekistan's countryside towards Shahrisabz. After two hours, they would reach the ancient city of Samarkand, and then they would turn south for the remaining three hours that would take them over a mountain pass.

"You think Jahongir's going to be pissed we went down to Shahrisabz to interview the widow without telling him?" Rex asked Daniel as their Land Cruiser left behind a trail of dust.

"He called me late last night just to mess up my sleep," Daniel retorted as he took a swig of Nescafe, the best coffee available from the hotel. "I'm not going to play by his rules."

"This will show him who's in charge," Rex said with a grin. "What's the skinny on Shahri-whatever? I'll call it Shock-town."

Daniel explained that Shahrisabz means "Green City" in languages with Persian roots. Ironically, the city is considered the cradle of Uzbek civilization, whose language is not Persian, but Turkic. The same Tamerlane commemorated by a statue in Tashkent was born hundreds of years ago in the old city of Shahrisabz. The gates of his palace still stand in Shahrisabz, one of the few ancient sites not "restored" by the Soviets but left mostly in its original condition. Nestled among mountains on several sides, the city served the Soviet Union a specific purpose in the twentieth century.

During WWII, the Soviet Union realized they had to keep their industry safe from German bombers. Accordingly, some of it was moved to their Central Asian republics, far out of the reach of the invading Nazis. The city of Shahrisabz became the proud host of a giant silk factory. This silk factory had a sole purpose: produce silk for parachutes for Russian paratroopers. It served its purpose well during the war, and after the war, it continued to function. After the Cold War, Uzbekistan was loath to lose assets from the Soviet times, and so the silk factory continued to operate in a reduced capacity.

Daniel finished the explanation as he veered the Land Cruiser south along the outer edge of Samarkand. The two rode in silence as they wound up and down a mountain pass before descending into the historic Green City. Daniel didn't have to ask around much to find the home of Dmitri Petrov. It seemed he was the lone remaining Russian in town, and the townspeople were eager to help Americans driving in a Land Cruiser.

By lunchtime, Daniel and Rex sat across from Dmitri's widow. They sat on the floor, and the woman waited for a younger relative to serve tea on the short table between them. Zuhro wore black, as did the other female relatives gathered to mourn with her. She was probably in her mid-forties, much younger than the Russian victim. Stricken by grief, she was also confused by the American visitors, one of whom spoke with her in Uzbek.

"America has a partnership with Uzbekistan," Daniel explained. "You already know about your husband's unfortunate death, and I am working with the *militzya* to understand why your husband died."

"Where is the *militzya*?" Zuhro asked.

"Detective Jahangir Barakatulla is busy in Tashkent at the crime scene," Daniel explained, "and he has much work to do up there."

"But I told him I would come up in a few days, and he agreed to that," Zuhro said.

"Would it be possible for us to speak privately?" Daniel asked delicately.

Zuhro gave a questioning look, but she said a few words to the other woman. Zuhro rose and motioned for Daniel and Rex to follow her. The other women sat in silence as Zuhro led the men outside to stand under an apricot tree.

"Was my husband murdered?" Zuhro asked when they were alone.

The question surprised Daniel.

"Why do you ask?" Daniel said. "Did you have reason to suspect something."

"The detective who called seemed too important to be calling me."

She sensed Jahongir is secret police, too, Daniel thought to himself. Daniel tried to translate for Rex as the conversation progressed.

"We believe your husband was murdered," Daniel said. "And we are also hoping that you can help."

"I don't see how, but—"

"Can you think of anybody that would have wanted to kill your husband?" Daniel asked. "Did he have enemies in Tashkent?"

"He didn't know anybody in Tashkent," she responded. "And he certainly didn't have any enemies in Tashkent."

"How did you meet?" Daniel asked.

"I worked as a cleaner at the silk factory," Zuhro explained. "Dmitri came at the end of 1987. I was unmarried, and I was considered too old to marry, but Dmitri thought differently. After we were married, I quit working at the factory. His pay was plenty."

"What did he do at the factory?" Daniel asked.

"Paperwork. I didn't work directly with him. I was a cleaner. And he never talked about work."

"Did he ever go back to Moscow, especially after the Soviet Union fell?" Daniel asked.

"He never went back," she said. "He was happy here, and he had a new life here. He only has two old pictures of his parents who died a long time ago. He never talked about his life in Moscow."

"Did he tell you why he went up to Tashkent?" Daniel asked.

"He didn't say. He just said he had to go. I could tell he didn't want to talk about it. He has his quirks, but he is a very patient and kind man. So what if he doesn't want to talk about one thing once in a great while?"

"Did he seem happy or upset to go to Tashkent?"

"No. He seemed... *normalny*."

After Daniel caught up translating for Rex, Rex observed, "She's not telling us crap."

"Were you suspicious back in 1987 about this man from Moscow coming here to work at a factory?" Daniel asked, digging into the past and hoping to get lucky. Daniel knew he was really fishing now. "I'm sure that anything you share can only help. Anything at all. He was murdered, so help us find out who's responsible. Remember, we're Americans, and we're new here, so things that you take for granted, we might have no idea about."

"It's a known secret," Zuhro explained, lowering her voice, "that the Russians had something nearby. Something that nobody ever talked about."

Daniel gave a questioning glance.

"Nobody was sure, but we couldn't ask questions. The Soviet Union taught us to mind our own business, and so we all pretended ignorance. But there were certain places you'd never go outside the city. There are large blank areas on maps. And Dmitri was not the first man from Moscow to come. Several others had come. But none of them seemed to like it here. We all figured that most, if not all of them, worked for the KGB or the GRU."

GRU, the military's intelligence service, a rival of the KGB, Daniel thought to himself.

"But you said Dmitri worked at the silk factory, correct?" Daniel pressed.

"He went to the silk factory, anyway," Zuhro said. "But the work that he did, and how much was actually at the factory, I can't say. He never wanted to talk about work. And I was fine with that."

"Did you ever overhear him talking with somebody else from work?" Daniel asked.

But now Zuhro was beginning to clam up, perhaps afraid she had already said too much.

"I hope you find the murderer, but I must mourn Dmitri's death," Zuhro said.

Daniel and Rex left, unsatisfied they were any closer to finding the murderer.

"Seems tenuous, but maybe there is a KGB or GRU connection to Dmitri's death," Rex observed as their Land Cruiser exited the city to take them back to Tashkent. "Maybe that's why Jahongir is so shifty."

Less than an hour later, Daniel and Rex were winding their way up the road past mountainside tea houses towards Samarkand and then Tashkent.

"And, we know the Soviets launched their space program out of Kazakhstan," Rex continued, "so maybe they had something top-secret in or near Shock-town."

"Perhaps," Daniel speculated. "And it's not far from Afghanistan, so maybe they needed something to support the Soviet-Afghan War."

"Maybe we should've gone poking around in some of those blank areas on the map," Rex said.

"Maybe we will someday," Daniel said. "But I'll bet it's mostly mountains and wild goats. Maybe we should have tracked down her twin sister."

Rex gave Daniel a questioning look. "Her what?"

"In Uzbek culture," Daniel explained, "twins are always given the same names. For girls, it's Fatima and Zuhro."

Just then, their satellite phone rang, and Daniel answered it.

Daniel listened intently for a few moments and then hung up.

He said to Rex, "That was Edwards at the US Embassy in Tashkent. He said Ambassador Fitzpatrick didn't want him to tell us yet, but it turns out that our Russian friend, Dmitri, visited the US Embassy the same morning he was murdered."

———

THE TWO MEN SAT opposite each other, each eager to display his drinking prowess.

Although both held considerable power, the bald man was not only physically stronger, but he also held the trump card. He carried instructions from his master, whom everybody feared above all.

"Why this unusual meeting?" the dark-haired man asked the bald one.

"Are you not happy to drink vodka with me?" Pavel replied.

"I would never pass up the opportunity. But this is... *irregular*."

The two men were speaking in Russian at a *diskoteka* in Tashkent after lunch. It had closed at about two in the morning, and employees had recently arrived to clean and prepare for the next night's debauchery. Both men had business interests in the nightclub, but they were discussing something else entirely.

They paused as a waitress placed six shot glasses of vodka on their small, circular table. Three for each of them. Both watched the waitress walk away.

"It is irregular," Pavel conceded, finally turning his eyes back to the other. "But for a good reason. You know of the upcoming international security conference here? Misha is convinced the Americans will attempt something. This is merely a courtesy call to remind you to be ready. Your immediate service may be required on short notice."

"Of course," the man replied. "It's always that way."

Each man grabbed a shot glass and downed it.

"Also, this American must be kept safe at all costs. Even if we must kill others, this one is to remain. He is vital for Misha's purposes."

Pavel slid a small photograph across the table to the man. He looked at it and nodded. Pavel knew he didn't have to explain his master's reasoning. Pavel put the photo back into his pocket.

They each took their second shot of vodka.

"What about the SNB?" the dark-haired man asked, referring to the Uzbek secret police. "They don't seem as cooperative. If we have to take extreme measures—"

"You don't need to worry about them," Pavel said with a wink. "Lastly," Pavel continued, "not a word of this to that filthy wife of yours."

"Never," the man replied. "I assure you that we agree on that."

They each took their third shot of vodka.

Pavel rose, said goodbye, and left, guessing the other man was going after the waitress. Pavel hoped he would have his own opportunity with a woman that night.

Even more, Pavel yearned for violence and bloodshed. He reassured himself that it would come soon enough.

7

"I WAS RUINED," PATRICK RILEY CONFIDED TO DANIEL AND REX that night at dinner in Tashkent. The Intercontinental Hotel restaurant was a favorite for Westerners, and Daniel figured it must have been on the cleared list for security. Edwards had arranged the dinner for Patrick, Daniel, and Rex. Edwards and another man would be joining them later. "After Bishop went missing, I didn't know what to do. Agent Bishop was the highest KGB asset we had."

"And that's the man who was stabbed to death and then bombed in Tashkent just the other day?" Daniel asked.

Patrick Riley gave a nod. Now in his late forties, Patrick Riley had grown a beer gut, and his slightly red hair had taken on some more gray, but he still had the same convictions about the evils of communism that he had when he worked in Moscow. The only difference now was that everybody was convinced that since the Berlin Wall fell, communism was no longer a problem. Patrick felt otherwise.

"I'm positive that the man in the morgue is Agent Bishop," Patrick said. "I don't think you realize how big of a deal Agent Bishop was. When he sent the urgent meeting message about fifteen years ago, I couldn't believe it. I didn't know what the message meant, but I was nervous as hell when I went to the meetup.

"When he was a no-show for that, and then there was nothing at the backup dead drop, I didn't know what to do with myself. Forcing myself to keep my cover as a journalist was nearly impossible. I felt I had lost Agent Bishop. It was like losing a loved one. The worst was that I didn't really know what happened. The urgency of the meeting called for was such that I feared Soviet tanks were gonna roll across East Berlin into West Berlin and then WWIII was going to begin. Or, perhaps the prime minister of England was going to be assassinated by a KGB hitman. It seems crazy now, but back then, if Agent Bishop had a message of that urgency, that's the type of thing I was looking at."

Daniel could see Patrick's mind wander into the past as he looked about and took a long drink of his beer before continuing.

"Of course, none of those things happened. I figured maybe the emergency was diverted. But deep down, I feared that the urgent message was that he needed to get out. But there was a different signal for that. But maybe he panicked. I couldn't stand the thought of him being tortured and killed by the KGB. I stuck it out as a journalist for a bit, but then I was posted all over the former Soviet Union, mostly Eastern Europe. I did very little work for the CIA then. I truly was a journalist. I listened in on some Russian conversations in the field, but I was never given another agent to handle. I think somebody higher up was ticked off that I confronted the KGB guy I encountered when I was trying to meet with Agent Bishop. I just arrived in Tashkent to support the war in

Afghanistan, not as a journalist, but finally as a real embassy worker with the foreign service."

"You're not just here for the security conference?" Daniel asked.

"I'll be there," Patrick said. "Along with Billy. Edwards is coming in just for the conference. Of course, Ambassador Fitzpatrick, the jerk, will make an appearance."

Daniel wondered if those were Edwards' top suspects for the mole. Rex jumped into the conversation before Daniel's question raised any suspicion from Patrick.

"That must've been gut-wrenching, not knowing what happened to Agent Bishop," Rex observed. "Where were you when the bomb went off?"

Patrick Riley took a sip of his beer and continued his tale. "I was at my new place here in Tashkent. I didn't even have anything unpacked when the bomb went off. I was phoned and informed to stay in my house until the all-clear was given. After just a few hours, I was given the clear signal to come to the embassy for work, which I was anxious to do because I wanted to get out of my packed-up house."

"And when you got into the embassy, that was when you found out that Dmitri, or Agent Bishop, had paid you a visit?" Daniel asked.

"I got a message that a man who called himself Dmitri and said he was an old friend had come and wanted to talk with me and play chess," Patrick answered.

"Did you tell anybody about this?" Daniel asked.

"Yes, I told Billy, my boss," Patrick answered. "I could hardly contain myself. I knew Billy back from Moscow. Billy was a good guy back then, and he still is. It's the CIA guys above him that were horrible, especially his boss, Fitzpatrick. He was a real douche. Still is, as ambassador here. He never said as much, but I got the feeling from Fitzpatrick that he thought he was running the hottest spy network in all of Moscow. Damn. That arrogant prick couldn't run the treadmill." Patrick finished his beer and raised his hand for another.

"Billy doesn't seem like somebody who would want Dmitri dead," Daniel observed.

"No, I wouldn't think so," Patrick agreed. "I'm sure Billy passed news of Dmitri's visit up the chain, so he's not the only one who knows."

"But the timing is a bit fast," Daniel said. "If a man unexpectedly came to visit you, the information was passed on to Billy, and then he passed it on to somebody—"

"What are the odds," Rex said, jumping in, "that somebody up the chain could've gotten the information fast enough to both stab Dmitri and then also bomb him?"

"Unlikely, I agree," Patrick said.

"I think old KGB ghosts finally came back to haunt Agent Bishop," Rex observed.

"Did you learn anything about my poor Agent Bishop in Shahrisabz?" Patrick asked. "He feels like a lost uncle to me, and I've always wondered what happened to him."

Daniel and Rex shared what they had learned in Shahrisabz from Zuhro about Dmitri's past in Uzbekistan.

"So, he started a new life, found a new girl, and started a new job?" Patrick wondered out loud. "I guess there's no way he could've contacted us. I wonder if he was still gathering information, even if he didn't have a way to pass it on. Or, maybe he was completely out of the game. I would almost envy that possibility myself."

"What kind of information could he have gathered at a silk factory?" Daniel asked.

"Why would the KGB send men to work at a silk factory in the middle of nowhere?" Patrick countered. "Sure, the KGB liked to keep their eye on everything, but for a skilled KGB man from Moscow, going to Shahrisabz would've been about the worst thing imaginable."

Patrick's next beer arrived. He hesitated to lift it for a sip.

"Did you remember something about Agent Bishop?" Daniel asked. "Something triggered by what we told you?"

"There were always rumors, and we always wondered if the Soviets had secret facilities spread out all over their empire."

"They launched the rockets for the space program from the middle of nowhere, Kazakhstan," Daniel said.

"And Shahrisabz has their geological science location, plus the industrial silk factory. It would make the perfect cover for weapons research, or even production," Patrick said. "And if there is an accident that contaminates or kills a lot of people, then it's a lot easier to cover up than if it happened in Moscow."

"It looks like our next item for investigation is finding more about what's really happening in Shahrisabz," Rex said.

Daniel and Rex exchanged a knowing glance, having already discussed the possibility.

"I'd like to meet Agent Bishop's widow when she comes up here tomorrow," Patrick said.

"I'm sure that can be arranged," Daniel said. "How much will you tell her about her husband's past?"

Patrick shrugged helplessly and began to reach for his new beer. He looked up to welcome the final two members to their dinner party.

Daniel turned and recognized Edwards with his slicked-back

hair. The other man reached across the table for Patrick's beer and said, "Thanks for getting me one."

"Billy," Patrick chided as he shook his head from side to side.

———

EDWARDS AND BILLY sat down with Daniel, Rex, and Patrick.

The waiter came by and said, "The entertainment will begin soon."

"Bring me and my friend a beer," Edwards said to the waiter. "*Baltika Three*, please." After the waiter left, Edwards continued, "I'm sure you have already told the others, but Billy said you had an interesting visitor today. Who was it?"

"My visitor was Agent Bishop," Patrick answered. Daniel saw surprise register on Edwards' face. "Remember? I handled Agent Bishop in Moscow. You and Fitzpatrick can try to take all the credit for everything that happened in Moscow in the 80s, but I was the one who got all the gold from Agent Bishop."

"Don't use a codename in a public place like this," Edwards warned Patrick with a lowered voice. "It's because of such sloppiness that he disappeared."

A new party was arriving at the restaurant, demanding a pause in the conversation. Even in the dim light, they saw a hulking man enter wearing a perfectly tailored suit. Daniel guessed he possessed a chiseled physique in his prime, but he had gained some girth along with his age. His collar hardly contained what passed as his neck, which was as thick as his bald head. Daniel wondered what tattoos hid under his collar and cuff-linked sleeves. A few younger men followed him and sat with him. All the American men noticed the brunette who also sat with them.

Daniel was sure she was the reason Billy whistled under his

breath. Daniel overheard their conversation, and he could tell it was in Russian. The woman was displeased with something, but her complaint didn't appear personal. She wasn't bickering with a boyfriend; she was arguing with a coworker.

Patrick ignored the newly arrived Russians and continued with Edwards.

"Who cares about codenames?" Patrick asked bitterly. "The man is dead, and the codename was from fifteen years ago. And don't lecture me about being careful, because I handled Agent Bishop perfectly."

The waiter arrived with the beers for Edwards and Billy. Daniel and Rex asked for bubbly water with lemon, explaining they didn't want to drink while getting over jet lag.

Edwards took a sip and smiled as if surrendering to Patrick. "Okay. I'm not going to lecture you like Fitzpatrick. He's the stickler for protocol who would be throwing a fit about using codenames, even if it is dated."

"Quit the arguing. I need to drink," Billy said before taking a long swallow of his beer.

"How can you be certain this man was you-know-who?" Edwards asked Patrick.

"Who else could be an old friend named Dmitri who wanted to play chess?" Patrick answered.

"Rex and I spoke with his widow earlier today," Daniel said. "His arrival to Uzbekistan perfectly matches the timeline of his disappearance from Moscow."

"And what else did he write in the note?" Edwards asked.

"What note? The duty officer told me the message. He didn't say anything about a written note."

"He probably assumed you would find it on your desk. I did, just before coming here."

Patrick's mouth hung partially open.

"You read the note on my desk? What did it say?" Patrick demanded.

Before Edwards could answer, the lights dimmed to nearly complete darkness, and rhythmic music began blaring in the restaurant.

As promised, the entertainment had begun.

HORNS BLARED as the drums and tambourines pounded out the rhythms through the speakers.

A new entrant into the restaurant drew everybody's eyes. A belly dancer wearing a black veil stood at the front, slowly undulating her hips while swirling her hands in the air.

"*Woohoo!*" Billy called out while clapping. Others in the restaurant were enjoying the entertainment, but none cheered like Billy. Patrick was agitated, desperate to hear what was written in the note left by Dmitri.

The belly dancer worked her way down the center of the restaurant. Soon, she was between the table of Americans and the table of Russians. Billy no longer yelled. Instead, he watched in silence, as if hypnotized by the veiled woman's secrets. With her back to them, she approached the table of Russians. Her hips shook faster now.

The bald man turned slightly at his table to enjoy the entertainment as the belly dancer drew closer to him. Daniel caught him reach into his pocket for something. He couldn't be sure, but he thought he might have passed something to her.

Probably money, Daniel guessed.

Just as he noticed the brunette watching on with a bored

scowl, Edwards jabbed Daniel in the ribs and began yelling into his ear, the only way to communicate with the loud music. Daniel felt Edwards press something into his hand under the table. It was a metal key.

"The key to Dmitri's apartment," Edwards explained. "Use it for a thorough search."

Daniel gave Edwards a look as if to say, "Where did you get this?"

"From the morgue, but Fitzpatrick would throw a fit. Protocol, and all," Edwards responded. Daniel gave a nod of understanding.

Most people in the restaurant impatiently waited for the belly dancer's interruption to end.

But first, she came to the table of Americans. All but Billy looked away in embarrassment. Billy rose, clapping his hands, and approached her to dance along. Her hips now moved so rapidly, they appeared to be vibrating.

"Didn't he just start drinking?" Rex yelled to Daniel.

The belly dancer didn't allow Billy close, and she slinked out of reach. Her gyrations slowed as she went farther away, and finally out of the restaurant. When she was gone, the music faded, and the lights slowly came up.

Daniel looked over to the Russians and thought he noticed the bald man looking away after giving him an icy glare. Daniel guessed tattoos would have revealed he and his entourage were part of the Russian mafia. Daniel noticed that the brunette was gone. She must have left during Billy's attempted co-belly dancing.

"What was in the note?" Patrick hissed, leaning forward across the table towards Edwards.

Billy slumped back down into his seat, disappointed.

"I quote: 'I learned how to beat the French Defense,'" Edwards answered. "Whatever that means. If you ask me, anybody can beat the defenses of France."

"My God," Patrick said as he unsteadily placed his beer on the table, hardly managing to prevent it from spilling. "He learned the identity of the Wolf. The French Defense is from chess, and it was a code we set up. I had been pushing him, more than anything else, to obtain the identification of Russian agents. That was the hardest and riskiest. He passed mountains of other excellent intelligence, and yet I continued to push for the identities of Soviet spies. He finally uncovered the identity of the Wolf."

Patrick rose to leave and said they would talk later. Billy followed after finishing the last sip of his beer, stumbling slightly on his way out.

Once they were gone, Edwards took Billy's seat so that he sat across from Daniel and Rex.

"Who the hell is the Wolf, anyway?" Rex asked impatiently.

———

"THE WOLF WAS what all intelligence services fear most," Edwards explained to Daniel and Rex.

"The office had been plagued by a leak for years," Edwards continued. "A mole. But the mole never gave away information specific enough to nail down his identity. Or, at least, the Soviets never took action on enough specific information. We always feared it was somebody high up because they had enough flexibility and discretion to get varied and high-level intelligence."

"And you're here to catch a mole, aren't you?" Daniel asked. "And that's the Wolf."

"Over the years, we have had three people who could identify the Wolf," Edwards said. "The problem is, they all ended up dead before they could tell us anything. That told us that the Wolf had to be high up. If they knew somebody was about to defect, they could make sure the KGB got rid of them before they did so. The last one was found dead in an unused subway station in Berlin, days before the Wall came down. If he had waited a few days, he could've walked right into our embassy and told us who the Wolf was."

Both Daniel and Rex shook their heads in disbelief.

What a difference a few days could've made? Daniel thought to himself.

"But there's no way anybody could have known the Wall was going to come down, could they?" Edwards continued. "After it was clear to us that the Soviet Union was falling apart, we realized we had to make sure that this collapsing behemoth didn't cause even worse problems throughout the world. We stopped focusing on the Wolf and intelligence operations against the Russians. We had to prevent their top scientists from becoming mercenaries. The Soviet Union surely had weapons all over the world that had to be secured. If the Soviet Union completely collapsed, would there be millions upon millions of people starving to death, willing to do anything to eat?"

Daniel didn't say anything, but he wondered about the failure to secure weapons, having recovered a lost Soviet nuke just months before. The remaining Russians at the nearby table were getting up to leave. Daniel watched the confident gait of the bald man leaving while he listened to Edwards continue the tale.

"I thought we were going to get the Wolf after the Cold War ended," Edwards said. "A lot of very powerful people from the former Soviet Union were going to need our help. I met with Krushkov, who wound up being the last head of the KGB. I told him the Cold War was over. We would even let the Wolf go if they would only tell us his identity. And, of course, we would continue to help Russia survive, hoping to prevent all the previously mentioned problems that we both agreed would be catastrophic for the world."

"But that didn't work out?" Daniel asked.

"Krushkov called my bluff," Edwards said. "He agreed that the Cold War was over, but for him, it was really just a setback. Of course, Krushkov was a hardliner, and he later led the coup against Gorbachev that failed."

"And after that?" Daniel asked.

"I tried the same thing with the new KGB, which they so cleverly named the FSB," Edwards said. "Eventually, Putin became director of the FSB. I told him the same thing I told Krushkov. Russia was going to have some serious cleanup to do, and the US would help, but we wanted to know the Wolf's identity."

"And apparently, that didn't work," Daniel said.

"Not in the least," Edwards said. "Those Russians knew I was bluffing. They always seemed one step ahead, making the most out of everything, even if the world seemed to be falling apart around them. They were not going to give up the Wolf's identity. Of course, we always feared that the Wolf would uncover Agent Bishop, but it seems like he may not have until recently. Heck, not even I knew who Agent Bishop was until today. It seems that Agent Bishop disappeared years ago for entirely different reasons. And just when he claims to know the Wolf's identity, he dies? Surely Dmitri didn't take the Wolf's identity with him to the grave. He survived in the game too long to do that."

"And you think I might find something in Dmitri's apartment in Shahrisabz while his widow is up here tomorrow?" Daniel asked, referring to the key.

"I hope so," Edwards said. "Anything that can point me towards one of my three suspects."

"Who are...?" Daniel asked.

Edwards looked down at the table they sat at.

Patrick and Billy, Daniel thought to himself while giving a slight nod of understanding.

"And the ambassador," Edwards whispered.

Fitzpatrick, Daniel thought. *Damn. They all had long-standing careers dating back to Moscow and the Cold War.*

"Daniel can fill in my gaps of understanding," Rex said, "but we've got to pay somebody a visit tonight."

"Certainly," Edwards responded.

"I'll let you know if we find anything tomorrow," Daniel told Edwards.

Daniel and Rex left Edwards alone in the restaurant as they went to make a courtesy call to a tea house elsewhere in Tashkent.

———

"YOU SURE THIS IS A GOOD IDEA?" Rex asked Daniel as they got out of the taxi near the tea house. It was still before midnight. "She gave you a stiff warning last time you saw her here."

"I need all the help I can get," Daniel answered, not mentioning he wasn't sure this was a horrible idea. Part of Daniel wondered if he wanted to see her again to prove to himself he no longer loved her. That was, if she was still alive. Maybe the Russian mob had chewed her up and spit her out, but Daniel suspected she was too cunning for that.

Daniel and Rex entered the teahouse and passed two stocky men with bulges in their jackets. *Guns.* They headed towards the back room and its beaded door as they glanced at the patrons eating local meat shish-ka-bobs, *shashlik*, and drinking tea.

Two more men with bulges in their jackets moved in front of the beaded door as Daniel and Rex approached. They didn't say anything. Their body language said enough. You had to be somebody to get into that room, and they were nobody.

"Hey buddy, we just want to party," Rex said, acting like he was just another Westerner looking for a little bit more *oq choi*, tea mixed with vodka. But the two men didn't flinch. Others were drawing closer.

Daniel took a business-like approach.

"Tell Nigora that a good friend of her brother, Oybek, is here," Daniel said in fluent Uzbek to the man in front of him. The man looked at Daniel from head to toe. He tried to stare Daniel down, but Daniel didn't budge.

After what felt like a long silence, the man turned and went back into the room through the beaded door. Daniel and Rex exchanged a relieved look. The man returned moments later and allowed Daniel and Rex to enter.

The room was full of acrid cigarette smoke, and two younger men, about twenty, sat at the table. Directly across from Daniel sat Nigora, the woman who had almost outsmarted Daniel in Afghanistan, and had definitely outsmarted one of the most dangerous Taliban terrorists. Her hair and dress were as for a formal occasion. Her hair was pinned up with pearl accents that matched her dress. Beside her sat an Uzbek man who, Daniel guessed, was her husband. Daniel wondered if she had used her one million dollars from Afghanistan plus her marriage to cement her place in the game for power in the former Soviet Union. But did her husband know that Nigora's cunning and wits were her most valuable assets?

Daniel extended his greetings to each person sitting around the table in turn, continuing his perfect Uzbek. Rex stood back to keep an eye on the bodyguards in the room. Once the greetings were finished, Nigora's husband continued studying paperwork before him, ignoring the conversation in the room. Daniel wondered how much his massive gold watch cost, and how he had obtained it.

"I told you what would happen if you interfered in my business," Nigora said. She wore a smile, but her words were full of hatred.

"I am not here to interfere," Daniel responded.

"I can't imagine any other reason that you would be here."

Daniel hesitated a few moments as he recalled his history with her. He had lived with her family in Northern Afghanistan while he conducted linguistic research. Her brother had been his best friend before the Taliban killed him. Her father had been like a father to him, and Daniel had visited him in his last days. Her father gave up his life to kill several Taliban and saved Rex's life. Daniel wanted to plead with her and remind her of her gentle and kind father. He wanted to remind her of all the fun they had had with her brother, Oybek. He wanted to go back to the way she was.

"I think we can help each other," Daniel said.

"If you tried to help, you would be interfering," Nigora replied.

"You might not realize it," Daniel continued, "but you owe a lot to me."

"It's because of you that my family is dead," Nigora said. Her smile had disappeared.

"Do you remember when you left Afghanistan?" Daniel asked.

Nigora sat silently.

"As you drove north," Daniel explained, "to eventually come

here, an American jet flew overhead. Your car was in its bombsight."

"And you told them not to bomb me?" Nigora guessed.

"You're welcome," Daniel said. "I felt a duty to your father and your brother to let you live. But more than that, I know that you are a victim of the war and the Taliban."

"I'm nobody's victim," Nigora asserted. "Look around. I have everything I want."

Of course, Daniel thought to himself, *you've lost your father, brother, your conscience, and your soul. But what is that to somebody who's been ruined by war?*

"I need to ask a favor of you," Daniel said.

"What makes you think I would extend a favor?" Nigora asked.

"I assure you that it would be in your best interest to help me," Daniel answered. "Rex and I have power now, and we can use that to help you in a tight spot. But, for now, I just want to know something small and insignificant."

"And what would you like to know?" Nigora asked.

"A man was murdered the other day," Daniel said. "I want to know who did it."

"That is no small piece of information," Nigora warned. "It's not my normal line of business. Besides, the police here are most excellent at finding murderers."

"I wouldn't ask unless the circumstances were unique," Daniel assured her. "If you find anything, let me know."

"If I learn anything," Nigora said, and then paused before continuing, "and if the price is right, I might tell you."

"His name was Dmitri Petrov," Daniel said. "He was over seventy years old. He was stabbed and then blown up in the bomb blast I'm sure you've heard about."

Nigora shrugged as if she didn't care and then stated, "Your interference is over now."

"And don't you interfere with me," Daniel warned with a calm voice. "I'm fighting the War on Terror for the United States, and if you interfere with me, you make yourself an enemy of the US."

"Go well," Nigora said, ignoring Daniel's threat. Her husband also looked up and muttered a farewell wish.

Daniel and Rex turned to leave, and they walked warily out of the back room. Daniel wondered to himself if he truly was fighting the War on Terror, or if he was hunting for the Wolf.

It seems, Daniel thought to himself, *that Dmitri connects the two.*

As they exited the tea house, a woman brushed past them, heading towards the beaded door in the rear. The men with bulges in their jackets didn't hinder her.

"Hey, wasn't she...?" Rex whispered to Daniel after they were outside.

"She looked exactly like the woman at the Intercontinental Hotel with the Russians," Daniel agreed.

"But this woman was blond, not brunette," Rex said.

"You noticed?" Daniel asked. "I won't tell Jenny."

"Ha-ha," Rex joked as they waited for a ride to their hotel.

8

"Yes, that's him," Dmitri's widow, Zuhro, said before her knees went limp and she nearly collapsed.

"I'm sorry you have to see him like this," Detective Jahongir Barakatulla told her. He replaced the sheet over Dmitri's partially charred and mangled corpse.

"Who would do such a thing?" she said in shock.

Daniel and Patrick Riley were also at the morgue the next morning for the identification. Rex was waiting in the car in the parking lot.

"Perhaps we can leave here for someplace more comfortable," Patrick said in Russian to the widow. "I knew your husband when he was in Moscow, but then we lost touch. I want to know about the new life he found here." Patrick explained to Daniel what he was saying in Russian.

Zuhro nodded, and the group of them exited the morgue.

Daniel found the morning sun to be a welcome relief from the cool building full of death.

"How did you know my husband?" she asked as they made their way to their parked cars. "Not many had American friends."

"I was a journalist," Patrick explained. "We crossed paths a few times, played chess, and then he stopped showing up."

"He played chess?" she asked. "He never told me."

"Maybe he only ever played with me," Patrick said, and it appeared that he was trying to add some levity to the situation. When Patrick translated it for Daniel, it struck him as odd, and he had to pause and think about it. He also noticed the bags under Patrick's eyes.

What had he and Billy done after leaving the restaurant last night? Daniel wondered.

Rex was waiting in the car. Jahongir was about to leave in his police car with two of his men, and Daniel told Zuhro she could ride with him to the US Embassy where she could talk more with Patrick.

She nodded with understanding, but then raised her hand to her mouth. It stifled her scream.

Daniel turned to look, and the first thing he saw was blood.

Patrick fell to the ground, gasping. Blood gushed from his neck despite his hand grasping at it.

Daniel's first instinct was to stop Patrick's bleeding, but when Daniel reached his body on the ground, he knew it was too late.

Rex and Jahongir's two men had already started the footrace after the killer.

Daniel followed.

They entered a neighborhood with narrow streets that wound in every direction. Many were not wide enough for a car. Daniel knew they would be lucky to be able to keep track of the killer. After a few turns, he lost sight of the chase. Daniel slowed to a jog and looked around, realizing he was disoriented and lost.

Not exactly a pro move, Daniel chided himself.

About a minute later, Daniel encountered Rex in the maze of small streets. They exchanged exasperated looks.

"Surely he couldn't have stopped in this small neighborhood to hide," Rex said. "He would be trapped."

Daniel took a few deep breaths and thought. A major road was somewhere on the other side of the neighborhood.

"He's probably trying to get to the larger road beyond this neighborhood," Daniel said.

Resuming the chase, they wound their way along the path, always in the general direction of the main road that lay beyond.

Bursting out of the edge of the neighborhood, they came upon a four-lane street with cars clipping by at about thirty-five miles per hour. With multiple lanes, it didn't seem likely the killer would have crossed on foot.

Did he have an escape vehicle? Daniel wondered frantically. But there was no place to park on the shoulder and timing a pickup would have been impossible.

"There!" Rex yelled, pointing to a pedestrian bridge up the road that had chain-link fence reaching up on either side for safety. Several people were crossing it, including a young man who was hurrying, but not running.

Daniel and Rex ran towards the bridge, yelling after the man to stop. The passersby, well trained in ignoring emergencies, did nothing to stop the man who soon began running.

To Daniel's relief, Jahongir's two policemen appeared on the far end of the pedestrian bridge. Both had police batons ready to use. The sight of the policemen made the killer stop, but he turned to see Daniel and Rex coming towards him. The killer was younger than Daniel, fit, but Daniel couldn't tell where he was from or how well he was trained for such a situation.

"He still has the knife," Daniel said to Rex.

"I specialize in dealing with armed combatants," Rex said. "I'm always armed." Rex cracked his knuckles. "Stay out of my way, and I'll take care of him."

"We need him alive," Daniel reminded Rex.

The killer went towards Rex and Daniel, but he soon saw the look on Rex's face. Without another option, he began scaling the fence on the side of the pedestrian bridge. Daniel looked down and didn't think anybody could survive the drop, especially if they were struck by an oncoming vehicle.

Rex scrambled up after the man. Daniel watched from below. Rex grabbed the attacker's foot just as he crested the fence. Rex let go of the fence, releasing all his weight onto the man's leg.

The man struggled to support his weight plus Rex's while clinging to the fence with his fingertips.

He would soon fall onto the pathway.

Instead, a gunshot cracked, the sound coming from the pistol of a policeman who had just arrived and was standing next to Daniel.

The first shot in the man's back made him release his grip and fall. The second shot made sure he was dead.

"What the hell are you doing?" Daniel yelled, first in English, and then in Uzbek.

The policeman returned an angry look as if to tell Daniel he wasn't to be questioned about how to do his job.

Daniel cursed, not bothering to argue with the policeman. After he rolled the man over, he saw that he was already dead. Daniel guessed he was a teenager. Probably a desperate kid trained to do somebody else's dirty work. He would never reveal who had sent him to kill Patrick, or why, if he knew.

Daniel and Rex walked away in disgust. Daniel wiped Patrick's drying blood off his hands and onto his pants.

"Police work that bad can't be an accident," Rex said to Daniel.

"It only could have been worse if he had shot us," Daniel said. "I can't wait until we get to the bottom of this."

"At least we know Patrick, most likely, was not the Wolf," Rex said with sarcastic optimism.

"That leaves Billy and Fitzpatrick. But if the Wolf had Dmitri killed to protect his identity, why would he have Patrick eliminated?"

"Perhaps Patrick had a clue he didn't yet realize was significant," Rex speculated.

"I hope we find something in Dmitri's apartment later today," Daniel said as he felt for the key in his pocket.

———

It took Daniel and Rex about two hours to reach the ancient city of Samarkand in their black Land Cruiser before Daniel realized something.

"I don't feel so good about driving around in this vehicle," Daniel said. "Ambassador Fitzpatrick seemed a little too prickly about allowing us to take an embassy vehicle without telling him where we were going."

"We are an easy target to follow," Rex agreed.

"Dmitri was killed in short order, and then Patrick. It seems to me that the Wolf doesn't mind killing. He apparently didn't care that Patrick was with the US Embassy."

"But this Land Cruiser can get us away from anybody, and it has bulletproofed glass along with reinforced sidings," Rex countered. "And the heated seats are nice."

"I say we go into Shahrisabz a bit more discretely," Daniel said, remembering how much attention their vehicle attracted when they visited Zuhro the previous day. "Just to be safe."

"What do you have in mind?" Rex said.

On the outskirts of Samarkand, Daniel pulled over and talked with some of the shopkeepers. He got back in the car after a short discussion and said, "They told me where we can get a less conspicuous vehicle."

Another ten minutes later, and they arrived at the taxi bazaar that fed taxis to Shahrisabz, Kharshi, Tashkent, and Bukhoro. As always, it looked to Daniel like a mass of disorganized, parked vehicles with people milling about. He was amazed that people ever managed to drive their car away.

After parking several meters away from the fray, Daniel asked around for the taxis to Bukhoro.

"Aren't we going to Shahrisabz?" Rex asked.

"We are," Daniel said. "But I don't want anybody to see us asking around about Shahrisabz."

"Got it."

Daniel brushed off several pushy taxi drivers. Daniel even had to pull his arm back as some of them grabbed at his hand to drag him towards their vehicle.

It took Daniel about fifteen minutes to find the car that he wanted.

"A 1997 *Nexia*," Daniel finally explained to Rex. "That year was a good year. This car should serve us well."

Rex gave him a raised eyebrow.

"It even has power steering," Daniel said. Rex wasn't sure if he was serious or joking.

"Could I rent your car for a few days?" Daniel asked the driver.

"Where do you want me to take you?" the driver responded.

"You don't have to come," Daniel said. "I can do all of the driving. You just sit at home, drink tea, and enjoy the money that I'm going to pay you. Then, when I bring your car back after a few days, you will have made four times as much money than driving taxis, except that you got to sit at home, drink tea, and play with your grandchildren."

The man looked back and forth at Daniel and Rex. Daniel couldn't blame him. The deal surely seemed too good to be true.

"I just want your car for about four days," Daniel said. "You have a good car, and I can give you four hundred dollars right now. When I bring your car back, I will give you another five hundred." Daniel pulled out a wad of hundred-dollar bills to show he was serious.

"What's wrong with your car?" the man asked. "Why would you want my car?"

"Okay, I'll give you five hundred now," Daniel said, avoiding the question, "and I will give you another five hundred when I return your car. And, you can have the keys to my car while I'm gone. If I never bring your car back, then you can keep this one."

"Six hundred now," the taxi driver said, "and—"

"Six hundred more when I get back," Daniel said, finishing his sentence. "Agreed."

Minutes later, Daniel watched as the man pulled the black Land Cruiser into a detached garage in a nearby neighborhood, away from snooping eyes. The man didn't flinch while Rex moved gun cases and put them in the Nexia. Daniel was counting out the six hundred dollar bills as Rex did so. They said farewell and shook hands.

Daniel and Rex were soon heading towards the mountains in the south, and then on to the city of Shahrisabz over the mountain pass.

"Somehow, I don't think Fitzpatrick would approve of how we are ignoring protocol by temporarily trading an embassy vehicle for this hunk of junk," Rex said with a grin. "And do you really think we'll find a clue about the Wolf's identity in Dmitri's apartment?"

"He was a pro," Daniel said. "He wouldn't allow such information to go with him to the grave."

"But he was a pro because he never left clues behind," Rex countered. "Oh well, at least I can enjoy the non-heated seats before we go looking for clues that may not exist."

———

"I'VE GOT a bad feeling about this," Rex warned as Daniel jiggled the key into the lock of Dmitri's apartment.

"Well, I've got a good feeling," Daniel answered as he leaned into the door, trying to find the sweet spot at which it would grant access.

"It's just kind of creepy to search a dead guy's apartment," Rex whispered. The door creaked open. "And without his widow's knowledge or permission."

Daniel stepped into the entryway of the apartment and looked out onto the street. The apartment building was only two stories, with four units on each floor. Dmitri's apartment was on the first floor, probably because of his position within the KGB. Daniel noticed that he had a water faucet in the yard, not something everybody had. There was no indoor plumbing other than a toilet and bathtub with a showerhead. The street was dark. The neighbors were at least pretending to not notice their presence.

Neighbors learn to mind their own business when a KGB man is around, Daniel thought to himself.

Daniel and Rex clicked on their flashlights and scanned the apartment's interior. As expected, the apartment was sparsely appointed. In the entryway was a tiny kitchen on the left, and on the right was a raised sitting area with the traditional low table. Beyond that, a hallway led to a sitting room, bathroom, and two bedrooms. After they glanced through each of the rooms, they began searching. Daniel searched through the extra bedroom, which seemed more like a combination of an office and a library. Rex went to the main bedroom.

Rex commented, "There isn't much here to search."

"That's normal," Daniel said. Daniel searched through the desk drawers and leafed through several of the old Russian books that were meaningless to him. He did notice an old copy of *The Communist Manifesto* that made him chuckle for a moment. He checked behind the two pictures hanging on the wall. Daniel paused to gaze at the two photos, and he guessed they must've been Dmitri's parents.

Were those all that Dmitri brought from Moscow to Shahrisabz? Daniel wondered.

Daniel found a photo album, but it began with him and Zuhro. She didn't look much different. As was customary, neither of them was smiling in the pictures.

Except for one.

In that picture, Dmitri held a baby, and he couldn't hold back a smile. Daniel wondered what had happened to Dmitri's baby. Daniel made a mental note to ask Zuhro.

"I feel like a real a-hole going through the widow's underwear," Rex said from the other room. "Good thing nobody is searching through my room right now."

"Maybe Jenny is," Daniel joked.

"Not funny," Rex warned.

"I don't like doing this to a widow, either," Daniel said, "but I've got to think Dmitri left something that would lead us to the Wolf."

Daniel and Rex moved to the front of the house, and Daniel started going through the kitchen while Rex searched the seating area.

"Looks like a bunch of storage to me," Rex said as he lifted the door that exposed the area below the raised seating area. "They don't pay me enough for this." With a sigh, Rex got down on all fours and began pulling out old kitchen items. He then crawled under the seating area with his flashlight.

Daniel scoured the two kitchen cupboards that held the teacups, plates, and a few other dishes. There were no nooks or crannies in the kitchen to hide anything. Daniel halfheartedly pulled the refrigerator away from the wall to inspect it.

"Oh crap!" Rex yelled from under the seating area.

"What is it?" Daniel knelt at the entryway and shined his flashlight in. He jumped back as a rat shuffled by. It raced across the floor and disappeared under the kitchen cabinet.

Rex hurried out from the storage area and nervously tried to brush off the dust and dirt that clung to him.

"There is definitely no secret document down there," Rex said panting. "If there was, that rat ate it."

"Nothing in the kitchen either," Daniel said. They quickly searched the sitting room next, but it only contained a small television, two chairs, and a rug.

"We have to be more thorough," Rex concluded.

Daniel's shoulders sagged. Destroying Zuhro's furniture, pulling up floorboards, and busting into walls didn't sit well with him.

"I'm starting to think that if Dmitri left a clue behind, he wouldn't have left it in his home," Daniel said.

"I don't want to destroy what few belongings the widow has, either," Rex said, "but we've got to thoroughly search this place."

"Wait a minute," Daniel said, holding up a finger. He went back to the bedroom and picked up a book and declared to Rex, "*The Communist Manifesto.*"

"Didn't everybody have to own that?"

"Maybe, but this copy is well read. Look how the spine is bent, and the pages have been turned. A lot."

"Surely you don't think he wrote the Wolf's name in the book, do you?" Rex asked.

Daniel didn't answer, but instead pulled out a folded piece of paper. He unfolded it and told Rex, "Cyrillic cursive, probably in Russian. Doubly incomprehensible to me."

"But he couldn't risk anybody finding that," Rex protested.

"Unless it was in code, and this book was the key to the code," Daniel said. "That would explain why it's so worn, and yet I'm sure Dmitri didn't read and reread it for pleasure."

"Even if you're right and that is a coded message, and that book is the key..." Rex began, but he didn't finish.

They both knew.

Patrick Riley was the one man who would know how to use The Communist Manifesto *as a key to decode the message. But he was dead.*

"I'm not giving up," Daniel said, as much to Rex as to himself. Daniel pulled out the photo album. With a razor blade, Daniel began disassembling every page and peeling off stamps from postcards. He searched for microdots that could contain pages of tiny text in a dot the size of a pinhead.

"If anybody did that to my photo albums," Rex said, "I would kill them."

Daniel held the photos inches from his face and scanned it

with the flashlight, desperately hunting for a microdot. After frantically peering at photo after photo, Rex finally said what Daniel knew.

"There's nothing to find there," Rex said. "Part of being a good agent is knowing when to move on. If we're not going to bust this place apart, then it's time to go."

Daniel took a few deep breaths and finally agreed with Rex and said, "Maybe we should find Zuhro's twin sister and talk with her."

Rex didn't have time to agree because the front door of the apartment crashed open as an imposing and massive dog charged in and barked furiously at the intruders.

Daniel saw that the dog was on a leash, but he wasn't sure the owner would be able to restrain it.

9

THE MAN HOLDING HIS DOG BACK ON A LEASH YELLED, "WHO ARE you?" and waved a metal pipe in the air with his other hand.

Daniel and Rex moved away from each other, making it impossible for the dog to attack both of them.

The man swung the metal pipe at Daniel. Daniel dodged just in time to partially block the blow with his forearm.

Daniel lunged at the man to grapple and disarm him. He saw that Rex was trying to fend the dog off.

Daniel took the man down to the ground and knocked the pipe from his hand.

Daniel grabbed the pipe and ordered the man to call off his dog just as the animal saw his master in danger.

"Stop! Sit!" the man yelled in Uzbek.

The dog immediately sat and looked at him expectantly. The dog's puffy brown hair nearly concealed his dark eyes.

Rex brought over a flashlight and shined it in the man's eyes.

"It's okay," Daniel said to Rex while regaining his breath. "This guy is no assassin."

Daniel asked, "Who are you?"

"My brother-in-law and my sister-in-law live here," the man said. "I saw lights, and I knew that nobody should be in here."

"Then you know Dmitri and Zuhro?" Daniel said. "We're trying to solve Dmitri's murder."

"What happened to Dmitri?" the man asked. "We only know that he died in Tashkent. Why isn't Zuhro here?"

Before Daniel could explain, Rex said, "Ask him how he got an attack dog that's part brown bear and part Ewok."

————

ONLY MINUTES LATER, Daniel and Rex were seated on the ground and drinking tea in the middle of the night with the man. His own apartment was just a few minutes' walk away. The light was dim due to the electricity's low voltage, but it didn't seem to bother the man. Daniel learned that his name was Jamol and that he was married to Zuhro's older twin sister, Fatima.

After Fatima had prepared a meal, despite Daniel's protestations, and they were on the second pot of tea, they finally got to talking about what was on everybody's mind.

"What happened to Dmitri?" Jamol asked Daniel.

"I can't tell you much at this point," Daniel answered.

"Did you see Fatima's sister? How was she?"

"She was fine," Daniel said. "But Dmitri is dead. That's why we, unfortunately, had to search Dmitri's apartment."

"Something more must have happened for that to be necessary."

Fatima entered with another pot of hot tea and sat down.

"Is Zuhro safe?" Fatima asked.

Daniel hesitated before he answered. "We think she is safe. She has not done anything wrong."

"What is she asking about?" Rex asked Daniel in English, assuming the other two did not understand.

Daniel explained she was asking about her sister and whether or not she was safe.

"But we can't guarantee anything," Daniel said, switching to Uzbek. "If Dmitri told her something, or if she is aware of something, even if she doesn't know its significance, then your sister could be in danger. Tell me about Dmitri and Zuhro's relationship. You might know something that could help. Was there anything odd about their relationship?"

"They had a baby that died," Fatima said. "That made my sister very sad. But it only got worse."

"How so?" Daniel asked.

"They had another child, but then he died when he was two years old. It was an illness."

"Are you sure?" Daniel asked.

"Of course I'm sure," Fatima said defensively. "If you had seen the boy, you would've known he was sick."

"What about before they had children?"

Fatima bit her lip and looked away. She looked down and tried to hold back tears.

"Did she not want to marry Dmitri?" Daniel asked.

Instead of answering, Fatima got up, covered her face with her hands and walked out of the room to the kitchen.

"I'm sorry if I've offended her in some way," Daniel said to Jamol. The Uzbek man leaned over the table and told Daniel why Fatima had left crying.

"Her sister slept with Dmitri before they were married. She was married to another man."

Daniel sensed it was difficult for Jamol to say these words. An unfaithful woman brought shame upon the entire family.

As Daniel explained to Rex, he noticed a young boy, about ten or twelve years old, peeking in through a crack in the doorway from another room.

So Zuhro has lost all of her children, but Fatima had at least one, Daniel thought.

"Now we know of somebody other than the Wolf who has a motive to kill Dmitri," Rex observed. "Zuhro's first husband. And Zuhro lied to us. She said she had never married before."

Daniel nodded with understanding before continuing with Jamol.

"Thank you for telling me. I know it is not something Fatima would like to talk about. But if I did not know about it, it could end up hurting Zuhro in some way."

Daniel wanted to press for more details, but he had to do so delicately.

"Are you certain she had done such a thing?" Daniel asked.

"It was suspicious at first because she went to work on the weekend when she normally would not work," Jamol explained. "Her husband found out she wasn't going to her normal workplace. She was going to a place in the mountains. She said it was a *dacha* connected to work. But, of course, it was Dmitri's *dacha* in the mountains."

Daniel knew that such flimsy evidence was sufficient to convince an Uzbek husband of his wife's unfaithfulness, but Daniel needed more details. The fact that Dmitri had a country house in the mountains added another wrinkle to investigate. Sensing this, Jamol continued.

"She had no children with her first husband, but then after she started working at the *dacha*, she had to get rid of a baby before it was born. I don't know exactly what happened to her first husband. I heard that he went to Tashkent."

"Can you tell me where this *dacha* is in the mountains?" Daniel asked. Daniel then translated for Rex to catch him up.

"This country home is another potential hiding place for clues," Rex said.

"Traitors have been known to squirrel away classified information below *dacha* floorboards," Daniel said in agreement. "We may find just what we're looking for there."

"For Fatima's sake," Jamol continued, "I followed Zuhro to the *dacha* once. I will never forget its location."

Daniel retrieved a map from the car, and after a few moments of thought, Jamol pointed at the *dacha*'s location. It was just inside one of the large blank areas on the map, somewhere in the mountains. Daniel wasn't sure if that was a good sign or not.

His eyes were heavy, and Jamol rolled out mats onto the sitting room floor for Rex and Daniel to sleep on. Daniel gratefully stretched out and began to drift off to sleep. As he did so, he reminded himself to ask for the name of Zuhro's first husband before they left in the morning.

———

DANIEL WOKE AFTER SUNRISE the following morning. Rex was already awake, anxiously pacing about the room.

"Time to wake up, sunshine," Rex said. "We need to call in, now that we haven't been murdered in our sleep. Jamol gave me this." He handed Daniel a piece of paper with a name scribbled on it. It was Zuhro's first husband's name.

Daniel pulled himself up to the short table and rubbed the sleep out of his eyes. Rex handed him the satellite phone. He dialed Jenny in D.C.

"Glad to hear you two are still alive," Jenny joked over the satellite phone. "Guess who's here? Muhammad is working with me, and he's a great partner. Say hi, Muhammad."

Daniel heard Muhammad bashfully say hello in the background.

"By the way," Jenny said before Daniel could continue, "Ambassador Fitzpatrick knows you ditched the Land Cruiser. Its GPS says it's been sitting in Samarkand. He is super pissed. He told me to inform him of your position if I learn it. And he pointed me to classified material he wants you to know about. And Edwards has a message for you also."

"I've got a lot to tell you right away," Daniel cut in. "First, I found the location of Dmitri's *dacha* in the mountains." He read off the longitude and latitude from the map.

"I'll have Muhammad look at satellite imagery as we talk," Jenny said.

"Secondly," Daniel continued, "it turns out that Zuhro, Dmitri's widow, was previously married. Dmitri was an affair. Her first husband, last we knew, lived in Tashkent." Daniel read off the man's name for Jenny. "See if you can dig anything up on him before I ask around myself."

"Got it," Jenny replied. "More?"

"Lastly," Daniel began, but then paused for a moment. "We uncovered what we think might be a coded message. And we're guessing it used a book as the key. How do you feel about cracking a code?"

"That depends. What exactly do you have?"

Daniel explained the note he found inside *The Communist Manifesto*, which he hoped was the key to decoding the message.

"Normally, to encode a message," Jenny began to explain, "you would use a randomly generated key. Like static from outer space. Unless the message was long enough and a supercomputer used brute force to repeatedly guess until it arrived at a combination that formed intelligible language, such a code is unbreakable. But even then, that could take so long that by the time it was cracked, it wouldn't be useful."

"But what if the key is *The Communist Manifesto*?" Daniel asked.

"In that case, the key wouldn't be random, and so that could conceivably speed up the process, but it would still take too long."

"How long?" Daniel asked.

"If ever, it could take supercomputers days, weeks, months, or even years."

"I'll read the Russian letters to you, and you and Muhammad begin working your magic, okay? I don't know Russian so it could be more obvious than I'm guessing, too."

"Don't get your hopes up," Jenny warned.

Daniel took several minutes to read off the sequence of Cyrillic letters to Jenny. Once he was done, he asked about the intelligence Fitzpatrick wanted him to know about.

"Interestingly," Jenny said. "It's related to Dmitri's country home. And it looks like Muhammad has satellite imagery."

"Can you tell me anything about getting to the *dacha*?" Daniel asked.

"I'm sure you can see on your map the road into the mountain that takes you closest?"

"Yeah," Daniel confirmed.

"There's a building at the foot of the mountains, and then

there are two more along the road. At the second one, that's where you want to get out and go by foot into the mountains. Of course, I don't know what's in that building, though."

Daniel hoped it was empty, or a harmless tea house.

"But here's what Fitzpatrick wanted you to know. There's what we would call a 'black site' in those mountains, just north of Dmitri's *dacha*, apparently."

"Is it dangerous?" Daniel asked.

"Well, Fitzpatrick wants you to approach it with caution, armed, and with backup."

"What's there?"

"We don't know, but the Uzbek government gave Fitzpatrick their approval for us to use any means necessary to carry out our mission there."

"The Uzbek government doesn't know what's going on at their own black site?" Daniel asked with frustration.

"Or, they do know, but they don't want anything to do with it," Jenny said. "Officer Carter consulted with Fitzpatrick and Edwards about it, and they think it's controlled by the Russian mafia. The Uzbek government would be happy for us to clean up their mess without any cost to them. It looks like a few buildings with a heli-pad, all fenced in."

Rex gave Daniel a look as if to say, *What the hell? This is messed up.*

"Edwards ordered Gunner and Walters directly to K2 to support you," Jenny continued. Daniel remembered that those two were part of Rex's squad that raided a Taliban village to recover a nuke.

Rex was grinning now.

"And Edwards also ordered Tina to join you as well. She's already flown in to Tashkent and is already on her way to K2."

"Tina?" Daniel asked. He both anticipated and felt nervous about seeing her. Recovering from the surprise, Daniel said, "Send Gunner and Walters the coordinates of the *dacha*. We'll meet them there. We can't wait for them."

"You sure you shouldn't wait?" Jenny asked. "There is a reason you're getting more firepower."

"We need to search that place as soon as possible. We don't have time to waste."

"Don't get yourself killed before Gunner and Walters arrive," Jenny said.

"Tell them to keep as low a profile as possible." Daniel imagined the two special forces men, fully armed, cruising around the city in a Humvee and then going off-roading in the mountains.

"Give Rex a hug for me," Jenny said. "I will inform Officer Carter, Ambassador Fitzpatrick, and Edwards of your location and plan. Fitzpatrick and Edwards, though, will be busy at the security conference that's starting today in Tashkent. And I learned not to call the ambassador *Fitzy*, by the way. Let's talk again in twelve hours."

The communications link ended.

"She told me to give you a hug," Daniel said. "But I think you get the idea."

"You made the right decision," Rex said. "We don't have time to wait around here for the big guns. We need to get to that country home and search it immediately. If we have a chance of uncovering the Wolf's identity, we can't delay several hours."

Jamol's twelve-year-old son entered with a tray of tea and round bread. Daniel thanked him and devoured breakfast.

Minutes later, after promising Jamol and Fatima they would find answers for Zuhro, Daniel and Rex went to get into the *Nexia*. They paused to pet Jamol's dog, who now appeared as a giant teddy bear. Daniel drove with Rex towards the road into the mountains. He pulled over at the empty building at the mountain's base so they could prepare for their insertion. About fifteen minutes later, they proceeded up the road, their guns no longer in cases.

10

"YOU SURE WE CAN'T STOP FOR TEA?" REX ASKED AS THEY GOT OUT of the *Nexia* at the second building along the mountain road.

Daniel gave a look down to Shahrisabz below and said, "Maybe we can get some *osh* on our way back."

An elderly man sat on a raised platform, drinking tea in silence, but he watched Daniel and Rex pass to the rear of the building and then into the mountains. They carried their handguns in holsters, and their packs contained the other equipment they anticipated they might need. They hiked until the tea house was out of sight.

Surrounded by mountains in every direction, Daniel checked the map one last time.

"That way," Daniel said as he pointed up a mountain ridge.

A gentle breeze carried the bleating of goats. Daniel spotted the animals near their route up the mountain.

Daniel and Rex both instinctively took cover behind a boulder when they saw a man near the goats.

"You think he saw us?" Daniel asked.

"Have a look," Rex said as he handed Daniel a pair of binoculars.

Daniel studied the man from a distance for a few moments before reporting to Rex.

"If I had to guess, I would say he looks Russian but is posing as a goat-herder. He disappeared over the mountain ridge, but I don't know if that's because he saw us or not."

The two waited several more minutes, but the man didn't return. Coming out from behind the boulder, they continued their path up the mountain. They soon reached a steep incline covered with small rocks. Before the demanding progress that would require going up on all fours, they drank a few sips of water. Daniel tested the satellite phone.

"No signal," Daniel reported.

"Could be lots of reasons," Rex said. "Are the batteries dead?"

"Very funny."

"I'll keep my short-range radio on. We'll know as soon as Gunner and Walters are in range."

"Until then, it's just the goats and us," Daniel said as he began picking his way up the rocks. Rex followed, and they sent trickles of stones and pebbles tumbling down as they worked their way to the top of the ridge. Keeping his head down, Daniel focused on putting one foot in front of the other.

Daniel looked up to see if the goats were still there, or if the Russian had reappeared. Sweat got into his eyes as he saw that the goats had wandered away.

He went to put his next hand down, but the rocks shifted.

Daniel let out a short yell.

A tan snake slithered among the stones and right past his hand.

"Jesus!" Daniel yelled as he recoiled and slid down the rocks for several feet before regaining his hold near Rex. "I nearly grabbed a snake. It freaked me out."

Rex chuckled and continued his way up the ridge. Daniel looked about and saw nothing but mountains. Not even the goats were in view anymore. After a few deep breaths, Daniel resumed the ascent with Rex.

When he finally reached the top, Rex was crouching among the goats. Nobody else was in sight. They were on a shelf that led to another ridge after about one hundred yards. The flat area was about fifty yards wide, and to their left, the mountains continued their rise. To their right, the mountain dropped off. One hundred yards forward, and then they would have to climb again. Large boulders littered the flat area. A few were large enough to provide cover, though the sun was no longer low in the sky. Daniel slumped down in the sliver of shade and took another sip of water.

"Tired?" Rex said, looking down at him. "This is a warmup."

"Hey, I didn't bust you up for not knowing how to speak Uzbek with Jamol and Fatima," Daniel pointed out.

"Point taken," Rex said. He pressed a button near his ear and tried to hail Gunner and Walters. He waited and then shook his head in the negative. Pulling his Glock from the holster, he cocked it and confirmed he had extra magazines of ammunition. Daniel followed Rex's lead and checked his equipment.

"Ready for anything," Daniel said.

Daniel and Rex moved forward among the boulders along the shelf towards the next ridge.

———

"AFTER WE GO UP THAT RIDGE," Daniel said while pointing ahead, "the black site will be another ridge over to the left, and the *dacha* will be to the right. I'll lead the way." There were another fifty yards of flat ground before they would have to resume climbing.

Dust shot up from a nearby boulder. A bullet ricocheted away. The boom of the rifle registered in Daniel's ears as he instinctively fell to the ground.

"Sniper!" Rex yelled.

Rex lunged out from behind the boulder and pulled Daniel to cover.

"It could be the guy we spotted earlier," Rex said. "Or maybe he had friends. If we're lucky, he will think you're dead." As Daniel caught his breath, Rex looked at the boulders near them. "We're pinned down here. But we can work our way back the way we came among the boulders. Going forward, they aren't large enough to cover us. The sniper must be to our left somewhere."

"He already missed," Daniel said.

"Or, he's a pro and missed on purpose," Rex said. "If not, he'll get one of us in the next fifty yards. If we stay here, he'll wait, and he'll send his friends to get us. We've got to move, and that means heading back."

"We're too close to turn back," Daniel argued.

"Without my rifle, I can't effectively shoot back," Rex said. "You might get lucky if you press on, but we need to fall back and then move forward strategically."

"I feel we're so close to figuring out Dmitri and Patrick's deaths."

"I do too, but... Wait."

Rex paused and listened to his radio earpiece.

"It's Gunner and Walters," Rex responded. A smile came to Rex's face. "They're nearby, and they do have rifles. They'll unpin us from the sniper, and then we'll fall back, join them, and then we can press on."

Rex frantically relayed the situation to Gunner and Walters.

Moments later, they heard more gunfire erupting.

"One of them is firing while the other moves closer to the sniper. Once they spot the sniper, they'll root him out."

The gunfight continued for several more moments.

Then everything was silent. Daniel felt another mountain breeze. Again, it carried the bleating of goats.

"Sniper has fallen back," Rex reported after listening to his radio. "We're in the clear to hurry back and join them. Ready?"

Daniel looked about fifty yards towards the ridge he would have to climb.

"Follow my lead, and we'll be in safe company soon."

Rex braced himself and then crouched as he ran back to the previous large boulder. The gunfire resumed, and Rex paused to fire back with his pistol. Daniel waited.

Rex gave Daniel a questioning look from about fifteen yards away, waved at him to follow, and then hurried on.

Instead of following Rex, Daniel turned the other way.

Daniel ran from behind the boulder towards his next climb. The gunfire rattled on, behind him and to his left.

Daniel thought he heard Rex yell after him, but when he looked back, he saw Rex snaking his way among the boulders, intermittently firing his pistol towards the mountain.

About thirty seconds later, Daniel threw himself to the ground behind a boulder at the base of his next climb. His chest heaved as he peeked back at the firefight in the mountains. Rex and his men constantly shifted.

They fired, then moved.

Fired, then moved again.

Their adversaries were doing the same. Daniel thought they were in about equal numbers.

Daniel smiled as he realized the gunfight was slowly shifting farther away. Rex was strategically giving up ground to draw the firefight away from Daniel's position.

Daniel looked up, and he began putting one foot in front of the other as his legs pumped him up the mountainside towards Dmitri's *dacha* and the black site.

———

AFTER DANIEL HEAVED himself onto the top of the mountain ridge, he collapsed to the ground, panting. He had expected to be shot as he climbed, but he had made it to the top. The gun battle was fading into the distance. Daniel was confident Rex and his men could hold their own in a fight, but Daniel had to make sure their sacrifice was worth it.

Daniel looked to his left and spotted the next mountain ridge that would lead to the black site. If its guards were drawn out and engaging Rex, then this was the perfect time to inspect it.

Looking back the way he had come, he faintly heard the gunfire continue intermittently, but he couldn't see the combatants. Forward and to his right, the path sloped upwards in the distance. Daniel was drawn towards the *dacha*, and so he continued on the long upslope. The area was barren: no goats, no shrubs, and no boulders.

After thirty minutes of plodding, Daniel spotted a cabin nestled on a ledge on the side of the mountain. Daniel was out in the open. He scanned the surroundings but saw nothing of concern. Pressing on, he arrived at the *dacha,* which was now a short climb above him on the mountainside. Daniel picked his way carefully up towards the simple structure. He peered into the small window, but he didn't see anybody. It appeared empty.

Daniel put his sack down by the entrance and pulled his pistol. He took in one deep breath, turned towards the door, and kicked it in. Daniel's eyes darted about the dim room. The small window and now open door were all that allowed in the light. As his eyes adjusted, and he aimed his pistol around the *dacha*, he saw that nobody was there. The room held sparse furniture and a kitchenette. A doorway led to the second and only other room. Moving quickly into that room, he saw that it was empty as well.

Daniel lowered his pistol. The *dacha* was empty.

Daniel went back to the door and shut it. Dmitri's country home was a tiny, two-room affair. One room had a reading chair, sitting desk, and a kitchenette consisting of a sink and a counter not more than a meter long. Off of that room was the single bedroom that was just big enough to hold a double bed. A minuscule bathroom, without a shower, was attached to the bedroom.

Daniel wondered how many times Dmitri came here. The chess set on the reading desk hinted that he had come most recently without Zuhro. She hadn't known that he played chess.

Had America's most potent spy left a clue here as to the Wolf's identity? Or was this place only for Dmitri's thoughts and dreams, now just as dead as the Soviet Union itself?

Daniel rested for a few moments in the eeriness of the *dacha*. He felt he was paying respect to Agent Bishop, one of the most effective agents in intelligence ever, by leaving the place undisturbed.

After several minutes of waiting, Daniel finally forced himself to search for clues.

He rifled through the kitchenette and other furniture. It revealed little. The chess set hid nothing. There were a few family pictures of Dmitri and Zuhro. Another picture was that of a child about two years old. And canned fish graced the kitchen cupboard.

Daniel thought to himself, *if I were to lose a child, would I want to see a picture of him? Or, would I try to forget him?*

Daniel opened the door and pulled his gear sack in from outside. He took out the crowbar. It was time to look through every nook and cranny for anything Dmitri might have left behind. Daniel began working with the crowbar into the ceiling, the walls, and then the floor.

As Daniel tore away at the small structure, he wondered if Dmitri's ghost was trying to guide him towards something he had hidden. More likely, he was shocked by Daniel's destruction because there was nothing to find.

After hours of demolition, Daniel had found nothing, but he had worked up an appetite. Without a radio to communicate with Rex and the others, he tried the satellite phone again. It still didn't work. Daniel guessed that it was intentional, and it was because of the black site.

Deciding to wait until dark to approach the black site, Daniel forced himself to eat a can of Dmitri's canned fish from the kitchen. Then he stretched out on Dmitri's lumpy bed and tried to sleep.

As night fell, Daniel knew he was going to be on his own. He wondered if Rex and the others were okay. He didn't hear any more guns. He tried the satellite phone one last time. Again, it didn't work. Daniel was alone, unless Dmitri's ghost was with him.

11

DANIEL LEFT THE *DACHA* AT NIGHT, CARRYING EVERYTHING HE thought he might need to break into the lab site. Going up the first mountain ridge was slow because of the deep pitch black and uneven ground. Daniel couldn't remember the last time he had seen so many stars in the night sky, unpolluted by the glow from a city. When he reached the top, he scanned down below. There was more black emptiness. Beyond the next ridge was the black site.

Using night vision goggles, Daniel scanned the area for guards. Finding none, he proceeded cautiously into the valley. After a drink of water, he continued the arduous trek up to the final ridge.

At the top, he dropped to the ground, peered through a fence, and took in the sight before him. The complex of cement buildings below surrounded by fencing above looked just like the Soviet installation Daniel had expected. Each of the buildings had a single light out front, and a few armed men circulated among the buildings. But they weren't wary. They talked and moved casually.

Daniel spotted a single *Kamaz* truck parked near a gate. A helipad was at the far end, encircled with lights.

Something drew the attention of the men. They all focused on a man exiting the central building. Daniel zoomed in on him and recognized him immediately. The thick neck and bald head were unmistakable. Instead of the perfectly-fitted suit from the Intercontinental, he now wore combat boots and desert camos. A rifle was in one hand. If he wasn't the sniper, he was probably one of the men who had been in the gunfight with Rex.

Is Rex still alive? Daniel wondered as he frantically scanned the facility below him.

With the others gathered around the bald man, he spoke in an agitated manner. Daniel guessed that was good news. Hopefully, he was angry they hadn't killed or captured Rex. Daniel watched anxiously as the bald man continued giving orders. Something was about to happen, but Daniel didn't know what.

The clinking of rocks behind Daniel made him turn and draw his Glock. He jerked his head from side to side with the night vision goggles, looking for the new arrival.

Daniel exhaled deeply and cursed when he saw a small herd of goats nearby.

At least they aren't bleating, Daniel thought to himself. *Watch my back, guys.*

The rumble of the truck's engine below filled the valley, and Daniel refocused on the black site. The truck pulled through the gate and headed away. A single guard remained outside the central building, smoking.

I can handle one guard, Daniel thought to himself. Eager to unlock the secrets of the Soviet black site, Daniel pulled the bolt cutters from his bag and began cutting the fence in front of him.

———

DANIEL PEEKED around the building one last time. A plume of smoke rose from the guard's mouth. A cigarette was in one hand, a rifle in the other. Daniel hid behind the nearest building. The guard was about thirty yards away at the largest building in the middle. To Daniel, it appeared to be a prison or a barracks. The windows spaced along the wall didn't have glass. They were barred. Metal rebar bent into the shape of steps formed a ladder near the back to allow roof access for maintenance.

Daniel knew he would not be able to find answers inside the buildings if the guard was still around. Daniel rested his bag of equipment on the ground and pulled out one item. He hoped the crowbar would do the job and he wouldn't have to kill the guard. The Glock in his holster was backup in case the crowbar wasn't adequate.

Daniel silently closed the distance between the rear of the two buildings. He pressed his back against the wall when he arrived at the central building and held his breath.

He heard nothing. He still had the element of surprise.

The next part would be harder. If Daniel wanted to use the crowbar, he would have about ten yards to close by foot without cover before he could strike. Would the guard react too quickly?

If Daniel turned the corner with his pistol drawn, he could shoot the man from about ten yards with ease. But that would create noise and probably end the guard's life.

Daniel thought of a third option.

He went near the back of the building and began climbing the rebar rungs up to the roof. Daniel soon made his way on the roof to the front of the building. He peered down at the guard below.

If Tina could see me now, Daniel thought to himself. *Would she be impressed with the infiltration so far?*

Daniel knew Jenny would probably laugh. Rex would... Daniel hoped he was still alive.

Perhaps Dmitri's ghost was watching, waiting for Daniel to unearth one of his secrets.

Daniel looked down again. It wasn't a long drop. Probably less than fifteen feet.

Daniel waited for the cigarette's end to glow orange, indicating a deep drag.

With the crowbar gripped in both hands, Daniel dropped down from above. He aimed for the man's head, but he incorrectly judged his attack.

The guard turned slightly.

The crowbar missed and cracked into the guard's collarbone instead. They both crumpled to the ground.

Daniel rose, his ankle throbbing from the awkward fall, and he grabbed at the guard before he could recover and draw his weapon. Daniel put the guard into a sleeper hold, just as Rex had trained him.

The shock of the injury from the crowbar and the lack of oxygen soon knocked the guard unconscious.

Daniel took a few deep breaths and pushed himself away from the unconscious body.

Daniel got to his feet with adrenaline coursing through his veins. He grabbed the guard's rifle and his knife. Daniel pulled up his sleeve. He was no tattoo expert, but he recognized the Cyrillic characters and guessed the man had been in prison or was part of the Russian mafia. Or both.

He saw a large padlock on the front door. He found a matching key on the guard's belt loop. But Daniel was drawn to the building he had initially hidden behind.

Daniel ran over to the other building, but the door was fastened shut. A wax seal, like a big stamp, was pressed into the doorframe and door. Daniel couldn't read the Russian writing on the seal, but he guessed it was a dire warning to any who would dare to open the door.

After a few attempts with the crowbar, Daniel decided the door was not going to give way. Daniel went back to his equipment pack and pulled out explosives. He pressed them on the door as Rex had trained him, and he went around the corner to detonate.

Daniel covered his ears as best he could and pressed the button.

The boom shook Daniel. It rattled through his whole body. He knew he would never get used to that. But after the blast, the door was no longer connected to the building, and there was silence. Daniel drew his pistol and stepped over the fragment of the wax seal laying on the ground as he edged his way in. He scanned for attackers.

But nobody was inside.

Daniel had entered the office of Dmitri Petrov, former KGB archiving expert and intelligence supervisor of the black site. Daniel was the first visitor since Dmitri sealed it shut when the Soviet Union dissolved.

———

AFTER PASSING through a small foyer with an empty coat tree, Daniel entered another room about twenty feet wide and forty feet long. A wooden table ran its length, and a large wooden desk sat at its end. Lining the walls of the room were giant file cabinets.

Behind the desk, portraits of the Soviet Union's leaders glowered. On top of the desk, stacks of paper waited. The table also held several stacks of documents arranged in an indiscernible pattern.

Fitting, for an archivist, Daniel thought.

Everything was covered in a thick layer of dust, undisturbed for years.

Daniel went to the desk first. Many of the documents had a passport photo on the top right corner, biographical information on the left, and then the rest appeared to be a personnel report.

Were all these people prisoners here? Daniel wondered, unable to read the Russian text in the reports. But there were hundreds, if not thousands, of files. Even without entering the other buildings, Daniel guessed the black site couldn't hold more than a few dozen prisoners, let alone host the guards.

The only personal item of Dmitri's that Daniel noted was the chess set stored in one of the file cabinets. Daniel imagined Dmitri poring for hours over documents at his desk, pulling files from the cabinets, placing them on the table, rearranging them, and studying them.

Daniel realized that Dmitri must have been doing more than storing and sorting paper. He was analyzing files. But what, or whom, was he looking for? And for whom?

If Dmitri left a clue here, where would he leave it?

Surely not in a pile of paperwork.

Would he leave a clue here at all?

Daniel didn't know what he had hoped to find, but he grew increasingly frustrated with his lack of progress. He didn't know how long the guard would be unconscious, and he didn't know when, or if, the others would return. He couldn't stay here long. But he couldn't leave empty-handed.

Daniel forced himself to slow down and think. He assessed

what he had seen. There were several KGB files from the Soviet days. There were lots of personnel files from all over the former Soviet Union. Nearly all of them were men. Additionally, many of the files were military or intelligence-related. All the files covered people of some considerable rank, whether they were in the KGB, GRU (the army's intelligence), navy, or any other branch.

Dmitri was part of a manhunt, Daniel thought. *Prisoners of special interest were interrogated here, and then Dmitri analyzed and filed the information from the interrogations.*

Daniel wondered if Dmitri was part of the effort to hunt down himself, the vaunted Agent Bishop.

Daniel was about to leave Dmitri's office when he decided to check for one last thing.

Seconds later, he'd found what he was looking for. Dmitri indeed had a safe in his office. It rested on the floor beneath his desk. It wasn't hidden, but it was virtually impossible to move. Daniel quickly decided he would have to use the last of his explosives to blow the safe open, despite the risk of damaging its contents. He placed the explosives on the safe, went back into the foyer, and pressed the detonation button.

After a thunderous boom that echoed within the office, the safe opened and revealed its secrets.

From the safe, Daniel retrieved a file folder that looked like the other personnel files, but he knew there had to be a reason Dmitri kept it in the safe. On top of that was a single document. It seemed to be a certificate. Daniel could make out Dmitri's family name. Was it a marriage certificate with Zuhro? Daniel thought he deciphered a weight in kilograms, and he guessed it was a birth certificate of one of his children. But why would he keep this one?

Another item in the safe made no sense to Daniel. A black jewelry case held a diamond engagement ring. Though it was valuable, it offered no clues to Daniel. His mind went back to the birth certificate.

Daniel thought it was a curious item to keep in his office safe, but he didn't have time to think about it. Daniel shoved the file folder, the certificate, and several other random folders from Dmitri's desk into his pack. He had to get as much intelligence as he could out of this office. He slid the ring in its case into his pocket.

Daniel left the office with the key from the guard. He thought it might be for the large building that Daniel now suspected was a prison. Perhaps it would yield more clues than Dmitri's office.

———

DANIEL LOOKED BACK at the guard, still laying on the ground unconscious, as he wrestled the key into the lock on the central building. When the door finally granted him access, he discovered a small anteroom to a long hallway. Doors with bars stretched down the hall. Noticing handcuffs hanging on the wall, Daniel grabbed them and went back outside. After handcuffing the guard, he dragged him inside and cuffed him to one of the bars forming the barrier between the entryway and the prison cells. After taking another key hanging on the wall and flipping on a light switch, he entered the row of cells.

Daniel ran down the hallway quickly, peering into each cell in turn. They were all empty. Except for one at the end.

The last cell on the left held a man at least fifty years old, wearing a gray jumpsuit. Once he realized that Daniel wasn't one of his captors, he gave a broad smile that revealed more gaps than teeth.

Daniel began to unlock the door. As he did, he wondered if he was doing the right thing.

The man said something excitedly in Russian. Daniel gave an embarrassed look and listed the languages he did know: Uzbek, Tajik, Dari, and English. The man shook his head at each one.

"*Amerikansky?*" the man said.

"*Da,*" Daniel said, exhausting his knowledge of the Russian language. He pulled the cell door open.

The man stepped out of his cell and took in a deep breath. Daniel feared it may have been his first time out in a while. The man hobbled towards the exit, and Daniel followed. They were going to have to leave soon, especially if Daniel was going to guide this frail man back to friendly territory.

As they passed the man handcuffed at the front, the former prisoner gave him a kick and spat on him. A Russian expletive slipped from his lips.

Daniel peeked out the door to see if anybody had arrived. No, they were still alone at the black site.

But Daniel didn't know for how long. He turned and motioned for the man to follow him, but the man stood up straight and pointed to a side door.

"*Amerikansky,*" he said while pointing to the door.

Daniel waved his hand again. He wasn't sure how much more time they had until others came back. And if they came back to an unconscious guard, a missing prisoner, and a burgled office, they would hunt Daniel tirelessly. And if he was trying to flee in the rugged mountains with a weak former prisoner, Daniel didn't like his odds.

But the freed man was resolute.

"We've got to hurry then," Daniel said as he pulled the door open and looked down a staircase. The stairs wound downward into darkness.

Daniel had always heard that the Soviets had basements nobody ever wanted to go into, even if it wasn't the basement of the KGB headquarters in Moscow.

————

PAVEL JUMBLED up and down in the passenger seat of the Russian 4 x 4 *Niva*. The transfer of the cases taken out of the mountain facility had gone smoothly. First, the *Kamaz* truck moved them to their abandoned warehouse on the outskirts of Shahrisabz where they were placed in another *Kamaz* truck. Pavel sent his most trusted man with the shipment of cases to the north while he returned to the facility with the others.

Pavel had often wondered what was so important in those cases to his master. And why was his master just now ordering them to be relocated via truck to his mansion in the mountains north of Tashkent?

Pavel obeyed the order without question or hesitation, but it had come at the most inconvenient time.

Pavel and three of his men had been engaged in a gunfight. They had held the upper ground, and they had pursued their opponents throughout the mountain terrain in a dangerous game of cat and mouse. Pavel hadn't felt such exhilaration since his time in *Spetsnaz* special forces late in the Soviet-Afghan War.

Pavel knew that he and his men were engaged in a gun battle with challenging opponents. They moved constantly, fired expertly, and were much more challenging than the Afghans he had defeated so quickly years ago.

But Pavel and his men had steadily pushed them back. He

sensed that they were American, or at least a NATO-trained special force, but he didn't care. His orders had been clear. Deadly force was to be used on any who would approach his master's secret facility in the south.

But when Pavel's master ordered him to disengage to relocate the cases, Pavel knew the cases must have been of the utmost importance.

Pavel hoped he would have the satisfaction of re-engaging with the same skilled opponents in a gun battle soon, but he was convinced that this would be his last trip to his master's secret facility.

His master was cleaning up and closing it down.

"What about the prisoners?" Pavel had asked his master over the radio.

"Do nothing else until those cases are safely on the way to me in the north," his master had ordered.

"And then what shall I do with the prisoners?" Pavel asked.

"Execute them," the master said. "Dump their bodies into a deep ravine. They must never be found."

Pavel moved his head from side to side, cracking his thick neck as he pondered the grizzly task that awaited him back at the facility.

12

DANIEL DESCENDED THE METAL SPIRAL STAIRCASE TOWARDS THE basement of the prison. His eyes slowly adjusted to the lack of light. A solitary bulb burned dimly as it hung from the ceiling of the underground hallway. The floor was cement, and cinder blocks formed the walls. Metal doors with slits at eye level lined this hallway.

Daniel looked behind the staircase and saw a sand-covered floor with sandbags against the wall. Daniel knew that must be where they would execute prisoners. And he was sure it was no coincidence that it was done within earshot of the other prisoners in the basement.

"*Amerikansky*," the man continued as he pointed down the hallway.

"Hello?" Daniel called out. "Anybody there?"

Daniel heard a slight scuffle down the hall. One door rattled slightly. Daniel ran to it and looked through the tiny slit.

"Are you an American?" Daniel asked the man that he saw.

Like the Russian prisoner, he wore a gray jumpsuit, and he looked malnourished and pale.

The prisoner looked back through the slit at Daniel, without answering.

"You know I'm an American," the man finally answered quietly.

"I'm an American too," Daniel said. "And I'll get you out of here."

Daniel looked about the hallway for a key. Finding none, he motioned to the Russian prisoner with his hand, making a turning motion near the door. The Russian prisoner shrugged.

There had been no other keys in Dmitri's office. He took the guard's key for the front lock and tried, but it didn't even fit in the hole.

Daniel wished he had saved some of the explosives. He would have preferred to free a person instead of documents.

"I need to go find the key," Daniel said. "I'll be back." Daniel rushed back up the stairs and outside. The guard was still unconscious, attached to the metal bar, and Daniel ran out of the prison towards the other buildings he had not yet searched. At least one of them was, no doubt, barracks for the workers at the facility and the guards. Daniel ran to each one in turn. Each was locked.

Daniel kicked at the doors, but none gave way. All the windows were barred. Daniel raced to grab his crowbar, but that also was useless.

Instinctively, Daniel knew where the key was. It had to be with the bald Russian.

Daniel raced back into the prison. He hurried past the surprised Russian man who had come up the stairs and went back to the basement.

"I'm sorry," Daniel said as he gasped for breath. "The key isn't here. I'm going to try with this crowbar, but I don't think it will help."

Daniel pounded and pried at the door for several minutes, but the door wouldn't give.

"I can't get you out now," Daniel apologized, "but look at me. I promise that you will get out of here soon. As soon as I tell my contacts at the CIA and the US military that you are here, they will move mountains to get you out."

The American did not respond as Daniel expected.

"Stop trying," the man said. "You can't fool me. You're not American. You're just pretending to trick me into something."

"What the hell did they do to you in here?" Daniel said. "You think I'm part of an elaborate trick? By who? The Russians?"

The man didn't respond.

"Believe me," Daniel said. "I am as American as apple pie. I'm not part of a Russian trick."

The man looked up at Daniel and squinted.

"As American as apple pie?" the prisoner asked. "Okay. Let's pretend I will play your game. Prove to me you are as American as apple pie."

"I can't stay long," Daniel explained. "They could come back any moment."

Daniel saw the American shrink back. He still suspected Daniel was part of a trick.

"Okay, okay," Daniel said. "What can I say to you to prove that I'm an American? What's something that only Americans know? Apple pie! 'American Pie' by Don McLean. Everybody knows that song, even if nobody knows what in the world it's about." Daniel hummed the tune as his mind raced to think of more ways to prove he was an American.

Daniel thought he spotted a glimmer of hope in the man's eyes.

"You could have prepared that beforehand," the man pointed out. "Try this. Explain to me how to play American football."

Now Daniel felt he was on a roll.

"I know how the game is played. The offense has four downs, and they need to get at least ten yards to get another first down." Daniel began to speak faster. "Or, if they get the ball into the end zone, they get six points, and with the extra point, they can get a total of seven points from scoring a touchdown. Or if they don't get that far, they can punt on fourth down. Otherwise, the other team will get the ball. Or they can kick a field goal for three points. I can even do the Superbowl Shuffle for you."

"Oh my God," the American prisoner said. "You are an American. I don't believe it. How did you get here? What year is it?"

"2002," Daniel said. "Who are you?"

"My name is Michael Devers," the man said solemnly. "I work for the CIA, and I was captured in Leningrad, the USSR in 1987."

———————

My God, Daniel thought to himself. *1987?*

"Did we finally go to war with the Soviet Union?" Michael Devers asked. "Has NATO made it this far, and you're here to rescue me?"

"No," Daniel said. "We never went to war with the Soviet Union. The Soviet Union ended years ago. The Cold War is over."

"It ended?" the prisoner said, stumbling down onto the floor out of surprise.

"It basically ended in 1989 after the Berlin Wall came down,"

Daniel said. "Then it was mostly just things sorting themselves out. You didn't know the Cold War ended?"

The man shook his head, still unable to take it in.

"The Wall came down?" Michael mumbled to himself as he got back on his feet.

Not only has this man been in prison since 1987, but he also doesn't even know the Cold War ended.

"You are in what is now known as Uzbekistan, part of the former Soviet Union," Michael explained. "In a secret prison facility that nobody knew about for years. We Americans are here because we now have an air base in southern Uzbekistan to support the war in Afghanistan."

"Afghanistan?" the man said. "We finally became overt in our resistance against the Soviets in Afghanistan?"

"No," Daniel said. "Islamic terrorists took over Afghanistan, and then it became the launching pad to send terrorism all over the world, even to the United States of America."

As Daniel said this last sentence, a picture of the burning World Trade Center flashed through his mind.

"The worst terrorist act on American soil took place about a year ago," Daniel continued. "Islamic terrorists hijacked planes and flew them into the World Trade Center in New York, killing thousands of innocent civilians."

"And now we're going after them in Afghanistan?" Michael asked, struggling to keep up with the history lesson.

"I promise that once I get out of here, I'll send in the cavalry to rescue you. But I need to know about the Russians who worked here during the Cold War. Did you know a KGB man named Dmitri?"

Michael nodded. "I don't know if that really was his name. He always seemed nice, but I figured that he and the interrogator were just playing good cop versus bad cop."

"Did Dmitri ever confide in you?" Daniel asked desperately.

"No," Michael said. "I only encountered him a few times. I didn't get out much, being here in the basement."

"I'm going to have to go soon," Daniel said in a hurry. "Think hard. Is there anything Dmitri ever did or said that seemed a little bit out of character? Did you ever suspect he was trying to pass on a message?"

Daniel knew he was taking a shot in the dark, but he couldn't bear to leave Michael Devers in this hellhole for a minute longer and not get any closer to Dmitri's secrets.

Michael responded with a definitive, "No," as if the idea were preposterous.

"You said you work for the CIA?" Daniel asked. "Dmitri also worked for the CIA. He was our best asset within the Soviet Union for years, Agent Bishop. Until one day, right after he revealed he had something of the highest urgency, he disappeared. I now know that he disappeared because he was posted here. But he was on our side. He was recently murdered in Tashkent, just as he was about to tell us something vital."

"Dmitri was Agent Bishop?" Michael asked. "I was captured in Leningrad in 1987, trying to get a defector out. The defector was supposed to have credible information about a mole within the American intelligence community. I had heard of Agent Bishop. I knew we were afraid that this mole could reveal who Agent Bishop was. But just as I met the defector, we were captured. I was supposed to meet him and escort him to a dock where a SEAL was going to meet us with a lightweight inflatable boat to take us to an American submarine lurking off the coast.

"Moments more, and he would've given me the identity of the mole. I'll never forget the look of terror in his eyes when they captured us. They brought me here. I'm sure the defector was executed. This has always been my cell. For fifteen years, apparently."

"Who did you report to in the CIA?" Daniel asked.

"Billy," Michael said. "We used to call him Billy the Kid."

"Do you think...?"

"No," Michael said. "Billy wasn't the mole. He would never betray me. We were good buddies. He was a great guy. We'd had too many good times together."

Daniel pondered Michael's words for a moment, but he felt that a clock was ticking. How long until the other guards returned? And the bald man with the thick neck?

"Did anybody else know about the mission when you were captured?" Daniel asked.

"I'm sure others knew. It required a Navy SEAL and a submarine, but those two are extremely secretive and generally separate from the CIA. I wanted to tell Allison, but I didn't. Things were complicated between Billy and us. But she might have guessed I had a big mission coming up because I acted weird."

"Allison?" Daniel asked. But he knew who it was as soon as he said it.

"Allison Carter," Michael replied. "Is she still...? Do you know her?"

"She's still around the CIA," Daniel said, downplaying his working relationship with Officer Carter. His mind was racing, though, and he wasn't sure if he could risk more time with Michael. But Michael switched topics as Daniel began to consider if Officer Carter could be the mole.

"Now that I think about it," Michael began, "I do remember something Dmitri did. Dmitri was kind of a soft guy, but like I said,

I thought he was just playing good cop. But then, one prisoner, a Russian who'd been my cellmate for a while, was set free. Dmitri cleared his name. That was unusual for this place. It was cold out, and I remember that Dmitri gave him his old coat when he was released. That is my last memory of Dmitri. Agent Bishop. I can't believe it. My cellmate, the man he freed, was named Vasyli Fedorov."

———

DANIEL MADE it to the end of the basement hallway when it started.

Michael Devers gave in to panic and began yelling, begging Daniel not to leave him. But Daniel knew he had no choice. He had no way of releasing Michael Devers, and the best thing he could do was to get away as quickly as possible and send other Americans to rescue him.

Daniel raced up the stairs with the Russian prisoner behind him, and after he shut the door at the top of the staircase, Michael Devers' yells were silenced. The guard was still handcuffed in the prison entryway, but he was beginning to move and groan. He was coming to. It didn't matter at this point, though.

Daniel raced outside with the Russian prisoner and picked up the guard's rifle. He looked up to the mountain ridge surrounding the prison and picked out the spot where he'd already cut a hole in the fence. Daniel made his way up the steep and rocky incline with the Russian prisoner following close behind.

Without having to worry about stealth, Daniel forced himself to get to the top as quickly as possible. He repeatedly glanced back, constantly afraid somebody would return before he made it out of sight. Just as Daniel made it to the top and laid down with his chest heaving, he looked down and saw a set of headlights crawl into the black site.

Just in time, Daniel thought to himself. He recognized the make of the vehicle. A Russian *Niva*.

Daniel allowed himself one more deep breath and then pressed on and crawled through the hole in the fence. As he waited for the Russian to come through, he realized that, although he had left the facility just in time, it may not have been soon enough.

Daniel recognized the outline of the first man to exit the vehicle below. It was the bald man from the Intercontinental Hotel. Others got out of the driver's seat and the backseat, and the bald man's head jerked about as he took in the scene. Daniel knew the guard's absence must have alerted him. And perhaps he noticed the blasted door.

Daniel heard the man release a string of Russian yelling and orders to the others, and they began moving quickly.

Daniel knew it wouldn't be long until they found the other guard, discover that somebody had visited, and then come searching for him.

Daniel calculated that they had the off-road vehicle, more men, and they didn't have to worry about a weak prisoner keeping pace.

But they haven't started after me yet, Daniel thought to himself. *I'm still one step ahead.*

Daniel saw the bald man below with another man standing by him in the light in front of the prison building. A second man dragged the guard out and threw him on the ground before the others. He went back into the prison.

Daniel sensed that they were going to execute the defeated guard for his incompetence.

Daniel wanted to start running away, but he couldn't help but watch. He had to gather as much intel as possible.

Daniel pulled out his binoculars to get a better view.

He focused on the *Niva* they had arrived in, but he was unable to see if there was still somebody in the car. It wasn't clear. He waited. If the Wolf got out of the vehicle right then and there, this whole mess could end.

Would it be Ambassador Fitzpatrick? Or Billy? Or...

"Oh no," Daniel said quietly as he watched a fourth Russian pull a man out of the prison and thrust him onto the ground near the defeated guard.

The bald man placed the guard Daniel had knocked out and Michael Devers about fifteen yards apart from each other. He manipulated a pistol and then set it on the ground in between them.

Daniel guessed the game that was going to unfold. The two men would race towards the gun, which probably had a single bullet in it, and whoever got the pistol first would shoot the other.

What a sick game, Daniel thought to himself. *And even if Michael wins, they will kill him, anyway.*

The guard who had been pitted against Michael Devers stood up and began yelling in Russian to his old comrades. Daniel had no idea what he was saying, whether he was appealing to their humanity, or if he was begging those who had once been his friends to give him another chance.

Either way, the bald man had had enough. He feigned as if he were going to punch the guard, who then shifted away slightly.

The bald man, with incredible agility, instead took a step and then spun around with a vicious roundhouse kick that smashed his foot into the man's head.

The man crumpled to the ground. That blow to the head, plus the damage Daniel had previously done, knocked him out.

Now the other Russians were jeering, showing mock outrage that they had lost their opportunity at sport. The bald man held his hands out defensively as if to say, *What was I to do?*

Daniel was relieved that he wouldn't have to witness such a horrible game, but then he realized what was next for Michael Devers.

Daniel instinctively reached for his Glock, but at this range, the handgun was not going to be accurate. He took the guard's Kalashnikov rifle and looked through the scope downwards. Daniel felt little confidence in his aim. He had only fired a rifle like this once before. And this one felt different in his hands. Perhaps the Russian had modified it, or perhaps it had slightly different specifications.

Daniel paused.

Firing would give away his position. If he didn't get at least one lucky hit, the remaining Russians would hunt him mercilessly.

Daniel pulled his head away from the rifle's scope. He could leave now. He would have more time to make his escape.

And then I'll have to live with myself, Daniel thought. *I promised Michael that Americans would come back to rescue him. That will have to be me.*

Daniel put the crosshairs on the man with the bald head and decided not to wait.

Daniel pulled the trigger, and the crack of the Kalashnikov rifle sent a bullet sailing down.

The shot missed wide and buried itself in the dust several feet to the side.

Daniel cursed to himself. If he had cut off the snake's head with his first shot, his and Michael's odds of survival would have been much higher.

The Russians below realized what had happened as soon as they heard the shot, and they took cover against the buildings. Michael Devers tried to do the same, but the bald man gunned him down just as he rose to his feet. The other Russians began to fire back towards Daniel's elevated position.

As Michael began bleeding out on the ground, Daniel repeatedly pulled the trigger, raining bullets down. Anger blinded Daniel.

He wasn't sure if he was hitting anybody.

He didn't care.

He unloaded the magazine, and then he threw the rifle to the side.

Without saying anything to the Russian prisoner, he rose to his feet and began running.

Moments later, a herd of goats blocked his path, but Daniel remembered what Edwards had said: "The Russians always seemed one step ahead, making the most out of everything."

I'm one step ahead, Daniel thought to himself, *but I don't know if I can make it stay that way.*

An idea came to Daniel, and he drew his knife. He waded into the herd of goats. Daniel grabbed one of the larger goats and slashed at it with his blade. He dodged its angry kicks and made sure it dripped blood before shoving it away. He booted several other goats to send them running.

With any luck, the Russians will think they hit me and follow the trail of blood.

Daniel turned the other way and ran into the night with the Russian prisoner not far behind. He didn't stop until he reached the opposite mountain ridge and Dmitri's *dacha* was nearly in sight.

"Daniel?"

Thank God, Daniel thought at the sound of Rex's voice.

"We need to get out of here," Daniel said.

"Gunner and Walters will cover our escape," Rex said.

A few hours later, after rough hiking during which Daniel explained to Rex what he had discovered, Daniel and the others finally exited the mountains.

The injured goat had worked perfectly; neither Gunner nor Walters fought off any pursuers.

———

THE WOLF DESCENDED into the *Maxim Gorky* subway station in Tashkent. His black jacket made him appear as nearly every other man in Tashkent, and the black hat he wore was not uncommon. He held no bag, for the police loved to stop and search anybody who carried a bag onto the subway system. Of course, it was for security, but it was also to line the pockets of the subway policeman. Policemen were also on the lookout for any kind of recording device; cameras were strictly forbidden on the subway system, and this suited the Wolf's purposes well. The last thing he wanted was somebody producing photographic evidence of him meeting with somebody new on the subway.

The Wolf walked as slowly and confidently as he could, but inwardly, he felt the net tightening around him. He had felt it before, but the KGB had always eliminated the threats. Now, there were too many, and his FSB master had not seemed willing to flex his muscle.

Without glancing at the subway map on the wall, he

proceeded to the turnstile and placed a blue subway token into the slot and passed through. He was always careful to have a supply of subway tokens in his coat pocket. He could never risk a long line and a delay.

A policeman waiting near the turnstile approached the Wolf and pointed towards his hands in his coat pocket.

"Pockets? Security," the policeman said.

The Wolf was agitated by the slight delay. He had an important meeting. He did not comply. He looked into the policeman's eyes and said in textbook-perfect Russian, "I will forgive you for not knowing who I am this one time." He pulled his ID from his pocket and gave the policeman a split second to look at it before he carried on silently without revealing what else he had in his pockets.

Petty policemen, the Wolf thought to himself. *Nothing but trumped-up toll collectors.*

The Wolf descended several flights of steps and watched a subway train pull away. He would have to wait for the next one, though it shouldn't be long. He glanced at the clock. He would still be able to make his meeting. The Wolf recalled the route in his mind and the bench at which he would sit. To avoid drawing attention to himself by studying subway maps, he had committed Tashkent's subway map to heart long ago, just as he had memorized the subway maps of each major city he visited.

After a few minutes, he boarded a subway train and got off four stops later. With a glance at the large clock hanging over the subway platform, the Wolf found his bench and sat down, pretending to wait for his ride. He had a few moments to relax before his contact would arrive, and he breathed in deeply, taking in the cool air with the faint scent of motor oil from the subway.

The subway was not as busy as he had hoped. He felt somewhat exposed. There were not near as many people about as he would've liked to provide cover. With this few people, anybody arriving on the subway platform would take note of him. He only hoped they would forget him because he was dressed like every other man: black coat, black hat, and looking tired of life. And that was exactly how the Wolf felt now. He had been playing the game for a long time, perhaps too long, and he knew it was only a matter of time until the Americans, his own countrymen, got lucky and caught him.

They wouldn't catch him because they would beat him.

Oh no, even the most idiotic spies got lucky at some point or another.

They would catch him because even minuscule odds would catch up to him at some point.

The Wolf shut his eyes for a few moments, contemplating what he would say to his contact. He would have to make it as concise and urgent as possible. He opened his eyes when he heard the light clicking of high heels approaching. He couldn't help but look when a blond woman sat at the bench. There were a few feet between them, but the Wolf knew that his contact would never come to meet him like this. The contact would have to sit between the woman and the Wolf.

The Wolf cursed inwardly. Protocol dictated he would leave and go to the backup meeting.

But this is an emergency. There is no backup meeting.

His eyes went up and down the lithe woman sitting only a few feet away from him, her legs tightly crossed. Indeed, she had no other option but to tightly cross her legs, given the skirt she was wearing. It only made the Wolf curse inwardly again. His long career of treachery had taught him to never trust a woman. He knew his fellow countrymen would shake their heads in disgust at such a non-egalitarian and misogynistic outlook, but he had learned from experience and couldn't always afford to pay attention to what was politically correct.

Another subway car arrived. Maybe the woman would board it. Or a friend might get off and meet her, and then she would leave. But she appeared content to examine her perfectly manicured nails. The subway's doors opened as soon as the car came to a stop, and the Wolf knew this was the last opportunity for his contact to arrive. Then the window of opportunity would close. But the Wolf had to meet.

The Wolf slowly stood up and yawned, pretending he needed to stretch his legs. He wandered several yards the other way to another bench that was empty.

It was a risk.

It was the wrong bench. He hated to break protocol, but he hoped his contact would see the situation and sit with him at the incorrect location.

The Wolf had no other choice. He decided to move to the other bench as people started to hustle off the newly arrived subway car. The Wolf forced himself not to look about for the contact getting off the subway. To distract himself, his sweaty hand fondled the extra subway tokens in his pocket.

"Excuse me," the woman said in Russian as the last of the subway passengers straggled by. "Did you hear that the subway fare is going to increase soon?" Her voice made even such a simple question sound seductive.

Still continuing his charade of needing to stretch his legs, the Wolf returned to his original bench. He bit his tongue and considered what to say. Inwardly, he fumed that his master had sent a contact who would draw so much attention to him.

The woman leaned towards the Wolf slightly, a move that would draw any man's eyes down to her chest. "Don't worry.

Everybody will look away from the old man meeting with his mistress."

This only made the Wolf angrier.

Old man?

"Sometimes, when you call such an urgent meeting, improvisation is required," she said. She gave a slight smile and reached out and touched his knee lightly, and scooted a few inches towards him. She was playing the part of a mistress perfectly.

Everything within him told him that he should stand up and walk away. But he didn't have time for that. The net was being tightened around him, even if by luck.

"Once the master has tied up all the loose ends, I want out," the Wolf said simply. "I will be no good to the master dead or captured. But if I get out now, I will speak freely of all that I know."

The woman acted as if she had heard none of the Wolf's offer. Rather, she said, "The master requires just one more thing from you. Then, he says you can have whatever you want." She spoke this last phrase slowly and placed her hand back on his knee, but it crept up higher. The Wolf thought back to the last time he had been with a woman. Again, his instincts told him to get up and leave. But he figured it couldn't hurt to at least listen to the plan. She kept her hand on his leg.

With her other hand, she deftly placed a folded piece of paper into his pocket. She carefully explained the plan to him. She had provided login credentials with which he would steal a load of intelligence, and all with the perfect cover. It didn't take her long to tell him everything else that was going to happen and what was required of him. The Wolf knew that if he refused his master, he would have to suffer the consequences. And the master, he knew perfectly well, was an expert at making others suffer.

But his master also offered an incredible opportunity.

Besides, he couldn't stand the possibility of that upstart kid gloating at his defeat. He couldn't tolerate the idea of everybody in the halls of Langley cheering his capture, cursing him, and then proclaiming how they suspected it had been him all along.

The Wolf made up his mind quickly. The master's plan would grow his legend, and he would be the greatest spy ever. Aldrich Ames and Kim Philby would one day be considered small precursors to the Wolf, and they would never know who the Wolf was.

The ultimate triumph of the spy.

"Tell the master to make sure he ties up all the loose ends, and I will do my part."

I will be the greatest, the Wolf thought to himself

The woman leaned forward once more, placed a gentle kiss on his cheek and said, "I look forward to your performance."

It was then that the Wolf recalled where he recognized her from.

They both got up, and the woman boarded the first subway to leave while the Wolf ascended to the street. With his master's plan in place, he welcomed the net tightening around him. He would use it to his advantage. He was no longer frightened, but confident that he would be perfectly protected from the United States intelligence community for years to come while he destroyed America from the inside.

13

Karshi-Khanabad Airbase (K2), Uzbekistan.
About 4 AM.

NONE OF DANIEL'S shots were accurate.

He rubbed his eyes from exhaustion after putting the rifle down at the shooting range at the K2 Airbase in Southern Uzbekistan.

Walters had turned the hour-and-a-half journey from the Shahrisabz area to the K2 Airbase into a drive that lasted just over an hour in a Humvee. Most of the ride had been spent with Daniel on the satellite phone with Jenny. A full briefing was scheduled for 8 AM, and Daniel had relayed the most vital information over the phone for Jenny and Muhammad to research before then. Investigating Michael Devers, Vasyli Fedorov, the bald man, and the fact that Billy looked more suspicious would keep both of them busy until then.

Daniel had decided not to mention to Jenny that he now suspected Officer Carter. Michael Devers had known her, and he may have been captured because of her. Officer Carter could potentially see any of Jenny's communications. Before Jenny signed off, she told Daniel that Tina should be at K2 by the time he arrived, and so he should be sure to see her.

But when Daniel finally arrived at K2 just before four in the morning, he had decided to wait to see Tina. Instead, he sent digital copies of the documents from the black site to Jenny, and then he went to the base's shooting range. He didn't want to encounter the complexity that Tina represented while he was in the field. He yearned for the simplicity of target practice.

But his next several shots revealed he was not improving.

How much more practice until I would have been able to make the shot and save Michael Devers? Daniel asked himself after each round. His aim was progressively getting worse. He couldn't get the picture of Michael Devers bleeding to death out of his mind. And the small dust plume from the bullet that missed the bald man.

A door clicked as somebody came into the shooting range.

"Daniel?" Tina's voice gently said.

"I'm here," Daniel said, trying to control his voice. He both desperately wanted to see her and avoid her at the same time.

"Why aren't you sleeping?" Tina asked as she approached Daniel. When she came into the light, he saw that she was wearing her favorite jeans and her Georgetown sweatshirt. Her ponytail made her appear deceptively sweet.

"I can't," Daniel responded. "You should be sleeping, too," Daniel said before Tina could dig more.

Tina gave a questioning glance to the rifle resting nearby.

Daniel remembered his last time at a shooting range with Tina and said, "Sorry about Saturday night. Work." He hoped Tina would allow him to joke.

"I understand the job," Tina replied. "Your aim still no good?"

But Tina's jab made Daniel's heart crumble. He looked away and could barely stand.

"I'm sorry. What's the matter?" Tina said as she took a step towards Daniel, sensing there was much more going on.

"I shouldn't be in the field," Daniel confessed as his throat tightened. "I missed, and an American is dead because of it."

He shut his eyes to hold back the tears.

Tina wrapped her arms around Daniel in an embrace. He lowered his head to her shoulder and began sobbing as he tried to explain to Tina.

"I shouldn't have left him... I should have found a way to get him out... I should have been able to make the shot..."

Tina didn't reply. She only held Daniel and reassured him it would be all right.

When Daniel finished crying after several minutes, Tina finally said, "Even the best don't win every time. What matters is that you get back up again and stay in the game. That's how you become the best."

Daniel gave a nod of understanding, stepped back and said, "Thanks."

He felt embarrassed, almost naked, in front of Tina.

"For what it's worth," Tina continued, "I think you have what it takes."

She stepped towards him and gave another hug to comfort him. Daniel took several deep breaths as she held him.

"Oh, and Jenny sent this for you," Tina said. She pulled out a folded note and handed it to Daniel. The paper was folded into a square, origami-style.

Daniel took it with a grin and said, "It's like she's passing a note in third grade. Why didn't she...?"

Daniel opened the note and understood immediately. The note read: "Billy and Carter connected??!!"

"What does it say?" Tina asked.

"I can't explain now," Daniel said as he refolded the note. Tina accepted his answer and didn't pry. Daniel realized Jenny must have uncovered something at least one day before. That allowed time for Tina's travel to Uzbekistan to hand-deliver the note. And Jenny didn't have another way to communicate her suspicions about Officer Carter to him without Carter becoming aware of it.

But Daniel's mind refused to work anymore, and he said to Tina, "I need to sleep. I'm exhausted."

Daniel and Tina walked hand-in-hand to Daniel's sleeping quarters where he immediately fell asleep until 7:55 AM.

———

"I WAS ABOUT to ask where the hell you were," Officer Carter said over the video feed in the briefing room at the K2 Airbase. Daniel entered just as the clock ticked to eight in the morning.

"Sorry, I—"

"No apologies necessary," Officer Carter said. "I've been briefed on what has transpired. Jenny has several items to report on first."

"Hi, guys!" Jenny said as she enthusiastically waved at the camera. Daniel, Rex, and Tina waved back. Daniel thought he saw

Rex wink at Jenny before she began her report. Everybody in the room sipped on coffee and munched on donuts.

"First, that prison-facility thing you encountered in the mountains. It was originally built to support the Soviet-Afghan War. The Soviets would send key POWs there for interrogation, torture, and possibly execution. It also became a convenient place for a few high-level KGB men to put their political opponents, anybody who crossed their path, or anybody else they wanted to make disappear without a paper trail. After the fall of the Soviet Union, the prison remained a convenient place for Russian oligarchs to put their garbage. It was also used by the president of Uzbekistan to get rid of his own political enemies in ways that he knew the general population wouldn't approve of, especially when it violated his newly enlightened and Western-friendly Constitution that came about after the fall of the Soviet Union. The prison facility continued to exist because of an uneasy alliance between the Russian FSB and the president of Uzbekistan and his own cronies. The president's political opponents, however, at least those who had so far avoided imprisonment, suspected that such a place existed and wanted to do away with it."

"How did you learn so much about a place we just learned existed?" Rex asked.

"A lot of help from that detective, Jahongir, in Tashkent," Jenny answered. Despite how surprising this was to Daniel, he decided not to interrupt.

"Whoever controlled it recently," Officer Carter said, "must have realized that the facility's days were numbered and has been trying to close shop. Daniel entered during its last hour."

"And about what you found at the facility," Jenny continued, keeping up her rapid-fire pace. "We have nothing on a man named Vasyli Fedorov. However, it matches the name on a report Daniel took from Dmitri's safe. Our translators are working on it now, but our preliminary guess is that Vasiyli had betrayed the Soviet Union. Dmitri hid the evidence in that report, and then set him free."

"Keep digging on Vasyli," Daniel said. "Dmitri may have told him something. Maybe even who the mole is."

Daniel looked to Officer Carter over the video as he mentioned the mole, but she didn't react visibly.

"Muhammad and I will keep looking into Vasyli, but I've still got lots to tell you," Jenny said. "The bald man Daniel encountered at both the prison facility and the Intercontinental hotel was in the CIA database. There's a file on him from Tashkent. Basically, he was a *Spetsnaz* soldier late in the Soviet-Afghan War, and then things get murky. There's speculation he was in prison, with the KGB and then the FSB, but he mostly disappears. Now, he's suspected of being connected to the Russian mafia. He goes by Pavel."

"And when he shot Michael Devers," Daniel began, "that confirmed he's a bad guy."

When Daniel mentioned Michael, he did see Officer Carter's eyes look down.

"Oh, and I almost forgot," Jenny said as she flipped through some papers. "The other document you found in Dmitri's safe was a birth certificate. For his son. Like I said, they're still translating all that was in the safe, so there could be more."

"I just think it's odd he would keep a birth certificate of his deceased son in his office safe," Daniel pondered out loud.

"Any news on that code you guys are trying to crack with computers?" Rex asked. Daniel had nearly forgotten about the coded message they had found in Dmitri's apartment.

"That's why Muhammad isn't here," Officer Carter said. "Basically, no, he hasn't cracked it."

"He wasn't able to find an old Russian edition of *The Communist Manifesto* to use as the key, so he's doing the best he can," Jenny added.

"I wonder... Never mind," Daniel said.

"So what's our next step, given all this information?" Tina asked. "We don't seem any closer to solving Dmitri's murder—or Patrick Riley's, for that matter—and finding the mole."

"The last thing I was going to mention," Jenny said, "was that the detective, Jahongir, told me more about Zuhro's first husband."

"Is he in Tashkent?" Daniel asked.

"Yes," Officer Carter answered. "And he's connected to the SNB in Uzbekistan."

"Who isn't a freaking spy in this mess?" Rex said out loud.

"And his expertise was explosives and bombs," Officer Carter finished.

"He would have the motive and the means to bomb Dmitri," Tina observed.

"You guys get back up to Tashkent to track him down," Officer Carter ordered, "and you also need to keep an eye on the International Security Conference. I don't trust Billy, Fitzpatrick, or Edwards."

Daniel noticed it was the first time she had mentioned Edwards as a potential mole. Previously, she had been eager for Daniel to leave and work with Edwards.

"Okay," Rex said. "All we have to do is solve multiple murders, take on the Russian mafia, and catch this mole who has evaded capture for decades. I think the three of us can handle it. We're the pros, after all."

Officer Carter added something that surprised Daniel.

"I want to tell the three of you that I knew Michael Devers before he disappeared. Honestly, I try not to think about him. It was a tough time for me and the CIA. But I can tell you that he was one of the best. Get up to Tashkent, and if nothing else, find justice for Michael Devers."

"Yes, ma'am," was the response in unison.

———

Tashkent, Uzbekistan.
US Embassy.
About 10:30 AM.

"UP YOURS, DANIEL," Tina whispered angrily as they walked down the quiet hallway in the embassy.

Daniel had feared this reaction his whole flight back up to Tashkent. It was why he hadn't slept as much as he had wanted to.

"You need me with you when you pound the pavement," Tina protested. "That's what I'm best at."

"No," Daniel responded. "I need you to keep an eye on Billy, Fitzpatrick, and Edwards at the conference."

"You want me to babysit?"

"Rex can't do it," Daniel said. "He's a knuckle-dragger. You, however, are savvy enough to keep an eye on those three. Besides, I suspect they will underestimate you. And I need Rex with me on the streets. Me, with a woman like you, trying to ask tough questions wouldn't work here in Uzbekistan."

"Why the hell not?" Tina demanded.

"I'm sorry, it's just how relatively young and good-looking

women are regarded," Daniel said. "Rex and I might need to get tough, and—"

Tina quickly veered into an empty conference room and shut the door after Daniel followed her inside.

Daniel was surprised she managed not to yell at him.

"I watched my partner get gunned down in front of me, and I got pretty damned tough in the toughest neighborhoods of D.C., so I think I can handle it."

Daniel knew Tina was right about that.

They each took a few deep breaths, and Daniel said, "I know you can handle it. I have to hit the streets because I can communicate in Uzbek. Rex doesn't fit in at the conference. Those guys won't do a thing if Rex is within ten miles. Those lonely old guys will open up to you."

"I'm not going to flirt with those dirty old men," Tina protested. "When I joined, I said I would never whore myself out."

"I'm not saying you have to do that," Daniel said. "I just meant that—"

The door swung open, and a man wearing a tweed suit entered.

"I thought I saw you go in here," Ambassador Fitzpatrick said as his eyes went back and forth between Daniel and Tina. "Am I interrupting anything between you two?"

Not now, Daniel thought to himself.

"Hello, Ambassador," Tina said with a smile. "And, no, you were not interrupting anything between us two. I look forward to seeing you at the conference. Perhaps you could show me around."

Tina brushed by Fitzpatrick and left him alone with Daniel.

Daniel wished he could have explained more to Tina, but he couldn't avoid Ambassador Fitzpatrick.

Daniel paused and wondered why Ambassador Fitzpatrick had followed him down the hallway.

A man who wears a tweed suit surely can't be the Wolf, Daniel thought to himself. *And surely he wouldn't do anything within the US Embassy.*

14

"About that Land Cruiser you abandoned in Samarkand," Ambassador Fitzpatrick started to say. Daniel stepped by him and exited the conference room, relieved that was all he wanted to talk about. Daniel continued down the hallway towards Patrick Riley's office.

"I forgot about that car," Daniel apologized. "It was necessary for the security of the mission."

"But it clearly violated regulations of the vehicle's use," the ambassador countered. Daniel ignored him as he listed all the infractions.

"And what are you doing here, anyway?" Ambassador Fitzpatrick asked when they arrived at Patrick's office.

Daniel opened the door and said, "I'm looking for a book Patrick said he would lend me." He studied the ambassador's face as he entered the office to see how he would react to the lie. But his face was still red from agitation over the Land Cruiser.

"And now I should expect you to fetch the vehicle personally so as not to waste valuable personnel from here. But I fear I should never allow you into another US Embassy vehicle. You amateur intelligence officers. I was once in the CIA, you know? And back then..."

Daniel only half listened as he looked around the barren office while Fitzpatrick rambled on.

Patrick had said he hadn't unpacked the boxes at his home. Only two boxes sat on the desk. Daniel opened one and rummaged through it. He soon found a book and went to leave the office.

"*The Communist Manifesto*?" Fitzpatrick asked with disgust when he saw the cover and translated it. "You don't know Russian."

"I might try to learn. Actually, it's needed to crack a code."

With a wink, Daniel walked away and left Ambassador Fitzpatrick in frustrated silence. Patrick had the exact same edition as Dmitri, strengthening Daniel's hypothesis that it was for a code.

Ambassador Fitzpatrick stepped out of the office and called after Daniel.

"Do you know where Billy is? He's supposed to go to this conference, but he hasn't been seen since yesterday. He ought to stay in better touch than this. Edwards is already at the conference."

"Sorry. I have no idea where Billy is," Daniel answered over his shoulder. He wondered if Billy's disappearance was something to be worried about, or if Fitzpatrick was being uptight about his rules.

Minutes later, Daniel dropped off Patrick Riley's old Russian edition of *The Communist Manifesto* with a secretary and gave clear instructions. He told the secretary to scan the whole book and send it to Jenny and Muhammad at the CIA in Washington D.C.

Then, he was to notify Daniel when they confirmed receipt, or, more importantly, if anybody interfered.

Ambassador Fitzpatrick studied up on me enough to catch that I don't know Russian, Daniel thought to himself. *Let's see if he gets in the way of my team cracking a code that could identify the Wolf.*

———

"BAD NEWS," Rex said to Daniel as they drove away from the US Embassy. Gunner and Walters rode in the backseat. "I got a message from Detective Jahongir. Zuhro, Dmitri's widow, was murdered last night. He said the Russian mafia is suspected."

"Maybe the Wolf is getting desperate and trying to tie up any potential loose ends," Daniel said.

"I challenged Jahongir on why his men shot the man who stabbed Patrick Riley, and he said they were dirty. Compromised by, guess who, the Russian mafia."

"Jenny said Jahongir had been very helpful in tracking down information about Zuhro's first husband," Daniel said. "Maybe he is a good guy, trying to clean out corruption."

"Let's hope so and that he's not leading us into a trap. And from now on, you need to keep these with you." Rex patted the satellite phone and Glock in the holster that rested on the console. "But hopefully, we won't need them, or Gunner and Walters."

"*Aww*, come on," both Gunner and Walters complained from the back.

Minutes later, Rex pulled off into a neighborhood.

"It looks like our man, Shahriyor, still has some power," Daniel observed as their black Embassy vehicle pulled up at the last known address of Zuhro's first husband.

Like most houses in Tashkent, the front of the property was a wall with a gate. But in this case, the wall was two stories high. The ornate gate was wide enough for two cars, and security cameras rested on the upper corners of the wall. A guard booth stood in front of the gate. An armed guard stepped out.

"Well, let's go knock on the door," Daniel said to Rex as he got out of the car. He left the satellite phone and gun behind. Gunner and Walters got out and stood by the car with their arms crossed.

The guard approached Daniel and Rex and said, "You need to leave. You can't park there."

"Tell Shahriyor that the US Embassy wants to talk with him. Let him know that getting on our good side can be very beneficial and profitable," Daniel said.

The guard hesitated. Daniel hoped the embassy vehicle and the extra show of muscle would sway the guard-and Shahriyor.

"Wait here," the guard said before going back to his guard booth and speaking into a radio.

"What if he tells us to get lost?" Rex whispered to Daniel.

"We'll let Shahriyor know he's implicated in the bombing from last week."

"Hopefully hardball will work," Rex said.

"If we can't talk to this guy, Tina is going to be pissed at me," Daniel said.

"Why?"

"I don't want to talk about it," Daniel said. The guard was still on the radio. "Hey, Jenny sent a note with Tina that she had uncovered a connection between Officer Carter and Billy."

"You don't think Officer Carter is involved with the Wolf, do you?" Rex asked. "Man, this guard is taking all day. Is Jenny in danger? Somebody already got to Max." Rex's last statement set in, and Daniel saw panic creep into Rex's eyes.

"Jenny's smart," Daniel said to reassure Rex. "She'll stay safe.

The best thing we can do to keep Jenny safe is to talk to Shahriyor."

Moments later, the metal door opened, and a man in a blue suit beckoned Daniel and Rex to enter. They exchanged relieved glances as they stepped forward. The man in the blue suit motioned with his hand for Gunner and Walters to stay outside.

Upon entering, the man frisked Daniel and Rex but found nothing. He led Daniel and Rex through a courtyard in silence and then through double-doors and into the home. Rex whistled softly at the wealth on display as they went up a marble stairway and finally into a long room paneled with dark wood. A long table made from matching wood stretched down the middle. A man sat at the desk at the end of the table. Daniel knew it was Shahriyor.

———

"I HEAR THAT YOU SPEAK UZBEK," Shahriyor said to Daniel. "Where did you learn it?"

"I've learned at several places," Daniel answered. "Including Tashkent."

"I hear there is something that can be mutually beneficial for you Americans and me," the man said open-endedly.

"One place I practiced the Uzbek language was near a city down south called Shahrisabz," Daniel said. At this, Shahriyor tensed and looked up at Daniel and Rex. The two guards by the side of the door also seemed to tense up.

"The man from Moscow, Dmitri, who came and stole your wife is dead," Daniel reported. "I know that you helped make the bomb that played a role in Dmitri's death."

At this, Shahriyor's face turned red, and Daniel sensed that the guards were getting ready to pounce on him.

Daniel continued quickly. "But I am not interested in whether or not you were part of Dmitri's murder. Dmitri was only a small piece of the puzzle. The CIA will protect you and give you immunity for this murder, but you must give us information. We need the bigger picture, and for that, we promise your safety. And of course, there will be ongoing benefits for a good relationship with the United States in the future."

"I'm not going to lie," the man said. "I'm getting too old to lie. I'm happy Dmitri is dead. I hate that man, and I'm glad the world is rid of him. But I know nothing about his death."

"Are you trying to tell me that somebody else in Tashkent made the bomb? If so, who?" Daniel pressed.

Shahriyor raised his hand and shooed his two guards away. He pulled out a cigarette and lit it. His hand shook as he began puffing.

"How can I know that you will keep me safe?" Shahriyor asked.

"Like I said, Dmitri is a small piece in the puzzle. The bigger picture is vital to the national security of the United States. We can keep you safer than anybody else. We think the Russian mafia is tying up loose ends. But maybe you already know that. I propose that we are your best bet for safety."

Shahriyor placed his cigarette into an ashtray and folded his hands.

"Let's say, hypothetically then," Shahriyor began, "that somebody did want a bomb to kill Dmitri. Hypothetically, it was unknown who ordered it, but it was known to be for Dmitri."

"Interesting hypothetical situation," Daniel said. "Surely there is more you can tell me. Will you take Zuhro back now that Dmitri is dead? Do you still love her?"

Daniel wanted to see if Shahriyor knew of Zuhro's murder the night before.

"That disgusts me," Shahriyor said. "I hate that woman. She was my wife first, and I loved her then. When we found out that a man, whom we knew must be from the KGB, was coming to the facility, we knew we had to keep an eye on him."

"Who is *we*?" Daniel asked.

"The GRU," Shahriyor answered. "The military's intelligence. We thought the best way to keep an eye on a lonely KGB man was with a woman. That woman was my wife."

"And Zuhro also was—?"

"GRU? Yes. We both worked for the GRU. Initially, neither of us liked the idea of her winning Dmitri's trust to gain information from him, but we didn't think she would have to do more than be kind to him. The GRU, however, continued pushing the relationship further and further until she was supposed to have an affair with him."

"You agreed to this?" Daniel asked incredulously.

"The possibility for advancement and benefits was huge," Shahriyor said. "And refusing wasn't an option. The GRU kept pushing for more. And a deeper relationship. I resisted it, but I began to suspect that my wife was beginning to enjoy it."

Shahriyor picked up his cigarette again and began puffing quickly as his story continued.

"She started to genuinely like the bastard. Zuhro claimed it was all an act for the job. I objected, of course, but I couldn't say no to the GRU. That would have meant my death. And it would have meant Zuhro's death. Once she truly did love Dmitri, her information became suspect and useless to the GRU. In the end, I whored my wife out to this man from Moscow for absolutely no benefit. The next plan from the GRU was even worse."

"What was that?" Daniel asked.

"When Dmitri got Zuhro pregnant, the GRU told Zuhro to

threaten to get rid of their child. They thought the threat of losing the child would make Dmitri do whatever they wanted. But, instead, Zuhro must have told Dmitri everything and that she didn't want to give up the baby. Their love for each other grew even deeper."

Daniel remembered the birth certificate in Dmitri's office safe. Perhaps they hadn't aborted the child. But it didn't make sense to Daniel to keep the birth certificate if the baby lived to be just a few years old.

"So if you wouldn't stand up to the GRU out of fear, how did Zuhro survive?" Daniel asked.

"The KGB must have been protecting them," Shahriyor said. "Dmitri was more valuable to the KGB than I thought. The GRU decided not to pick a fight over it. But I can't be sure."

"Is there anything else you can tell me about Dmitri?" Daniel asked.

"No," Shahriyor said. "But I am glad he's dead. It's all in the past. I moved on."

"What happened to the child they were to abort?" Daniel asked.

"I don't know. It wasn't mine," Shahriyor said. He placed the finished cigarette in the ashtray.

"Zuhro was murdered last night," Daniel finally revealed. He observed Shahriyor's reaction carefully.

Shahriyor blinked and said, "Like I said, I've moved on."

The surprise seemed genuine to Daniel.

"And just to be clear, you don't know who ordered the bomb? Hypothetically."

"The Russian mafia is my best guess," Shahriyor said. "But you didn't hear it from me. Now, have I been of assistance to the United States?"

"You have been most helpful," Daniel said. He rose to leave. "Your information regarding Dmitri may prove most valuable. I trust this is the beginning of a fruitful partnership between you and the United States."

As Daniel and Rex were escorted out, Daniel recounted the conversation to Rex that had taken place in Uzbek. They went back down the marble staircase, through the courtyard, and out the front gate.

On the street, Rex turned to Daniel and said, "All arrows point towards the Russian mafia keeping the Wolf safe. They must have a cozy relationship with the Russian government."

"I wonder if there's much of a distinction between the two," Daniel said as they approached Gunner, Walters, and the black embassy car. "But we still don't know who the Wolf is."

"I've got a message for you, sir," Walters said with a raised eyebrow. "A nice car drove up, stopped, and a woman in the backseat handed me this note before driving away."

———

"Nigora," Daniel said to himself after he opened the note to reveal the Uzbek scrawled in Cyrillic cursive. But before he could read it, the satellite phone next to him buzzed.

Jenny didn't bother with pleasantries.

"Max survived the attack in the sauna," Jenny reported. "He came out of his coma, and he is singing like a bird."

Daniel put the satellite phone on speakerphone so Rex could hear.

"Wow," Daniel said. He had assumed Max was dead.

"Max's handler went by Isaac. Max balked at carrying out an operation against Officer Carter. He thought it was too risky. He thinks Isaac moved to get rid of him when he wouldn't go against Officer Carter."

"Who is Isaac?" Rex demanded.

"Hi, Rex. How are you? I thought you might ask. *Um*, Isaac is unknown. Max says he hadn't seen him recently. Probably several weeks. He did say Isaac knew Russian, though."

"Okay," Daniel said. "Hopefully the name Isaac will ring some bells."

I wish I had known about Isaac a few minutes ago, Daniel thought. *I could have asked Shahriyor.*

"I'll let you know if Max says anything else," Jenny said. "Oh, and Muhammad says a big thanks for that old Russian edition of *The Communist Manifesto*. He said it should speed things up since it matches Dmitri's copy exactly, but nothing so far."

"Keep me posted," Daniel said before he hung up and turned his attention back to Nigora's note.

"Maybe that puts Officer Carter in the clear since she was targeted," Rex said. "But who is Isaac, and what does that note say?"

Maybe Nigora knows who Isaac is, Daniel thought.

15

"It's from Nigora," Daniel said slowly. "She wants to talk with me."

Daniel directed Rex away from their route back the embassy. Instead, they headed to a meeting spot Nigora indicated in the note. About twenty minutes later, they were on the northeastern edge of Tashkent. They stopped among a group of apartment buildings off the main street, behind a line of shops. One of the shops was a large supermarket. Daniel was supposed to meet Nigora in her car behind the supermarket.

"I don't like how this feels," Rex said. "How do we know she's not leading you into a trap?"

"We don't," Daniel admitted. "If she wanted me dead, though, this would be a bad way to do it. I'm sure she has her self-interests at heart and wants something from us."

"Protection?" Rex suggested. "Like Shahriyor? It must have really hit the fan if everybody is scrambling to cover their asses. Is it Isaac who's doing all the killing to protect the Wolf?"

"Maybe," Daniel said. "And maybe Nigora knows who Isaac is."

Daniel and Rex left the other two with the car and walked the last few blocks. They spotted a silver Mercedes Benz parked in the shade.

Rex hung back as Daniel approached the vehicle. Daniel peeked in and saw a female driver and a lone woman in the backseat.

Daniel got in and pulled the door shut behind him.

"I know where Billy is," Nigora said. She had bypassed all the typical Uzbek greetings and gone right to the point. "But I need you to promise me something."

"What's that?"

"The United States must protect me and take me to America if I tell you. And—"

Nigora paused when Daniel gave a doubtful look. Daniel wasn't sure he could promise that, even if he wanted to.

"It may be too late when you do find Billy," Nigora warned.

"Who do you need protection from?" Daniel demanded. "And why are you doing this?"

"They've turned my agents into simple whores. I can't let them do that."

Daniel thought about what Nigora had said. She hadn't told him who she needed protection from. The blond woman in the driver's seat caught his eye. He recognized her; the pieces came together.

"Your agent was with Pavel at the Intercontinental Hotel. She wore a brunette wig. Before that, she was—"

Nigora finished Daniel's statement. "In Washington D.C. Yes."

"And now you both need protection for the murder of Max, a CIA officer," Daniel continued. "And who is it that has turned your agent into a whore?"

"The Russian mafia. I've tried to take over, to reach the top, but..."

"You need protection from them. I need a name."

"I don't know. Somebody else very powerful from Russia is controlling the leaders here."

"I can't promise protection for you and your agent for a crime committed on American soil if the best you can do is point me to the mob," Daniel warned. "I need details, and I need a name."

"I'll tell you where Billy is," Nigora promised.

"Is he still in Uzbekistan?" Daniel asked.

"Yes, but I need more promises of protection before I say anything else."

"What was Max's involvement in America?" Daniel asked. "Did the mafia want him killed? Or the FSB? Who ordered your agent to kill Max?"

"I won't say more until you promise protection," Nigora said.

"If I promise, you must tell me where to find Billy, who wanted Max dead, and I also want to know anything you know about a man named Isaac."

At the mention of Isaac, Nigora paused before continuing.

"Agreed," Nigora said.

"And if you don't keep your word, the CIA will hunt you down to the ends of the earth."

"I understand."

"Okay, I promise that you and your agent will have protection and immunity for the attack on Max and any other previous wrongdoing. Now, where is Billy?"

"The Palm Island Hotel at *Lunacharsky,* in room 202. He's alone. Probably unconscious."

"And...?"

"The man named Isaac wanted Max dead. He's the head of the Russian mafia in Uzbekistan. And he's my husband."

My God, Daniel thought to himself.

"I don't recommend you go home tonight," Daniel warned.

He opened the car door and hurried back to Rex. They were soon back in their car, speeding towards the Palm Island Hotel.

———

"PALM ISLAND HOTEL." Daniel read the hotel's name out loud as they pulled in.

"Great name in a country that is double-landlocked," Rex joked.

It didn't take long to find room 202.

They didn't knock.

Gunner kicked the door in, and Walters followed with his weapon drawn. Rex went in after them, and it only took a few seconds for them to confirm that the room was empty.

Except for Billy.

Billy sat upright in the bed and was mumbling curses when Daniel walked in. Daniel pulled the door shut, and Rex opened the curtains. The daylight shone in and made Billy wince as it exposed his pale, white torso. The rest of him was only covered with bed sheets.

"What the hell is going on here?" Rex wondered as he looked around the room. Daniel had no experience in narcotics, but it didn't take an expert to see that drugs had been used in this room. Ripped lingerie on the ground indicated Billy hadn't always been alone. Daniel guessed it originally belonged to Nigora's blond agent.

Billy slouched over and held his face in his hands and tried to cry. But Daniel knew he was beyond being able to cry. The ability had probably left him years ago.

Daniel went for a glass of water and handed it to Billy.

"You need to tell us who you were with, and what you told her," Daniel said, gently yet firmly.

"I don't remember," Billy said after taking a small sip of water. "Can I put some clothes on?"

"Tell us something useful first," Rex demanded.

"I didn't tell them anything," Billy said defensively. "I never do. I'm not stupid."

"Not stupid?" Daniel asked. "You don't think there's any reason women would hook up with you other than to ask you about CIA operations?"

"Drugs?" Billy said weakly.

"You think a pasty old weakling like you is a catch for any woman, let alone the young and good-looking one I'm sure you were with last night?" Rex asked. "While I'm getting shot at, you're setting up your next hookup. Don't tell me you're not stupid."

"If you never tell them anything," Daniel pressed, "do you think they hook up with you for the drugs? Don't you think there are other ways for them to get drugs?"

Billy sat and shook his head from side to side, knowing he couldn't say anything that would appease anybody in the room.

"You don't even know when she left this morning, do you?" Rex demanded. "Or her name."

"Her name was Olga," Billy said.

"Right, and you told her your name was John Smith," Rex said.

"If you don't tell her anything, then somebody's blackmailing you, aren't they?" Daniel guessed. "How long has this been going on? How many women has it been? How many drugs?"

"I'm not sure when the first time was," Billy said hesitantly.

"Start thinking, real hard," Rex demanded.

"It was a long time ago."

"Whether or not you tell us anything," Daniel said, "whatever the blackmailer has on you is powerless now. You're already ruined. He can't do anymore. So, you might as well take the blackmailer down with you."

"I don't know who it is," Billy said. "Not exactly."

"When did it start?" Daniel asked.

"1985," Billy said.

"Jesus," Rex said. "You've been sleeping with whores and snorting since Reagan? You must have been brand new then."

Billy nodded dumbly.

"Although you're an idiot and a huge liability to the CIA," Daniel said, "you're not the Wolf. The Wolf wouldn't fall for this garbage. But the Wolf is involved. Do you remember a man named Michael Devers, from the Cold War?"

When Daniel said the name, Billy's face turned ashen.

"We found him," Daniel said, "about fifteen years too late. He was alive when I saw him less than twenty-four hours ago. But he's dead now, after fifteen years of detainment. No thanks to you. Now you had better help us find the Wolf."

———

"IT STARTED IN 1985," Billy confessed with shame in his voice. "But can I put some clothes on first?"

"Nope," Rex said quickly. "If you don't mind letting it all hang out for the enemies of the United States of America, you had better believe you're going to keep it out until we get to the bottom of this."

"I'm an American citizen," Billy whined as he composed

himself. "I want a lawyer."

"You're in the wrong country for that," Daniel said. "Besides, the Russians are tying up loose ends. Now that you're blown, they will want to make sure you don't talk. Cooperate with me now. Or, I'm sure the Russians wouldn't mind a shot at you."

Daniel watched the ounce of defiance leave Billy's face. Daniel knew he had him.

"Where in 1985?" Daniel asked. "And please don't tell me it was a beautiful woman with a Russian accent."

"It was in America," Billy said. "I had just gotten back from West Berlin. It had been damn stressful, and we weren't having any intelligence success at the time. We always felt like the KGB and the *Stasi* knew exactly what we were up to. So, when I returned to America, I needed to blow off some steam. Big time."

"How exactly did you do that?" Daniel asked patiently.

"I met a girl at a bar," Billy answered.

"What was she like?" Daniel asked. "Can you describe her?"

"And don't tell me she's a beautiful Russian woman, you dumb ass," Rex warned.

"She was a pretty good-looking woman about my age, with dark hair and dark eyes. Met her at a bar," Billy said.

"And you didn't think there was anything funny about a good-looking woman being interested in you?" Daniel asked.

"What drew me to her was how smart she was," Billy said. "She was an accountant at a big business, and she also clearly needed to blow off some steam. So did I. I went home with her, and it was the first time I had ever done that. But I didn't think anything could go wrong with me starting a relationship with an American woman. But then we got to her house. She did some drugs, and she offered some to me. I declined, but..."

"She was persuasive," Rex said, finishing his statement.

And what happened after that?" Daniel asked.

"I went back to work the following Monday like normal, but then when I went out for lunch, somebody slipped something in my pocket. When I went to look at it in the bathroom stall, I saw that it was a picture of me taking the drugs at the woman's house. Needless to say, I was scared, and I knew I would get in trouble, but I was going to report it as soon as I returned from my lunch break. But before I got back to the office, a man approached me."

"Who was this man?" Daniel asked.

"He eventually went by the name of Isaac, although I'm sure that can't be his real name. He didn't look like anything special. Just a pretty average guy, maybe about 5 feet 10. He looked kinda Mongolian, not too handsome, not too ugly, but he seemed fit enough and had on a pretty nice suit. He always wore a fancy watch. He explained that he needed to talk with me about the pictures in my pocket."

"Why didn't you run away, or attack him, or yell for the police, or anything other than allow yourself to be compromised?" Daniel asked.

"At first, he told me that the girl I had met was his sister, and he had been trying for years to break her of her addiction, and he just wanted to talk with me to see if there was some way we could help her clean up."

"And you believed that?" Rex asked angrily.

"It's obvious in retrospect now," Billy said, "but back then, I figured I was in America. I was in a safe place. I had simply been with a girl, and we did a few drugs. Thousands of Americans do that all the time. At the time, Isaac seemed sincere and trustworthy. But he eventually told me that he really wasn't her brother, but that he had to talk to me privately to tell me something. He apologized for lying."

"How kind of him," Rex joked sarcastically.

"Isaac told me he was with the *Mossad*. He said the *Mossad* needed a little bit of extra help, and I was the perfect man to do that."

"Why would he think you were the perfect man to do that?" Daniel asked.

"My parents had fled the Nazis," Billy said. "My parents gave me the nickname Billy so that people wouldn't guess that I'm Jewish. They didn't feel comfortable about how I would be treated, as a Jew, in America."

"So why didn't you report this, if it really was our allies and friends, the *Mossad*?" Daniel asked.

"He told me that the *Mossad* was working with the CIA on some things, but there were some things that the *Mossad* was more, shall we say, aggressive on than the United States could appear to be. He said the United States was too bogged down in bureaucracy, too bound to public opinion, and too worried about the Arab nations. He promised I wouldn't have to do anything to betray my country, just a few things here and there that could really help the *Mossad*."

"And you still didn't tell anybody?" Daniel asked. He couldn't believe how easily Billy had been compromised.

"I didn't want to throw my career away based on using drugs just one time," Billy argued. "But I decided that if Isaac ever did ask me to do anything other than harmless tasks, then I would report him."

"And did you ever see that woman again?" Daniel asked.

"No," Billy answered. "I never saw her again. But I kept seeing Isaac, even when I was posted at different places all over the world. He seemed to almost always show up, whether I was posted in Europe, Eastern or Western, and even in Moscow. Which didn't surprise me too much because he said he was with the *Mossad*. But things slowly began to snowball."

Daniel and Rex sat quietly, as Billy elaborated.

Isaac had begun providing Billy with women and drugs. Eventually, that led to gambling, and then Isaac would cover Billy's gambling debts.

"And how is it that nobody ever noticed that your life was falling apart with these addictions?" Daniel asked.

"Isaac helped me. He would cover up for me. He even gave me some tips that pointed me in the right direction that gave me success."

Daniel knew Isaac must have been feeding Billy small bits of intelligence in exchange for the big wins Billy was unwittingly giving Isaac. In the vernacular of intelligence, Isaac was trading chickenfeed for gold dust. Or worse, chickenfeed for a goldmine.

"And I never scheduled any of these romps with drugs or women when I knew a big mission was coming up," Billy said with a raised finger. "Only after."

"What did Isaac make you do?" Daniel asked.

"It was only ever harmless things," Billy insisted. "I was going to report him as soon as he asked me to do anything that would hurt Americans or the CIA. It was always pointless stuff. He would have me go to certain locations and then just sit there for ten minutes. The most he ever had me do was go to a park bench, wait, pick up a newspaper that had been laying on the bench, and then move it to another bench. It was harmless. Pointless."

"And since Isaac continued giving you women, drugs, and gambling, you felt like that was good payment for doing what you call pointless tasks?" Rex asked.

Billy nodded dumbly.

"I guess I could have been used as a diversion or something.

And of course, I soon suspected Isaac wasn't really with the *Mossad*, but he wasn't getting anything out of me," Billy said defensively.

"As long as the money, drugs, and women kept coming, you didn't care," Daniel added. "Tell me what went wrong with Devers. Do you remember the night he was supposed to get a defector out, and it went bad?"

"It was one of the worst nights of my life," Billy said. "I remember it like it was yesterday, and it is one of my nightmares. Michael Devers was supposed to get the defector and meet up with a Navy SEAL who would sneak them out to an American submarine. Devers left early to go on his route to lose any tails. He was good, so I'm confident he was able to get away clean. But then, he never came back that night. He simply disappeared. When we reported him missing to the police, they started a missing-person investigation. I'm convinced it was all for show. When we raised a little bit of a stink about it, we were told by a representative of the Soviet government, whom I'm sure was told this by the KGB, that we needed to keep a better eye on our agents."

"Who else knew about Devers getting the defector out that night?" Daniel asked.

"Me, Edwards, and the CIA chief of station at the time, Fitzpatrick. But I am the only one who knew that the defector was coming out on that specific night. Everybody else only knew that he was coming out within the next thirty days or so. I didn't trust anybody else with Devers and the defector, so I was intentionally vague. I communicated directly with Langley about the submarine and the Navy SEAL."

"You would claim that you never told anybody outside of Langley about that specific night, am I right?" Rex said.

"No. I never told anybody. Not even Fitzpatrick. I always

figured losing Devers was bad luck. We can't win them all. At the worst, I feared that our encrypted communications with Langley were compromised, but I never suspected it was somebody at Langley itself."

"And you don't think Isaac figured it out?" Daniel asked.

"I didn't tell Isaac," Billy insisted. "He didn't even ask me about any operations. So it's not as though he tricked me into telling him something. I didn't tell him anything."

"When was the next time you saw Isaac after the debacle in Leningrad, or, St. Petersburg?" Daniel asked.

"Not for a long time. I don't remember exactly how long, but I think I next saw him on a short stint in Vienna."

"You didn't suspect Isaac at all?" Daniel asked.

"Not at all," Billy said.

"When did you have your next romp, as you call it, after Devers disappeared?" Daniel asked.

"The night after," Billy said. "Originally, I had planned it as a celebration of getting the defector out, and whatever commendation or promotion I might receive from it. Instead, I was trying to escape and drown out my problems."

Daniel and Rex sat quietly, but Billy slumped over and began crying. Tears did come this time.

"I had a romp Sunday night. Just the other night," Billy said through his crying. "After I left you at the Intercontinental Hotel. Patrick caught me. He confronted me. And then..."

"Patrick was murdered the next morning," Daniel said. "You were compromised by Patrick, so Isaac had Patrick killed."

Billy nodded his head up and down, and he continued crying. "Patrick was my only friend. My only friend. And now he's dead because of me."

"Let me guess," Daniel said to Billy. "The woman was at the Intercontinental and wore a brunette wig."

Billy managed to confirm Daniel's guess despite his sobbing.

After a few moments, Daniel tossed Billy his clothes and said, "Get dressed. You're getting on the next flight to America."

Daniel and Rex stepped out of the room to talk privately. They were waiting for an embassy vehicle to arrive and take Billy away. Gunner and Walters stayed inside to keep an eye on Billy until then.

"It seems to me that Billy fell prey to a false flag operation," Rex said to Daniel. "He was intended as a diversion. If the Wolf ever came under fire, they had Billy framed up to be taken down as the Wolf. The harmless tasks were just to make him look suspicious, if need be."

"I think you're right," Daniel said. "But we still don't know who the Wolf is. It may be down to Fitzpatrick and Edwards."

"Edwards?" Rex asked.

"Can't rule him out," Daniel explained. "And it doesn't look like Dmitri left a clue behind. Unless Muhammad cracks that coded message, I think we've only got one lead left."

"Isaac, Nigora's husband?" Rex asked.

"Yes," Daniel confirmed. "Isaac had good reason to suspect that Billy had a big mission the night Devers disappeared. Billy had planned a romp. Besides, now that we know Isaac is involved in the murder of Patrick Riley and the attempted murder of Max on US soil, I say we go after him hard."

"I like the sound of that," Rex agreed. "If Russia is using Isaac and the mafia to protect the Wolf, we'll make sure Isaac tells us who the Wolf is."

———

THOUGH some lesser men would have complained of an impossible task, Pavel viewed it as a challenge. On Misha's orders, he and his men had to abduct three Americans.

And since all three are connected to the US Embassy, they are coddled, Misha thought to himself as the final, large SUV pulled into the warehouse on the outskirts of Tashkent. At a minimum, three would be necessary, but five would be ideal. At least one SUV had to survive the altercation to get the Americans away to safety.

Although Pavel knew it was best to use finesse to quarry the Americans, he secretly hoped he would have to use the force of violence. That unfinished business in the mountains to the south had left him disgruntled, and he thought a rough fight followed by a kill would make him feel better.

Except for that American, Pavel reminded himself. *Misha wants him to survive at all cost. But all others are expendable.*

Pavel watched his men prepare the SUVs. An armed driver in each one plus three armed passengers not only provided enough firepower to capture the Americans, but it also allowed seating to get away with them.

Although it was against his habit, he tried to guess what Misha's plan was with the Americans.

And those cases I had sent all the way up here.

But Pavel soon gave up. Without knowledge of the cases' contents or why the American must survive, he contented himself with the pleasure of carrying out orders and the anticipation of inflicting pain on others.

16

DANIEL WOKE FROM HIS NAP WITH A START. JET LAG PLUS STAYING UP nearly all night in the mountains near Shahrisabz had destroyed his sleep cycle. He rolled off the office couch at the US Embassy and checked the time. Just after 10 PM.

Officer Carter should be sending approval for the mission to get Isaac soon, if she hasn't already, Daniel thought to himself.

Moments later, Daniel walked down the hall and knocked on the door. Just in time, he remembered to use the secret knock: *Shave and a haircut, two bits.*

Rex unlocked and opened the door from inside for Daniel to enter. Rex quietly shut and relocked the door.

"Can't allow anybody to see what we're up to," Rex said as he motioned towards the model he had constructed out of paper and office supplies on the table. A schematic and floorplan were drawn up on a whiteboard.

"Did Officer Carter call with approval yet?" Daniel asked.

"Not yet," Rex said. "But she will. It might take longer than usual since we must keep it secret from Edwards and Fitzpatrick. She thought Peters would be able to get approval without alerting anybody who could inform them."

"Where are Gunner and Walters?"

"They're getting equipment ready for tonight."

"What's your plan so far?" Daniel asked.

"Basically, I've got a diversion planned, and then we'll sneak in, grab Isaac, and get him out of there."

"Please tell me your plan is a little more detailed than that," Daniel said.

"While you were sleeping, I did the best I could to reconstruct the layout of Isaac and Nigora's home. There's some guesswork involved, especially on the interior, but I'm confident we can get in and snatch Isaac before his bodyguards cause any real problems."

"What should I be ready for?" Daniel asked.

"About that," Rex said. "You won't be going in with me on this one."

"I'm not going to let you do this again," Daniel argued. "What do you think I've been training for? You've trained me yourself. What's the point of all that I've busted my ass for if I don't use it on a mission?"

"You've come a long way," Rex said calmly, "but you're still not ready for a mission like this. You're better than you were, but you're still no pro."

Daniel tried another tactic.

"You will need me to communicate with Isaac."

"From Billy, we know that Isaac speaks English, not just Uzbek and Russian," Rex countered. "And if anything goes wrong on this mission, then you and Tina can still catch the Wolf."

Daniel considered pulling rank and insisting that he join Rex on the mission when a chime on a laptop indicated an incoming call.

"That could be Officer Carter," Rex said as he pressed a button on the laptop.

Officer Carter filled half of the screen and Muhammad the other.

"Greetings, gentlemen," Officer Carter said. "I have approval from the top to extract Isaac, and then we'll bring him to the US. If successful, we'll learn who it is that he's been protecting for the Russians. This is all outside of the normal extradition process, so if you get caught, we will disavow you. Understood?"

"Yes, ma'am," Daniel and Rex said in unison. Rex gave Daniel an annoyed look before Officer Carter continued.

"Peters was cautious and gained approval without doing anything that could alert Edwards or Fitzpatrick to this unique mission. It's vital that you maintain that secrecy. If the Wolf learns about it, he'll surely tip Isaac off, and then we'll have a mess on our hands."

"We'll be careful," Daniel said. He was about to plead his case to Officer Carter to gain her endorsement to go on the mission when Muhammad jumped into the conversation.

"Jenny is digging into Billy's past more now, but I found something suggestive in Max's past. Max knew Fitzpatrick, and had met him on a few occasions when Max was in the Peace Corps. If Fitzpatrick is the Wolf, that could be how he first ensnared Max. Previously, there was no known connection between Max and Fitzpatrick."

"Suspicious," Rex agreed. "But I think we'll know the truth by tomorrow morning if my mission succeeds tonight."

"That will be vital because Muhammad uncovered more about Max and Fitzpatrick," Officer Carter said.

"Around lunchtime in Tashkent," Muhammad began to explain, "somebody used Max's credentials to access top-secret information. Lots of it. Suffice to say, we know it wasn't Max because we're holding him here. They used the computer in Patrick Riley's office in the US Embassy in Tashkent."

The pieces began to fall into place for Daniel.

"Riley is dead, Max is here in D.C., and so it must be the Wolf getting one last intelligence dump before he flees and disappears forever," Officer Carter said just as Daniel figured it out.

"I was with Fitzpatrick in Riley's office just before lunch earlier today," Daniel thought out loud. "Fitzpatrick was then at the conference. Tina was keeping tabs on him and Edwards. We need to let her know one of them is probably going to disappear."

"And you need to help her watch those two," Officer Carter ordered Daniel.

Daniel gave Rex a look and knew he wouldn't be joining Rex on the raid to Isaac's home.

"I don't like us being spread so thin," Daniel said.

"It will work," Rex reassured Daniel. "If you and Tina can keep your eyes on Fitzpatrick and Edwards, we'll learn from Isaac who the Wolf is soon enough."

"I just hope it is soon enough," Daniel added. "And I hope Tina stays on her toes. The Wolf could kill her in order to get away. I didn't make her too happy about babysitting at the conference."

"She might not have liked your orders to be at the conference," Rex said, "but she's a pro and will handle herself."

"You're right," Daniel conceded. "By this time tomorrow night, the Wolf—"

Several hard knocks came at the door.

"Daniel? Daniel?"

They recognized the voice. It was Edwards.

Rex abruptly ended the call and shut the laptop.

Daniel opened the door a foot.

"What's up?" Daniel asked. "How has the conference been going?"

Edwards squinted as he briefly tried to look past Daniel and into the room.

"Uneventful," Edwards said. "I was looking for you to see if you wanted to grab a drink. I could tell you my newest theory about the Wolf. Besides, Ambassador Fitzpatrick and Tina were going out for dinner and a drink together, and I didn't want to feel like the third wheel. Hopefully, Tina knows what she's doing."

"Tina can handle herself," Daniel said. "But yeah, sure, I'll join you for a drink. I think Rex was just going to bed, though."

Daniel looked back to Rex as he left the room to go with Edwards.

He hoped Rex was right about Tina and that she stayed alert.

"Let me grab a few things first," Daniel said as he went to get his Glock and the satellite phone.

I think that either Tina or I is having a drink with the Wolf tonight.

———

"I THINK you know why I wanted to talk to you," Edwards said to Daniel. They sat at Edwards' favorite Western restaurant, which was next door to the Intercontinental Hotel. "You've been busy."

"I'm just an analyst," Daniel said sheepishly as he picked at his food.

"Come on," Edwards said with a slight smile. "While I've been sitting at a conference and listening to politicians blow smoke up everybody's ass, you have uncovered Michael Devers at a secret facility, and you caught Billy with his hand in the cookie jar."

Daniel shrugged nervously, as if it had all been luck.

"How close are you to solving the bombing?"

"You know I'm not really supposed to talk about the bombing, even with you," Daniel said.

Edwards shrugged and took a sip from his beer.

He said, "I've been hearing that one for years. It seems like nobody can ever talk about anything. But I know where you're coming from. I hunted the Wolf for years. It was kind of my obsession for a long while. I wish you luck with him. But after this conference, I'm rethinking things. There has been absolutely zero suspicious activity at the conference. And I've thought a lot about what you said. Maybe I am a bit dated in this business. I must let you know that, honestly, I think the Wolf might be a ghost, a concoction made up by the KGB during the Cold War to intimidate us. Most likely, my feeling is that the Wolf is really just a combination of a few sources that are made to look like one mighty powerful spy to frighten us."

"Really?" Daniel asked. "You thought the Wolf was more important than the War on Terror about a week ago."

"Yeah, but the Wolf's information has been from all over the place. It could be a bunch of lower-level sources all over the world. If one occasionally hits the jackpot, it can make the Wolf look like a highly placed spy. If we clean up all the little leaks, we'll discover that the mythical Wolf may disappear - because he never existed."

"Hey, I'm the one who argued that last week," Daniel reminded Edwards. Daniel wanted to keep Edwards talking. He gave the senior officer an opportunity to gloat. "You've been around the block a few times, and you've been with the CIA since the Cold War. If you're so sure now that the Wolf is fiction, what did it feel like when you got closest to him?"

"I'll never forget the defector we were bringing across the

Berlin Wall back in the day," Edwards said as he swallowed a mouthful of beer. Daniel mimicked Edwards and sipped his drink. "The defector said he would deliver the identity of an agent code-named Wolf. 'The time has finally come,' I had thought. The *Stasi* and the KGB have been kicking our asses all over Europe, especially in Berlin, for years. They were always one step ahead of us, it seemed, and we could never get one over on them. When this man said he could hand us the Wolf, we thought we were about to get rid of all our problems. But first, we had to get the defector across the Wall. He wouldn't talk until he was safely in the West."

"What happened?" Daniel asked.

"All the defector had to do was go to a deserted warehouse. We had uncovered an unused utility passageway that would lead him near one of the subway stations where we would pick him up."

"That doesn't make sense. It couldn't have been that easy."

"This wasn't just any subway station. This was one of the ghost stations. You see, when East Germany put up the Berlin Wall, it's not as though the Wall was a perfectly straight line. It wound its way through the general center of the city, but parts of it even ran east and west, not north and south. More confusingly, some of the subway lines, while underground, would pass from West Berlin into East Berlin and then back into West Berlin. Obviously, the *Stasi* couldn't allow East Berliners to board the subway on one side of the Wall, ride, and then get off on the other side. So, they shut down the subway stops that were in East Berlin on Western subway lines. These stations were called ghost stations."

"But you found the utility passageway for the defector to get into a ghost station, and then you just had to use the Western subway line to get him out?" Daniel said.

"Basically," Edwards confirmed. "There were guards at the ghost stations, but they hadn't covered all the secret passageways. I never had any problems before that night." Edwards stared off into space as he said, "God, those were the days. So much happened in those tunnels."

Daniel wondered what Edwards was thinking about before he continued.

"But when I got there, the defector was dead. They had killed him and cut off his lips. *Rigor mortis* had not set in, and his body didn't feel cold. They had recently killed him."

"Did you think of going through the passageway to chase the killer?" Daniel asked.

"I thought about it. Believe me, I wanted to run and kill whomever I encountered. But my orders were clear. Get the defector and bring him back. If I had given chase, I would've been on my own. Even if I did catch the killer and kill him, I would've gotten in big trouble for disobeying orders. And worst-case scenario, the *Grepos* or *Stasi* would've captured me. Who knows what they would've done with me? I was in East Berlin, after all."

"So that was the closest you ever got?" Daniel asked. He began to lift his glass, but he froze.

Daniel thought he saw Ambassador Fitzpatrick enter the restaurant with Tina.

But he was mistaken. The man's suit was brown, but the woman was too tall.

Daniel brought his glass to his lips and took a sip.

Wherever Tina is, I hope she's safe, Daniel thought. *If one of us doesn't make it out of this alive...*

"The defector was dead with his lips cut off," Edwards said, seemingly unaware of Daniel's break in concentration. "The worst part is that the Berlin Wall came down just a few days later." Edwards finished his beer and placed it on the table. He leaned towards Daniel and said, "If he had just lain low for a couple more days, he could have walked under his own power into West Berlin, entered any NATO building and yelled at the top of his lungs who the Wolf was, and he would have been fine."

"Or, maybe, the Wolf was never real, and that was all part of the KGB's plan to inflate the Wolf's legend," Daniel suggested.

"I'm beginning to think that is likely," Edwards agreed. "The conference has been a bust in terms of uncovering the Wolf."

"But Billy seems to be cover for the Wolf. Did you ever suspect anything was wrong with Billy?" Daniel asked.

Edwards waved his hand, calling for another drink, and then answered. "No. Sure, he wasn't perfect, but he did do a lot of good things, most of which I can't even tell you about."

"It seems Billy hoped he was getting really close to the Wolf's identity in St. Petersburg," Daniel said.

"Leningrad," Edwards said, almost as if to himself, mentioning the city's name before it was changed in 1991. "That whole Devers affair was messed up." Edwards pulled out a lighter and began lighting up a cigarette.

Daniel's mind raced as he tried to decide if Edwards should have known about Devers in St. Petersburg.

"I guess it shouldn't surprise me," Edwards continued. "Everybody in this game deals with the stresses differently. Some of them turn to alcohol, drugs, women, and gambling. And I know that some of the agents we've had from the Soviet Union were like Jekyll and Hyde. They were straight-laced military guys by day, but by night, they could crave some bizarre stuff. But Billy was smart enough to keep his binges outside of working hours to conceal them. Perhaps Billy was just one of those little leaks that contributed to the myth of the Wolf." Edwards shrugged as he shook his cigarette over the ashtray. "There's a lot of secrets I won't know the answers to in this life. The dots don't always connect so nicely like they do in the movies. Lots of dead ends. Lots of uncertainty."

"Lots of uncertainty," Daniel agreed.

"But let me be straight with you," Edwards said, pulling Daniel back into their conversation. "I need sharp men. Hell, I won't be around forever. In case you haven't noticed, I'm an old hand, and now I've lost Billy." He paused for a moment. "Tell me about yourself."

"Well," Daniel started nervously, "You know about the MDF team that I'm heading up. In reality, I'm a linguistic analyst, and Rex does most of the fieldwork. And Tina was with the FBI, so she's usually in the field too. My adventure here in Uzbekistan is making me think I belong behind a desk."

"Can I talk you into becoming a field guy in my unit?" Edwards asked. "I have better funding than Officer Carter, which means more pay for you. And I have the best unit, so we get the best missions. Maybe you do belong behind a desk, but I think you have potential."

"I'm just a linguist and an analyst," Daniel said. "It would be a waste if I was doing anything other than that."

"I understand," Edwards said. "Not everybody is cut out for the field. Amateurs in the field only get people killed. Believe me, I've seen that too many times."

Daniel sheepishly agreed. He thought as he chewed. *Edwards wants me closer to him in the future*, he realized.

But before he could think about it more, he felt the buzz of his satellite phone.

"Hello? I'm just enjoying a drink with Edwards—"

They have to know I can't talk openly, whoever it is.

Officer Carter's voice sharply replied: "Tina hasn't checked in, and we can't get in touch with her."

"Edwards said Fitzpatrick and Tina were having dinner and a drink," Daniel said. He gave a momentary smile to Edwards.

"I think Fitzpatrick is making a run for it," Officer Carter said. "Find him and Tina."

"Okay. I'll go back to the embassy and start working on it," Daniel replied. He ended the call.

"Duty calls," Daniel explained to Edwards as he rose to leave.

"I understand," Edwards said. "I might as well come with you."

Daniel forced himself to remain calm and purposeful as he exited the restaurant. Inside, Daniel wanted to run to find Tina, but his instincts told him to not fully trust Edwards yet. He continued to act as if he was heading back for another extremely late night at the office.

Please God, don't let anything happen to Tina...

"WHAT TIME IS IT, ANYWAY?" Daniel asked Edwards as the driver slowed for a U-turn that would take them to the US Embassy.

"It's about one in the morning," Edwards said after a glance at his watch. Daniel knew Rex planned to start his raid at one in the morning. "Are you sure you don't want to be a field spook in my unit?"

Daniel was about to answer when his satellite phone buzzed again.

"Jenny?" Daniel said after he answered the phone.

"No, it's Muhammad," came the reply as Daniel gave a smile to Edwards as if to apologize for taking the call.

"You're not going to believe this," Muhammad continued.

As Daniel listened to Muhammad's report, a roaring engine

and squealing tires turned Daniel's attention to another large SUV that was accelerating on a perpendicular intercept course.

The large SUV smashed into the front driver's side of the US embassy vehicle carrying Daniel and Edwards. The last thing Daniel remembered was the disorientation of the car repeatedly spinning and then flipping over from the collision.

Pavel had made his move.

17

REX CHECKED THE TIME. IT WAS JUST BEFORE ONE IN THE MORNING.

Rex knew he and Gunner and Walters wouldn't have to wait much longer.

I hate waiting, Rex thought to himself as he gazed at Isaac and Nigora's fortress-like home from a block away.

As if on cue, a gray car with license plates from the British embassy pulled up to the guard tower in front of Nigora and Isaac's house.

"The party is getting started," Rex told Gunner and Walters quietly. Rex was anxious to put their elite skills to use. He ran through the plan one more time in his head. Satellite imagery had revealed a large courtyard inside the walls, with a pool surrounded by decorative vegetation in the back. A second-floor balcony was probably connected to the bedroom in which Isaac was sleeping. Rex hoped Nigora had followed Daniel's advice to not return home. Rex didn't trust her; she was too much of a wildcard.

Rex watched as the guard in the booth exchanged angry words

with the man at the steering wheel. A man got out of the backseat of the car and took a few stumbling steps. Rex chuckled at the sight of his MI6 buddy playing drunk.

The guard barked an order at the Brit.

The drunken man stepped aggressively towards the guard and began yelling at him.

"Pretty good acting," Rex observed.

Two more guards came to the front gate to assist the first.

The show of force didn't make the drunk back down. Instead, he lunged at the first guard and swung dramatically with a looping haymaker. The guard dodged easily and doubled him over with a blow to his midsection.

The drunk backed away and reached into his pocket as he straightened up.

All three guards drew their weapons and pointed them at the drunk and began yelling more orders.

"You're going to owe your MI6 friend big-time for this," Walters said to Rex.

"Nah," Rex disagreed. "Jeremy owed me from before. He's doing a good job, though."

Jeremy raised his hands into the air, revealing a cigarette and a lighter.

The guards stood steadfastly and motioned with their weapons towards the gray car. Jeremy complied and climbed back into the British embassy vehicle. Moments later, it backed away slowly. The guards didn't stand down until the gray car was out of sight.

"Hopefully that's enough excitement for them for one night," Rex said. "Now we know there are at least two men inside. We just need to wait for them to lower their guard. They can't stay on high alert forever."

"I'm glad Jeremy didn't get himself shot," Walters said.

"He played it perfectly," Rex said. "I reckon I owe him a pint now."

Rex rechecked the time.

I hate waiting, Rex thought to himself. *But I need to let them stew a bit longer.*

————

ABOUT FIFTY MINUTES LATER, Rex thanked God it was finally time.

"Go time," Rex said to Gunner and Walters. "But remember, we can only use lethal force on Isaac, and that's only if necessary."

"We always appreciate a challenge, sir," Walters said with a grin.

Their dark camouflage concealed them under cover of darkness as they exited their observation post and approached Isaac and Nigora's house. They crouched behind bushes and Rex pulled out the radio detonator.

Rex pressed the button.

An explosion boomed about a block away. The electric transformer for the whole neighborhood exploded, and the street went black.

There wouldn't be much time until backup generators in Isaac's mansion kicked in.

Rex and his men dashed to the back wall of the house and tossed up their grappling hooks. They scaled the wall in less than thirty seconds and looked with their night vision goggles down into the courtyard.

Rex counted several more than the two guards who had helped greet Jeremy earlier. All but one of them left, presumably to examine the exploded transformer elsewhere in the neighborhood. The one guard remained near the pool, smoking, but he was facing the front of the house and the activity in that direction.

Rex led the way for his men as he stealthily hurried across the top of the wall. Soon, they were directly across from the second-floor balcony.

Nobody had spotted them yet.

But the distance to the balcony disheartened Rex.

Rex looked back to Walters and Gunner, but they both made the letter X with their hands, indicating the jump wasn't possible.

Not much time could remain until the backup generators turned on. The courtyard would surely be flooded with light.

Damn, Rex thought. *Good thing I have a plan B. I just need to figure out what that is.*

Rex directed the men to retrace their movements towards the back.

They soon stood at their original point of infiltration.

The only thing I hate more than waiting is wasting time on a mission, Rex thought to himself.

The lone guard still stood by the pool, smoking.

Rex saw the orange light of the cigarette tremble. Jeremy's ruse, plus nearly an hour of waiting, had frayed the guard's nerves. And the cigarette's glow ruined the guard's vision in the dark.

Rex and his men pulled up their ropes from the outside and used them to silently lower themselves inside the courtyard. Gunner made it down behind the bushes first, followed by Walters, and then Rex.

After a thumbs-up, Rex grabbed a pebble and threw it towards the opposite end of the pool.

The guard turned instinctively towards the noise, and this allowed Walters the time he needed to take the guard from behind. A brutally quick chokehold, and the guard was soon unconscious. Gunner helped Walters drag him back behind the poolside bushes.

Rex hurried with the other two behind him, past the pool and towards the house's back door.

Still not detected, Rex thought to himself as he approached to kneel under the windows next to the back door.

A rumble indicated that somebody had finally coaxed the house's generators to life, and floodlights around the pool lit up.

Spoke too soon, Rex thought. *But we still have the element of surprise.* He lifted his night vision goggles out of the way. They would be useless now.

Rex pulled the door handle down and eased the door open. Walters entered in a crouch with Gunner behind him. The interior was still mostly dark; the generator must have only powered minimal circuits. Rex crossed the threshold, and Walters pointed to a stairway that would lead them up to the master bedroom.

A voice in Russian called out from a nearby room on the ground level.

Rex could only guess that somebody had heard the back door open and assumed it was the pool guard. Rex turned towards the voice and saw what appeared to be the security room, filled with small TV monitors.

Rex rushed towards the room as a man came out. Rex struck him in the larynx before he realized something was wrong. Gunner applied another chokehold, and the man soon went limp.

We still have the time we need to get Isaac, Rex thought as he headed towards the stairs. *But I don't know about getting him out.*

Rex and the others raced up the white-tiled staircase as more lights came on. A hallway with three doors greeted them at the top.

Yells in Russian erupted elsewhere in the house.

Somebody found the immobilized guards, Rex thought. *Time's up.*

But there wasn't time to search behind all the doors.

Remembering that the balcony had been just beyond their ability to jump to it from the wall, Rex chose the center door.

He pushed the door open enough to allow the three of them into the black room. He flipped down his night vision goggles to scan the darkness for Isaac as Gunner pulled the door shut.

Before the goggles adjusted, a musky, feminine perfume filled Rex's nostrils.

This is definitely Nigora and Isaac's bedroom, Rex thought.

———

AN UNEXPECTED CLICK of a light switch and the lights came on in the room, blinding Rex and his men with their night vision goggles.

Rex felt panic creep into his chest, and he threw up his night vision equipment.

Where is he? Rex thought to himself. *He was waiting for us.*

"Don't move, or I'll blow your brains out," a voice said to Rex's left. There was a second click, but this time, it was the cocking of a gun.

Rex lowered his pistol to the floor and slowly raised his hands. Gunner and Walters did the same. Rex turned his head towards the voice and recognized Nigora's husband, Isaac, whom he had seen in the teahouse just a few days prior. His expensive watch matched his fine suit.

"My darling, take their guns from them," Isaac said. He repeated it in Russian.

Nigora rose from the opulent bed, dressed in a white night-gown. Her dark hair tumbled down past her shoulders. She walked towards Rex, unashamed of the little she was wearing besides the smirk on her face. She bent down and picked up each of the Americans' guns. She placed two on her bed, but Rex watched as she held his pistol at her side.

"My wife thought we would have visitors tonight," Isaac told Rex.

Anger replaced panic in Rex. He and Daniel had tried to help Nigora, and she, in turn, had led Rex into a trap.

"No harm has been done," Rex said carefully. "None of us wants an international incident. We can all walk away from this. It's just a big misunderstanding."

"Misunderstanding? I have nothing to walk away from," Isaac said. "It looks to me like some American terrorist broke into my house to murder my wife and me. What would any husband do in self-defense?"

Now the anger was focusing Rex's thoughts to discover a way out. He knew Isaac was right. Isaac could kill the three of them and get away with it.

Rex decided to bluff his way out.

"There's more going on than what you know," Rex warned. He only needed to make Isaac hesitate.

Nigora spoke to Isaac in Russian. Rex didn't understand, but her warning tone was clear. She pointed Rex's gun at Rex. She sidestepped towards her husband.

"You know who the American spy is. The one they call the Wolf. You've been killing people to keep him safe. You will be next."

"Not possible. I don't think you realize who I am," Isaac said.

"The Russian mafia in Uzbekistan is nothing compared to Moscow and the FSB," Rex said. "Now that you've tied up all the other loose ends, you will be next."

Isaac's left wrist twitched, making his watch jiggle, as he pondered what Rex was saying.

"That's why I came here," Rex said. "We came to get you out of here safely so you can tell us who the Wolf is before they kill you."

Nigora raised her voice again in Russian at her husband.

"Think about it. Don't be too proud to think they would let you live even though you know the Wolf's identity."

Nigora shrieked at Isaac in Russian now, the gun trembling in her hand.

This just might work, Rex thought to himself.

"If you kill us now or deliver us to your master, he will thank you and then kill you."

Isaac's left wrist continued to twitch as he kept his pistol trained on Rex.

"If you come with us now and tell us who the Wolf is, you can be safe in America. You know how powerful the Russian mafia is. Because you know the Wolf's identity, where else can you live without fear of being hunted down? Come with me peacefully, and you can survive."

Rex saw Isaac's wrist stop twitching. His grip on the pistol loosened.

Nigora yelled at her husband. Rex knew she must have feared Isaac would flip.

Without warning, Isaac swung his left fist in a backhanded motion. It smashed into Nigora's face. She shrieked and collapsed to the ground. She raised her left hand to shield herself.

Isaac turned and angrily yelled down at her. After several moments, Nigora was curled up and sobbing on the floor. Isaac turned back towards Rex and lowered his gun.

"I think we can reach an arrangement that will suit all of us,"

Isaac said to Rex calmly. "I will tell you who the Wolf is once I am safe in America."

"*Nyet!*" Nigora yelled. Nigora raised to one knee with Rex's pistol. She aimed at Isaac and fired Rex's pistol three times into her husband's body. Isaac dropped to the ground.

Rex sprang into action.

Rex went to Isaac, who was bleeding out on the floor.

"Who is the Wolf?" Rex yelled at Isaac.

He looked up and saw Nigora pointing the pistol at Gunner and Walters, keeping them away from their guns resting on the bed.

"Who is the Wolf?" Rex repeated.

Isaac's lips moved. He gasped.

Rex watched Isaac's life depart as his eyes went blank.

"Why did you do that?" Rex yelled at Nigora as he rose to his feet. "You both could have come with me safely."

Nigora returned a steely glare. Rex realized she didn't understand English.

The bedroom door swung open. Rex felt another wave of adrenaline rise as two more security guards came in through the door, but the last man to enter caught Rex off guard.

————

DETECTIVE JAHONGIR BARAKATULLA walked into the bedroom and looked about. Two more policemen were with him.

Rex's relief at still being alive switched to confusion and fear. How would the Uzbek police handle his presence?

And Isaac was shot with my weapon, Rex thought to himself.

"It appears to me that everything played out just as Nigora envisioned," Jahongir said to Rex.

"What do you mean?" Rex asked.

"Nigora just made herself the new head of the Russian mafia in Uzbekistan," Jahongir explained.

"And you... What?" Rex stumbled to say.

"The Russian mafia had become too powerful and problematic here," Jahongir said. "I was eager for new leadership. New leadership that could cooperate with the government."

"So now you're on good terms with the new head of the Russian mafia?" Rex asked.

"We have an understanding," Jahongir replied. "Now come with me. We should leave here quickly. We still have much work to do within the next twelve hours. You must help me with something. Otherwise, I would hate to report this horrible incident."

Rex, Gunner, and Walters left Nigora's opulent residence with Jahongir and wondered what Jahongir had been talking about regarding the next twelve hours.

If Isaac could have just said the Wolf's name before he died, Rex thought to himself. He gave one last look back to the house before Jahongir drove them away.

18

DANIEL'S HEAD HURT WHEN HE CAME TO.

He quickly rose to his feet but fell back down onto the ceramic floor. He felt faint. As he took stock of his body, he realized that, though he was sore, he wasn't seriously injured.

Where am I? Daniel wondered to himself.

The walls were tiled to match the maroon tiles on the floor, and a drain was in the center of the room. A small window with frosted glass near the ceiling allowed in the only light.

Is it morning? Or, has it been more than a day?

Daniel noticed only two other items in the room: a bucket and a bottle of water. After several more deep breaths, Daniel rose slowly this time and turned the bucket over. He stood on it and attempted to pry the window open. The window was immovable.

A scream from outside his room turned Daniel's head towards the doorway.

The commotion ended with two gunshots. Daniel guessed it was in a nearby room or down the hall.

Remembering the sandbags in the prison's basement for executions, Daniel wondered if he was in the same prison Michael Devers had been in. But no. Those cells weren't tiled.

This feels more like an empty storage room in a basement, Daniel thought to himself. The bucket and bottled water gave Daniel some encouragement. Why would they bother to hydrate somebody destined for execution?

Daniel tried the door. As expected, it was locked. But it wasn't a prison-type lock. Though heavy-duty, the lock was that of a residential home. Desperate, Daniel began searching for loose tiles or anything else that would allow his escape or give him more information.

Only minutes later, Daniel decided there were no faults in his cell. He wasn't going to be able to get himself out. He sat and leaned against the wall and tried to remember all that had happened before he had blacked out.

The last thing he remembered before the car wreck was a call on the satellite phone.

Was it Officer Carter again?

Or Jenny?

No, Daniel remembered. *It was Muhammad, but what did Muhammad say?*

Daniel pressed his palms over his face and tried to pry the secret memories—if any—from his mind.

"Oh no," Daniel said alone in his cell. "Tina's in danger." He remembered she'd gone missing.

Now panic began to swell in Daniel's chest. He yanked at the door's handle and kicked.

He pressed his ear against the door and waited.

Frustrated, he slouched back onto the floor.

A low rumble made his room vibrate. Several more blasts

erupted in the distance, and then gunfire came. A gunfight had started elsewhere. Probably upstairs.

He heard footsteps coming down the hallway, and Daniel rose to his feet.

A key began working in the lock from the other side. Daniel grabbed the closest thing he could find to a weapon: the bucket.

He pressed against the wall next to the door, ready to strike whoever entered.

"Daniel?" a voice called as the door handle went down. Daniel recognized the voice. "Are you in there?"

The door opened. Daniel swung the bucket down, but Edwards blocked it with his arm and moved out of the way.

"*For Chrissake!*" Edwards said as he entered the cell and backed away from Daniel. The Glock in Edwards' hand drew Daniel's eyes. "That's a helluva way to thank somebody for rescuing you."

Edwards extended the Glock, handle-first, towards Daniel and said, "Jahongir and the SNB are mounting a raid on the Russian mafia. Even your friend Rex is helping."

Daniel exhaled deeply, dropped the bucket, and gratefully took the gun from Edwards.

"Where are we?" Daniel asked.

"The Russian mafia's mountain *dacha*, north of Tashkent," Edwards answered as he handed Daniel his satellite phone. Daniel clipped it to his belt.

"*Dacha?*"

"Mansion, more like," Edwards said. "Try not to be an amateur and shoot me in the ass while we escape." He stepped to the doorway and looked down the hallway as he began to explain. "After the wreck, the mafia brought us here. Lucky for us, Rex and his men are working with the Uzbek secret police to raid this place. The Uzbek government finally had enough problems from the Russians and decided to clean house." Daniel followed Edwards down the hallway and towards a set of stairs. "An Uzbek policeman freed me, gave me a gun, and then I recovered your stuff and said I'd get you out. There's a fierce gunfight upstairs, but we can get out of here."

"Is Tina here?" Daniel said.

"I'm sorry," Edwards said as he started up the stairs towards the gunfire. "I don't know. I do know Rex agreed to help because the ultimate mission was to rescue Ambassador Fitzpatrick."

Ambassador Fitzpatrick is here?

There was no time for another question because Edwards and Daniel exited the basement to the mansion's main level where the gun battle raged between the secret police and the Russian mafia.

———

DANIEL AND EDWARDS crouched behind a large sofa as bullets flew around them. Several policemen in body armor were in the room, carefully acquiring targets and firing. One policeman was next to them, intermittently peeking over the sofa and firing. The Russians were on the opposite side, more keen to expend ammunition in the general direction of the invaders.

As the bullets put divots and cracks in the marble floor and walls near Daniel, Edwards yelled, "Follow me. They told me to go out through a hole in the back garden wall that they created in the raid."

Daniel didn't want to just escape with his life, though.

If Fitzpatrick is here, then maybe Tina is too.

Daniel risked a peek over the sofa. Directly in front of him, the cavernous living area of white marble accented with large animal skins gave way to a broad panel of shattered windows that looked out to the majestic mountains in the distance. Russians hid behind furniture and returned fire, but now they were trapped.

To the left, Daniel saw that the home opened up to the outdoors and a courtyard or garden. The police were moving out there.

"Rex!" Daniel yelled as he spotted the stealthy movements of the SpecOps warrior. He wasn't sure, but he thought he saw Tina in front of him, just as they went out of sight to the outdoors.

A bullet shattered the wooden frame of the sofa, and Daniel had to duck back down.

"Come on!" Edwards urged Daniel as he motioned away.

Daniel looked up and saw that the staircase to his left led to a balcony from which a Russian was firing down.

Daniel fired but missed.

The policeman next to him fired, and the man on the balcony slumped down.

Daniel turned to leave with Edwards, but then he saw a man with a rifle run along the balcony above.

The man entered the first room off the balcony and shut the door.

Daniel knew the room undoubtedly overlooked the courtyard below, and he would use his rifle to pick off Rex and Tina from above.

And Daniel had encountered this bald man before.

It was Pavel who had toted his rifle to the room above to fire upon the police and Daniel's friends.

"Come on!" Edwards urged Daniel again.

Daniel ignored him and spoke to the Uzbek policeman next to him.

"Cover me. I'm going up."

Pavel had already killed Michael Devers, and Daniel was not going to allow him to kill Rex and Tina.

The policeman released a heavy stream of fire and gave Daniel the precious seconds he needed.

"No!" Edwards yelled after Daniel. "We need to get out of here!"

Daniel turned away from Edwards and ran up the stairs to the room Pavel had entered with his rifle.

———

As Daniel flew past the final steps on the staircase and approached the door, he imagined himself bursting in and shooting Pavel in the back of his thick head as he looked over the courtyard with his rifle.

A moment before impact with the door, Daniel remembered his training.

I can't run in blindly.

With a single swift motion, he pushed down on the handle and swung the door in to enter. He scanned the nearest corner and dropped to a knee to take in the rest of the room. The wall to his left was lined with built-in bookcases that housed books and souvenirs from all corners of the world.

As Daniel turned to his right, he spotted a wooden desk on which the rifle rested.

Before Daniel could finish his visual sweep of the room, the door swung back at Daniel and knocked him towards the bookcase.

Pavel charged like a rhinoceros from where the door had concealed him.

Daniel fired, but he was too slow. The shot went wild.

A solid blow in Daniel's stomach weakened his grip on his gun, and Pavel knocked it away with the next strike.

Daniel rolled away as Pavel's meaty fingers grasped at him. Daniel sensed he would be no match for the hulking Russian in close hand-to-hand combat. He spotted his Glock on the floor, but he would have to go through the Russian to get to it.

Daniel cast about the bookshelf on his side, desperately grasping for anything to be used as a weapon. He only found thick books, which he threw at Pavel. But that wasn't slowing Pavel's advance much.

Finally, Daniel's hand wrapped around a metal cylinder, and he pulled it from the shelf. Daniel saw that he had grabbed a telescope that was as much for show as the books had been.

Pavel straightened up slightly and laughed. He said something in Russian that Daniel didn't understand. Pavel reached to the bookcase and pulled down a sword that had been resting near a painting of a Napoleonic battle.

Daniel lowered his telescope slightly and cursed to himself. His mind raced for a solution. The gunfire inside the house had now transferred to the outside. Gunshots rang out in the courtyard below and behind Daniel's back.

At least baldy isn't picking them off like fish in a barrel with his rifle, Daniel thought to himself.

Pavel pulled the blade from its scabbard and sliced the air with it.

Daniel searched frantically for another weapon on the bookcase. The best he found was a ceremonial dagger.

Why not a samurai sword? Daniel thought ruefully to himself.

Daniel wielded the telescope in his right hand and the short blade in his left.

Pavel grinned, approaching him slowly as his sword cut

through the air. Daniel backed towards the balcony and heard something unexpected.

The roar of a helicopter's engines coming to life felt all-consuming; the gunshots were mere accents of noise. The thunder of the machine filled the room and shook Daniel's body. He guessed this mansion in the mountains had a helipad to match the one in the facility near Shahrisabz. But he didn't have time to think about that. Pavel was ready to shed Daniel's blood.

A quick attack, disengage, dodge, and then go for my Glock, was the best plan Daniel could concoct. He felt his only advantage was that Pavel was overconfident; he didn't appear skilled with a sword.

Pavel said a few more words in Russian, spat, and then rushed at Daniel with the raised sword.

"This is for what you did to Michael Devers," Daniel said as he met Pavel's charge.

———

DANIEL FEINTED to his left and then dashed back to his right.

From a crouch, he threw the telescope at Pavel's face, hoping to blind him just long enough.

As the telescope flew, Daniel prepared the dagger in his right hand.

The telescope struck Pavel harmlessly, and Daniel threw the dagger, leaving him unarmed.

The dagger glanced off Pavel's midsection.

Daniel couldn't wait around to see the results.

He made one lunge towards his Glock, but before his hand reached it, Pavel's sword came crashing down.

The sword smashed into the wooden parquet floor between Daniel's hand and the Glock. Daniel instinctively retracted his hand, and Pavel used his sword to flick the Glock out of Daniel's reach towards the door.

Pavel laughed again, said a few more Russian words. And then he raised the sword above his head to strike Daniel.

Daniel was frozen between fleeing and attempting to go hand-to-hand with Pavel, but a new Russian voice came from the doorway.

Daniel looked and saw Edwards, now holding Daniel's Glock.

Three gunshots rang out.

Daniel watched as Pavel fell to the ground. The sword clattered at his side harmlessly.

Before Daniel could thank Edwards, he heard more gunshots and yelling from the courtyard. He barely caught Rex's voice over the gunfire and the roar of the helicopter.

And he heard Tina's voice.

"We need to get out of here," Edwards yelled over the noise. "There's too many mafia."

But Daniel rushed to the balcony to witness the carnage.

19

THE COURTYARD BELOW HOUSED AN EXPANSIVE GARDEN, REPLETE with walkways, fountains, flowerbeds, and trees. But now it also contained dead bodies. Several dead Russians lay scattered about, but so did the bodies of police wearing body armor. Daniel guessed the garden was as large as a football field, surrounded by a wall. At the far end was another house, perhaps for servants. Daniel wondered if Ambassador Fitzpatrick was there, or if only more mafia were waiting for the fight.

Daniel finally spotted Rex, with Gunner on the left. They were advancing steadily through the garden. Far to Daniel's right, he saw the raised helipad connected to the same level on which he stood. The helicopter was preparing to take off. A Russian in a gray suit and sunglasses walked from the house and onto the helicopter. Daniel couldn't be sure, but he thought he could see one other man in the helicopter beside the pilot.

Daniel was about to exit and run down the hallway to the room that opened out to the helipad when he heard Rex yell out.

"Gunner! No!"

Daniel looked below frantically.

He spotted a Russian who had outflanked Rex and Gunner.

Daniel saw Gunner laying on the ground, motionless.

Rex quickly repositioned to take out the flanker, and Daniel ran to the wooden desk.

"What are you doing?" Edwards asked. "We need to get the hell out of here. You're an analyst."

Daniel ignored him and carried Pavel's rifle to the balcony in time to see Rex take down the man who had killed Gunner.

But there was gunfire elsewhere.

He scanned the courtyard, looking for a target.

He heard yelling from his right by the helicopter.

Daniel considered leveling the rifle at the chopper to make sure it didn't get away.

But then he spotted what he feared most.

Tina was in the courtyard below to Daniel's right.

She was in the fight of her life.

Two Russians lay dead nearby, and she was now grappling with a third.

Daniel guessed the Russians had underestimated her and planned to have fun with her.

The crosshairs rested on Tina and her attacker. The two were locked in a struggle.

It's not a clean shot.

Tina and the Russian twisted as they each grappled for an advantage.

An unexpected change, and Daniel could accidentally shoot Tina.

The Russian took Tina down to the ground.

Daniel knew a rain of blows would follow.

It also meant the Russian was on top of Tina.

I hope my life is never on the line when you're shooting, Daniel remembered Tina saying.

The Russian struck Tina on the head. She lay defenseless, momentarily stunned.

The Russian was about to strike the fatal blow.

Daniel recalled his embrace with Tina at the shooting range at the K2 base.

You have what it takes, she had said.

Daniel pulled the trigger.

Through the scope, he saw the Russian slump over on top of Tina.

Thank God, Daniel thought to himself as he exhaled deeply.

Daniel gave a quick wave to Tina, but then he spotted movement in his periphery near the helicopter. He lowered the rifle and turned to look.

It was Ambassador Fitzpatrick.

"Fitzpatrick! No!" Daniel yelled.

The ambassador must have heard something and hesitated.

Gunshots erupted from the helicopter at Daniel. They forced Daniel off the balcony and back into the house.

Daniel ran past Edwards, and out of the room into the hallway, the rifle still in his hands. The room that led out to the helipad was down the hallway.

I can't allow Fitzpatrick on that helicopter, Daniel thought.

———

DANIEL IGNORED EDWARDS' calls to come back and instead burst into the room that led out to the helipad.

This room was a mirror image to the one he had fought Pavel in, but Daniel didn't have time to examine the historical souvenirs.

The man in the gray suit had gotten off the helicopter and pulled Fitzpatrick towards it, but then he whispered something into his ear.

Fitzpatrick's not getting away, Daniel thought to himself.

Daniel took a step towards the two to stop them, but then the man in the gray suit backed away, pulled a gun, and fired several bullets into Fitzpatrick.

What the hell? Daniel wondered as he ran at the man and raised the rifle.

Unfamiliar with the weapon, Daniel fumbled with the gun as he struggled to chamber the next round. The failure allowed the man in the gray suit to jump into the helicopter just as it began to rise.

Daniel threw the rifle away out of frustration and ran at the helicopter as it pulled away from the helipad.

After passing Fitzpatrick's dying body, Daniel leaped into the air and grasped the helicopter's landing skid.

He clung on and strained to pull himself up.

Russian shouts Daniel didn't understand came from the helicopter, and he looked up to see a perfectly polished black shoe come down onto his fingers. He caught sight of not the man in the gray suit, but another Russian he had never seen before. His dark hair was nearly black and full of gray streaks. Aviator sunglasses concealed his eyes.

The man stamped with his foot and forced Daniel to release his grip. Daniel fell back down onto the helipad.

Daniel looked up and watched the helicopter pull away into the sky.

Daniel stumbled back towards Fitzpatrick, who was bleeding out on the ground.

"What did he say to you?" Daniel yelled as he observed the man's multiple gunshot wounds.

Fitzpatrick mumbled something in Russian.

"What does it mean?" Daniel demanded.

Fitzpatrick repeated the Russian phrase.

Edwards approached from the room slowly as Daniel screamed at Fitzpatrick for the meaning of the Russian.

Edwards stood nearby and said, "It means, 'Your usefulness is over.'"

Daniel slumped over onto the ground near Fitzpatrick, exhausted. His head felt like it was spinning.

Fitzpatrick's glassy eyes went to Edwards and then back to Daniel as if there was more to say, but then he went lifeless.

"I need to call this in," Daniel said as he reached for the satellite phone on his belt.

"Let's get the hell out of here first," Edwards insisted. "If the Russians win the gunfight, we'll be lucky if they only kill us painlessly afterward."

"I can't argue with you this time," Daniel agreed.

Edwards handed Daniel his Glock and said, "Here's yours. I took Pavel's gun."

Edwards readied the gun and hurried back into the house. Daniel followed.

———

DANIEL STUMBLED as he struggled behind Edwards and into the house. Pain was replacing adrenaline in his body.

"I must have hurt my ankle when I fell from the chopper," Daniel said to Edwards.

Edwards positioned Daniel's arm over his own shoulder, and they stumbled out to the hallway that overlooked the palatial living area below. A few policemen had stayed behind, keeping the surviving Russians pinned down.

Edwards fired from above and provided cover as Daniel dropped to the floor and crawled to the stairs. Moments later, both were hurrying down the stairs on all fours as the policemen provided more covering fire.

When they reached the bottom, a hail of gunfire erupted from outside, and Daniel guessed the Russians had reinforced themselves from the other building and were making another push.

Daniel crawled behind Edwards, past the couch and basement door, and continued towards another. Once they were each through that door, Edwards explained, "The police told me there's a smaller garden out this way, and at the end, there's a hole in the wall. It was one of the police's breach points. It's closer than their breach point at the main gate."

"Got it," Daniel said, wincing from the pain in his ankle.

"I'm out of bullets, so—"

"I can't have many left," Daniel said. "I'll make sure they count if I have to use them."

Edwards left his gun on the ground and moved in a crouching position through a final door and into the mansion's side garden. Daniel followed and held his breath as they silently pressed on. Beyond the rosebushes and walkways, Daniel thought he spotted a break in the wall about one hundred feet away.

While hurrying behind Edwards, Daniel gritted his teeth and tried not to yell out in pain as he dragged his foot behind him.

A shot rang out from nearby, and Daniel instinctively dropped to the ground.

Daniel felt about his body.

I'm not hit, Daniel realized.

Edwards had done the same as Daniel, but he was now peering over the bushes and looking for the attackers.

"Russians," Edwards whispered to Daniel. "Probably posted here to seal it off after they realized there were multiple points of entry. They're moving in on our position."

Daniel handed his Glock to Edwards. "I can hardly..."

Edwards took the gun and peeked again.

Daniel considered using the satellite phone to report Ambassador Fitzpatrick's death.

A memory struck Daniel.

He remembered the call he had received from Muhammad just before the car collision.

The code. Muhammad had made progress on Dmitri's coded message. *But what was it?*

Daniel's mind churned as he tried to remember what Muhammad had told him about the coded message.

But he didn't have more time to think about it because Edwards fired at the Russians and told Daniel, "We need to move. *Now.*"

Despite the pain, Daniel used his three working limbs to hurry towards the hole in the wall. The moans of the Russian hit by Edward's shot filled the garden.

Although it was less than a few minutes later, it felt like an eternity to Daniel when he and Edwards finally stopped behind a bench at the edge of the garden. The hole in the wall left by the secret police was about thirty feet away.

But there was no cover for that last thirty feet.

"I can't go fast enough for us to get away," Daniel said. He felt as if his face must have been completely white. "If I try to get through the hole, they'll see us and gun us down."

"You think this is my first rodeo?" Edwards said jokingly. "I'm going to get you out of here alive and in one piece. Maybe that way you'll join my unit. Besides, you won't be any good to me dead."

Edwards gave a grin and wiped away a wisp of his usually slicked-back hair.

"You enjoying this, sir?" Daniel asked.

"I haven't done anything this fun in years," Edwards replied. "Watch, and you might learn a thing or two from this dinosaur."

"Just in case I don't make it," Daniel said as he reached for his satellite phone, "give Officer Carter in D.C. a call and update her. I can hardly think straight."

Edwards took the phone and handed Daniel his Glock.

"Hopefully you can shoot straight. Give me the number, and you shoot any *Russkies* that get too close."

———

"No luck," Edwards reported after trying the satellite phone. "No satellite connection." He handed the phone back to Daniel.

Without taking it, Daniel pulled the trigger from behind the bench and dropped one of the Russians who was methodically moving through the garden, hunting for him.

Daniel knew they had no choice but to go for the hole in the wall now.

Daniel took the phone and said, "You first."

Edwards started the dash across the final thirty feet to escape.

Daniel moved after him, willing his body to run as many steps as possible before stumbling to the ground.

Looking back, he fired in the direction of one of the Russians.

He fired a few times rapidly, hoping they would take cover, not knowing he had the lone gun.

Daniel struggled on. He looked up and saw Edwards through the hole. He had made it out. Looking down to the ground, Daniel shut his eyes and forced his body onward.

"Come on!" Edwards encouraged from the other side of the wall.

Daniel heard several more shots, and cement splintered from the wall near the exit.

He turned, fired, and emptied his magazine. Daniel pushed down on the Glock's slide release and threw his body through the hole in the wall with a final lunge.

Rapid gunfire shot past Daniel and Edwards.

"They've got reinforcements," Edwards yelled. He rose to his feet and motioned for Daniel to put his arm around his shoulder again. Daniel shoved the Glock into the back of his waistband and reached up with his arm to accept the assistance.

"The more distance between them and us, the better," Edwards said.

At least Tina was alive when I last saw her, Daniel thought to himself as he replayed in his mind the shot that had saved her life.

Now I just need to stay alive.

In a moment of clarity, Daniel marveled that he had survived this long. Though he had needed Edwards' help to defeat Pavel, he had survived the brawl with the human tank. And though Fitzpatrick was dead, at least the Wolf could no longer share America's secrets with the Russians.

Daniel looked around at the bleak mountain desert that surrounded them as he staggered several steps forward with

Edwards. Snow-tipped peaks rose in the distance, but a ravine dropped below them to a dry riverbed with scattered boulders.

Another flurry of gunshots came through the hole in the wall, and Daniel reflexively tried to drop to the ground.

Instead, it made Daniel stumble, and Edwards tried to catch him.

Edwards braced himself and reached after Daniel as he began to teeter over the edge. Edwards grasped at Daniel's belt, but he only succeeded in dislodging Daniel's Glock and sending it down into the ravine first.

Edwards made another lunge to grab Daniel, but it was too much.

They both tumbled down the steep and rocky side of the ravine towards the dry riverbed.

A final volley of gunfire thundered through the hole in the wall above.

20

DANIEL GROANED IN PAIN ONCE HIS BODY REACHED THE BOTTOM OF the ravine. He struggled to roll over onto his back.

When he finally did, he looked up into the clear blue sky. He occasionally heard a gunshot in the distance.

At least I won't be shot, Daniel thought to himself.

He moved his hands in front of his face and wiggled his toes. He didn't want to know what he looked like, but he did not feel as badly as he had expected. His ankle still throbbed from his drop from the helicopter, and one of his ribs had hit a boulder awkwardly, but he was confident he could eventually walk away from the tumble.

Looking about, he spotted Edwards about twenty-five feet away, gathering his wits. After sitting up, he looked around again and saw the satellite phone resting in the dirt.

His body was shaking slightly, and Daniel thought he might be going into shock.

Am I injured in a way I haven't noticed? Daniel thought to himself, fearing he would look down to see that his knee was bent ninety degrees the wrong way.

But no, Daniel rose to his feet slowly and noticed no other significant injuries. He went to grab the satellite phone, but a sharp pain in his side made him wait.

"Daniel?" Edwards called out in pain. "Are you okay?"

"Doing better than Fitzpatrick," Daniel called back. "As long as somebody rescues us from this ravine, I think we will be able to celebrate."

Edwards stood up, sat back down, crouched over, and then said, "You think Fitzpatrick might have broken protocol a few times as the Wolf? That bastard." Edwards sat back up and rose to his feet. "Well, I finally got the Wolf."

"What now?" Daniel asked. He picked up the satellite phone and asked Edwards, "You going to retire now and play golf?"

"Probably spend a little extra time at the driving range," Edwards replied. "I don't hear any more gunfire from above. Hopefully, the police called in backup and cleaned out the Russian mafia."

"Hopefully," Daniel agreed. He gave a funny look and pressed the satellite phone to his ear after hitting a button.

"Damned reception," Daniel mumbled as he turned away from Edwards.

He pressed the phone firmly against his ear.

Daniel listened.

He stood up straight and froze.

"Edwards?" Daniel said into the phone. "You have proof?"

Daniel nodded slowly as he held the phone to his ear.

He pressed a button and lowered the phone to his side.

He turned his head slightly in both directions, scanning the area around him.

"Are you looking for this?" Edwards asked.

Daniel turned toward Edwards.

Edwards was pointing Daniel's Glock at him. He was less than ten feet away.

"Drop the phone," Edwards commanded.

Daniel allowed the satellite phone to slip from his fingers and land on the sandy riverbed with a thud.

"You're the Wolf," Daniel said, both as a statement and as a question. "But Fitzpatrick...?"

"All of this was to make it look like Fitzpatrick was the Wolf," Edwards explained. "And I was going to have the best cover in the world. I had been captured by the enemy, rescued, then saved you. I had wanted you to live, but that won't be possible now."

"They already know the truth about you in D.C.," Daniel lied.

Nobody had been on the satellite phone.

It had been a final test for Edwards, and he had fallen for it.

"But I still have to kill you," Edwards said grimly.

"How did you do it?" Daniel asked, not willing to plead for his life.

"What I told you before was close to the truth," Edwards said. "The best kind of lie. What I gave to the Soviets was then intermixed with information from other sources, but it was all made to look like it came from one agent. Although I have no doubt that I was the best agent for the Soviets, and then the Russians, my *mythos* was only enhanced by my codename."

"But the Wolf gained information that you didn't have access to," Daniel objected.

"Billy was far more compromised than he knew," Edwards said. He took several steps closer to Daniel. "He couldn't admit how deep he was into his addictions. And Fitzpatrick was too easy to frame. Nobody liked him, and making it look like he was trying to flee after stealing classified information using Max's credentials was easy. All my master had to do was kill him and tell him his usefulness was over."

"And I thought his usefulness as the Wolf was over for your master," Daniel said. "And that's why Pavel didn't use his pistol on me. He was under orders that I must survive so I could vouch for you rescuing me. And that's why the man in the gray suit, though he shot Fitzpatrick, didn't shoot me."

"Not bad, kid," Edwards remarked snidely.

"And who is your master?" Daniel asked.

Edwards paused for a moment before answering. "Nice try. You won't be able to make me talk, amateur."

"But why did you do it?" Daniel asked as he stared down the barrel of his own gun. "Why did you do it all these years? For money? You aren't tempted the same way that Billy was."

"Let's just say that I always pick the winner, because I am a winner," Edwards said. "The Soviets were tougher, smarter, and they were always winning the Cold War, doing whatever it took to win."

"But the Soviet Union fell apart," Daniel stated flatly.

"Outwardly, it would seem that the Soviet Union failed. But that will ultimately only make Russia stronger. They went astray when they became a geriatric bureaucracy. But what rose from that is powerful. Russia is already stronger than you know."

Daniel knew Edwards was ready to pull the trigger.

"It's ironic that you will die from your own gun, the very gun your father gave you," Edwards said as a grim smile crept onto his face. "I'll pass along my condolences for your death when I finish him off in the future, as I'm sure my master will command."

"Then let me give you a piece of advice before you face my father," Daniel said.

Edwards gave a quizzical look before Daniel explained.

"Spend more time at the shooting range."

Edwards squinted and readied to pull the trigger before Daniel added, "You're an amateur at handling a gun."

Daniel rushed at Edwards.

The Wolf pulled the trigger several times, but only clicks came.

Daniel struck Edwards squarely in the face. A second blow sent the older man to the ground.

Daniel rushed on top of him, grabbed a nearby rock, and smashed it into his skull.

When Daniel was sure the real Wolf was unconscious, he fell over onto the dry riverbed and grabbed his Glock away from Edwards' limp hand.

"If you are anywhere near as good as you thought you were," Daniel said to the unconscious Edwards, "then you would've felt that your gun was light and that the magazine was empty. I had pressed down on the slide release to make it appear loaded. *Amateur.* Who's the winner now?"

———

THE NEXT HOUR was a blur for Daniel. But he wasn't sure if that was because much time had passed or because it had passed rapidly.

As Edwards had lay unconscious on the ravine floor, Daniel paced about in shock for several moments. The gunfire up in the mansion had intensified, but it quickly died down. The sound of an approaching helicopter had put Daniel on edge until he saw the iconic silhouette of a Blackhawk approaching. Somebody must have spotted Daniel in the ravine waving his arms. After it descended into the narrow valley and Marines who had been posted at the US Embassy loaded the still unconscious Edwards and Daniel, Daniel made sure they radioed an urgent message to the embassy, Officer Carter, and Peters in Washington DC.

Everything continued to be a blur until he struggled off the helicopter and onto the helipad at the mansion and saw Rex and Walters inspecting the carnage. They stood over Ambassador Fitzpatrick's lifeless body. Medics from the helicopter checked the ambassador first. After confirming his death, they proceeded to treat Rex and Walters. Daniel noticed that the mansion was now swarming with Uzbek police.

Jahongir came out to the helipad from the house and approached Daniel, but Daniel ignored him as he limped towards Rex. Daniel was concerned by the haggard look on Rex's face. Rex had seen more combat than anybody else who had been at this mansion, Daniel knew. And he had already lost more friends than any of the Embassy Marines had lost combined. And yet, Rex still wore a worried look.

"Edwards is the Wolf," Daniel said simply. "I tricked him at the last moment."

But Rex ignored Daniel.

"Gunner is dead," Rex said calmly.

"And we lost contact with—" Walters began before Daniel cut in.

"Where is Tina?" Daniel demanded impatiently.

"We don't know," Rex said.

Daniel looked down from the helipad towards the courtyard below. He spotted where he had shot Tina's attacker with the rifle. Daniel guessed Tina must have continued towards the house that was at the far end of the garden.

Daniel attempted to hurry out of the room to go search, but his injuries did not allow him.

"Come with me, sir," one of the medics said as he approached Daniel. "We'll get you fixed up."

"Later." Daniel pushed the medic aside. "Help me get to the far end of the courtyard, and then you can do whatever you need to do."

"Sir," the medic continued. "You're injured. The best thing you can do is—"

"Help me get over there. Now."

"You best do what the man ordered," Rex said, coming over to help.

The medic conceded, and along with Rex, they helped Daniel out of the room, down the stairs and into the courtyard.

Daniel grimaced with discomfort as they stumbled through the bullet-ridden garden and past the dead. When they finally reached the door at the opposite end, Daniel thought he was about to pass out from pain.

The medic sensed this and gave him a shot of morphine. All the windows were broken, and bullet holes pocked the wall and door.

Rex pushed the door open.

"Tina must've made her way in here," Daniel explained.

The entryway beyond the door had a small staircase that led upstairs, and directly in front of them was a kitchenette. To the left was a living room with a TV that been destroyed by the gunfire that came to the windows.

Servants quarters, Daniel thought to himself as he took in the scene. This is probably where the reinforcements laid in wait until they were needed.

Daniel pointed to a door to the right, and the medic helped him over. When they opened the door, they discovered a staircase that angled downward.

"We've got to go down there," Daniel said.

"This area has not been cleared yet, sir," the medic explained.

"We're clearing it out now," Rex said as he stepped down the first step with Daniel.

The medic followed down the stairs, and they entered a hallway that matched that of the basement in the main house in which Daniel had been imprisoned.

The first door off the hallway was open, and Daniel stumbled in. Four bodies littered the floor. Three of them were Russian men in plain clothes, but the fourth was wearing body armor.

"Tina!" Daniel yelled as he fell to the ground and rolled her body over.

Tina's eyes opened slightly, and she mumbled, "Daniel?"

"You came looking for me?" Daniel said. A lump formed in his throat as his heart swelled.

"No, I just enjoy kicking down doors."

She still has her wit, Daniel observed with relief.

Tina shut her eyes and relaxed.

"Painkiller will kick in soon," the medic said as he gave Tina an injection.

Daniel looked around and realized what had happened. Tina had come looking for him. She had guessed that Daniel was being held prisoner in the basement of this building. She had been wrong, of course, but in the process, she had killed the men she encountered in the basement.

Most importantly, Tina was still alive.

"I'm alive, Tina," Daniel said urgently. "And you're going to make it out of here too."

The medic continued working, searching for her injuries and reassuring her that she was going to make it out okay.

Daniel didn't interrupt but allowed the medic to do his job.

Several minutes later, the medic gave Daniel a nod.

Daniel knew what it meant.

The medic thinks she's going to make it.

Daniel slumped down onto the floor out of relief.

She's going to get back up and fight again.

Daniel heard footsteps and then voices upstairs as other Marines came to clear the final portion of the mansion.

———

OTHER MARINES ENTERED the basement and helped the medic move Tina. Another helped Daniel up the stairs.

As they moved across the courtyard and back to the main house, Jahongir approached Daniel again.

"I am sorry you lost your friend, Gunner," Jahongir said. "I lost several men as well. The nation of Uzbekistan is indebted to you and your friends."

"I don't understand why Rex was involved in a raid by the secret police on the Russian mafia," Daniel said, "and I'm too tired to worry about it now."

"You will leave by helicopter from this place, and you must never speak of this event again. Understood?"

"Same with you," Daniel replied. But curiosity got the best of him. "What did happen here?"

"Russia was increasingly exerting its power through the Russian mafia," Jahongir began to explain. "Although the mafia had always existed here, there had been a balance of power. A respect between the mafia and the government of Uzbekistan. But the mafia got too big for its britches, you Americans would say."

"So you were willing to use Rex and his men to help clean out the Russian mafia?"

"And in exchange, you Americans would be able to recover your personnel."

"Other than whoever that was in the helicopter," Daniel said, "it looks like to me the mafia was wiped out."

"That man was from Moscow," Jahongir said, "and he was part of the plan. He needed to clean house some, and there is a new head of the Russian mafia in Uzbekistan, but she is much more willing to coexist in a mutually beneficial manner with the President."

Daniel almost asked who *she* was, but then he remembered. Nigora.

Jahongir stopped before entering the house. Daniel would be on the last helicopter out from the scene of the raid. Jahongir extended his hand, and Daniel shook it firmly.

"My son marries next week," Jahongir said. "We would be honored by your presence at the wedding. Will you be there?"

"Will the music be loud?" Daniel asked with a grin.

Jahongir smiled and answered, "Bring earplugs."

Rex helped Daniel the rest of the way inside and up to the helipad.

When the Blackhawk carried Daniel away from the mansion in the mountains, he thought about the Russian man who had smashed his fingers, forcing him to fall from his helicopter.

Who was he?

Jahongir had mentioned he was from Moscow, but he didn't say that he was mafia.

Was he the Wolf's master?

Daniel realized that if the master's plan had succeeded, then Edwards would have had the perfect cover, and all the Russian mafia who knew the Wolf's identity would have been dead.

Jahongir had needed to clean up the Russian mafia, and the

mafia had been a willing participant in restoring the balance of power to protect the Wolf.

"How did you know Edwards was the Wolf?" Rex yelled to Daniel over the roar of the chopper's engines.

"I didn't," Daniel said. "Not until he was pointing my gun at my face. But I think Muhammad called me to tell me just before the car wreck."

"Muhammad cracked the code," Rex confirmed, "but it wasn't about the Wolf."

21

One week later.

Thursday, September 26, 2002.

DANIEL AND REX knocked on a door in Shahrisabz. It was the door of the apartment of Fatima, Dmitri's widow's older sister.

"Maybe nobody is home," Rex suggested after their knocking was met with silence. "Their dog isn't barking, anyway."

Daniel leaned over to the window and peeked in, but he didn't see anybody. He tapped the glass lightly.

Daniel pounded on the door again, harder this time.

Daniel heard noise inside, and after several more seconds, he could hear the locks on the door coming undone. The door opened a crack, and Fatima's husband asked, "What do you want this time? This is a hard time for us."

Daniel greeted Jamol in Uzbek and said, "My friend and I are paying one last visit to this historic city." Daniel could hardly continue because of his broad smile. "And I do have some good news for you, Jamol and Fatima."

Jamol gave a pained look, as if good news mixing with the grief from Zuhro's death could only bring more pain.

"I don't think they want to see us," Rex said to Daniel. "Maybe this was a mistake, and we need to head back."

But Daniel pressed the conversation. "I can assure you that if you faced any hardship because of our previous conversation, that trouble has passed. What I have to tell you is only good news."

After looking him up and down, Jamol opened the door a bit further and invited Daniel and Rex in.

Daniel and Rex sat down on the floor mat, and Daniel exchanged greetings again. Daniel watched as their son, who was about twelve years old, served them tea.

"Somebody did visit us after we talked with you," Jamol said calmly. "Ziyo scared him off."

"Ziyo?" Daniel asked.

"Our dog," Jamol explained. "The man left, but we feared he would return with more men."

"And... he hasn't?"

"Thankfully, no," Jamol said. "But they still may."

"The matter involving Dmitri and Zuhro has been resolved," Daniel explained. "You shouldn't be bothered anymore. As I said, we do have good news for you."

"What?" Jamol asked.

"There's lots to explain," Daniel said with a look to Fatima, who had joined them for tea. She still wore black to mourn her sister's death. "Zuhro had a challenging life, but I want you to know more about the truth concerning your sister."

Daniel patiently told Fatima and Jamol Zuhro's story as best as he understood it: that she had been with the GRU, and that her behavior may not have been what Fatima would have expected from her sister.

"How do you know she was with the GRU?" Fatima asked.

"I spoke with her first husband, Shahriyor," Daniel said. "He also was with the GRU."

"Did Dmitri take advantage of my sister?" Fatima asked.

"Initially, I believe," Daniel began, "the GRU, including her own husband, forced Zuhro to keep an eye on Dmitri. But I believe she ended up genuinely loving Dmitri. Dmitri did not go after her and take advantage of her. Dmitri genuinely loved her. They ended up loving each other, even if their relationship started for the wrong reasons."

"Why did you come so far to tell me all of this?" Fatima asked. Her husband looked at her with a concerned look.

"You're good people who deserve the truth," Daniel said. "You haven't known the truth about your sister and Dmitri for all these years, but you deserve to know it. Her relationship with Dmitri didn't start or proceed because she was immoral. Initially, she had no choice."

"Is that all?" Fatima asked. Daniel knew that she was insightful. She knew that he had more to add to the story.

Their son reentered the room, now with some warm bread in the traditional round shape, and placed it on the table. Daniel thanked him and watched him leave the room.

Instead of taking the bread, Daniel leaned over and asked them quietly, "Does your son know that Dmitri is really his father?"

Both the husband and the wife stared at Daniel in shock. Neither could say anything.

"I found the boy's birth certificate," Daniel explained. "At first I didn't know what it was. But after I figured it out, it didn't make sense because I thought that all of Dmitri's children died. The birth certificate itself did not seem like a large priority in the investigation. But included in the documentation was the boy's legal name change. To your family name."

"Yes, it is true," Jamol admitted, as if Daniel had uncovered a shameful secret.

"Tell me if I'm wrong, but you couldn't have children," Daniel continued. "And when Zuhro was found pregnant with Dmitri's son, she wouldn't abort it. Instead, she followed your ancient custom of one fertile couple giving their baby to an infertile family member. And then you raised Zuhro's child as your own son, and you were the only ones who knew about it."

Although they were silent, Daniel knew that he had hit on the truth.

"I love him as my own son," Jamol said. "I had even forgotten that he is not my biological son." The words were heavy. "But this is just a sad reminder. What other news did you speak of?"

"I found the birth certificate and legal name change hidden in Dmitri's safe," Daniel said. "But why would Dmitri want that information to be kept secure?"

"I don't know," Jamol answered. "Nobody has ever questioned whether he was our son."

"It only made sense if Dmitri wanted to be able to prove that the identity of your son is, in fact, his son," Daniel continued. "We've uncovered a coded message that Dmitri left behind." Daniel was referring to the code Dmitri had inserted in *The Communist Manifesto* that Muhammad had cracked about a week earlier.

"What sort of coded message did this KGB man leave behind?" Jamol asked cautiously.

"It pointed us to legal documents, stored safely in Switzerland, that stipulated that his son, *your* son, should inherit his wealth upon his passing. And his wealth in the Swiss bank accounts is considerable." Daniel had decided not to explain how the CIA had paid into Agent Bishop's Swiss bank accounts for several years, and that the man had never touched a single penny.

Jamol and Fatima sat in stunned silence.

"I know it is in no way compensation for the loss of Zuhro, but Dmitri's forethought will provide for you and your son more than you could have imagined. I've worked with the US Embassy to ensure that local lawyers properly handle the details for you."

Jamol and Fatima still silently.

"My friend and I must leave now," Daniel said as they remained speechless, "But I wanted you to know the truth. Zuhro was a victim, forced onto Dmitri, but then they did find true love with each other. And when you tell the boy the truth about his biological father, he should know that his father, Dmitri, was a brave hero who fought for freedom without regard for personal gain. He eventually died for it, but not before providing for his son's—your son's—future. But that is all I can tell you about Dmitri's heroics."

Jamol managed weak words of thanks in response.

Daniel asked the father to say the traditional prayer before guests leave, which he only did reluctantly.

"Will you not stay at least one night?" Fatima asked. "It is a long journey back, and you should stay until breakfast."

"I'm sorry," Daniel said, "but we must attend a wedding in Tashkent tonight."

"Ask them where their dog is," Rex whispered to Daniel as they got up to leave.

Daniel asked about the large dog, and when Jamol answered,

he said, "Ziyo got out and killed a neighbor's chicken, so we sent him to a relative in the countryside until the neighbor calms down."

Daniel translated for Rex, who said, "We had a rough introduction, but I kinda liked that big ol' dog."

As Daniel and Rex left, Jamol and Fatima urged them to return again.

I just might come back, someday, Daniel thought to himself. *I have friends in Central Asia again.*

———

LATER THAT NIGHT, Daniel and Rex could hear the music's bass from several blocks away.

"You know," Rex said to Daniel, "that I only get in trouble whenever I encounter Nigora?"

"We've got to see her one last time," Daniel said.

"What the hell for?" Rex asked. "And why do you think she'll be at the wedding?"

"If she's the new head of the Russia mafia with a renewed 'understanding' with President Karimov, then she'll be there. More importantly for me, I owe it to her father and brother to give her another chance out. It was her father's dying wish."

"Fine," Rex said. "I guess I can finally attend one of these supposedly epic Uzbek weddings."

When Daniel and Rex entered the wedding reception hall - there was even a second-floor balcony overlooking the entertainment - the spotlight was on a boy breakdancing to throbbing, loud music. Rex gave Daniel a grin of approval. The tables were filled with wedding attendees clapping along with the beat and then roaring in applause when the song finished.

The spotlight switched to a speaker near the wedding party at the front. The groom, who shared Jahongir's long nose, smiled broadly. The bride, however, only looked down with a sullen face, despite the festivities around her. Daniel spotted Jahongir's father sitting near the front. They exchanged a nod, and Jahongir whispered something to a man nearby.

Moments later, the man approached Daniel and Rex and asked them to follow him. Daniel and Rex followed through the smoke-filled hall, past the wedding party seated at the front, and through several large doors to another, more intimate, ballroom. This one was dimly lit, and Daniel knew Jahongir had planned it for special guests to attend to special business, whatever that might be. Some could be finalizing a business deal, others bribing an official for a piece of paperwork, and still others trading their youngest daughter in marriage for a political favor.

There were two women in the room. One was the head of the Russian mafia in Uzbekistan. The other sat by her side, dressed in a red cocktail dress with matching high-heels and lipstick.

Daniel and Rex sat at the same table as Nigora. As if on cue, the other three men at the table got up and left. Two others, probably Nigora's bodyguards, moved closer to the table. Though Daniel had initially known Nigora as a village girl with long black hair, she now wore her hair up in an elegant do and a *zamonaviy* dress made of shimmering, silver fabric. Daniel wondered if she had intentionally worn a dress made from the same cloth he had offered her as a gift months ago when he still hoped she would go to America with him. But she had refused the gift.

Not that long ago, Daniel knew that he would have felt the sting of bitterness at seeing her, but he didn't feel it now. He had business to conduct with Nigora. Besides, even though Tina was still recovering, she would pull through.

Tina already killed three men trying to rescue me, Daniel thought to himself.

"Shouldn't you be mourning your late husband?" Daniel asked.

"Business doesn't stop for the dead," she said nonchalantly.

"I want to start by thanking you for telling us about Billy," Daniel said. It was hard for him to say it, but it was necessary. "Without your help, we never would have made the break in the case."

"Consider yourselves indebted to me," Nigora said.

"You said you were upset about how they used your women," Daniel continued, with a look to the blond woman seated next to Nigora. "Is that no longer a problem now that you've taken over your husband's business?"

"It is no longer a problem," Nigora confirmed.

"You can have a better life than his," Daniel said. "Your husband wasn't planning on dying last night. You can fall victim to the same type of treachery."

"Is that a threat?" Nigora said playfully.

"This isn't a game," Daniel said. "You still have the chance to leave with me. You already helped us get Billy. You still know a lot more that can help America. Come with me. You can help us, and you can have protection. You won't have to live in fear of the next rising star among the Russian thugs. Your father and brother are dead. You don't have family here. You can make a fresh start, a new and peaceful life."

"Don't think you are doing me any favors with such an offer," Nigora said. "Yes, I lost my husband, but I have a way of outgrowing them. Right now, I am so powerful that nobody would dare to touch me."

"That's what your husband thought," Daniel said. "That is,

until you and that other Russian sold him out. Whoever was above your husband and is now above you will someday do the same to you."

Nigora smirked and said, "I was the one who stole the nuke in Afghanistan, and I was the one who took down Isaac and gave you the break you needed here. How about you let me know the next time you need my help? I have not needed yours."

"Then help me with this," Daniel said. "Am I right in saying that your master was at the mansion in the mountains? He escaped in the helicopter. It was all part of the plan that you would betray the man named Pavel and his men to Jahongir, you would kill Isaac, and then that would leave you to run the business in Uzbekistan."

"Not bad," Nigora said coolly. The woman in red released a sigh, but Daniel wasn't done.

"Do you really think your master wanted you to replace Isaac because you are better? He had to get rid of Isaac, Pavel, and the others because they knew the identity of his most powerful spy. He replaced them with you to protect his most important asset. He's not reluctant to dispose of even the best servants if it suits his larger plan. Everything that has happened has been to protect his spy."

"That sounds like an intriguing plan," Nigora said.

"But it didn't work," Daniel said. "I caught his spy. He got rid of all those men for nothing. He made a big sacrifice, and it didn't pay off."

For the first time, Daniel thought he saw Nigora considering what he was saying.

"Come with Rex and me to America now. We can keep you safe. You only have your position because your master had to sacrifice those above you. But because that sacrifice didn't work, I think you are in a very tenuous position."

After a pause, Nigora continued her cool act.

"Like I said, you're the one who has needed my help. I haven't needed yours. So, I think I'll decline your generous offer once again."

"Then help me one last time," Daniel said. "Who is the man who is pulling all the strings?"

Nigora smirked.

"The CIA must really be desperate," she said. "Everybody knows the name Misha."

Daniel nodded as if to say, "Of course," and rose from the table. He took a step to leave, but then turned back to Nigora and said, "Tell your agent that, next time she visits the sauna, she must be sure to enter the women's sauna. Doing otherwise can be dangerous."

Daniel didn't wait to see the reaction. He left with Rex behind him. They re-entered the main wedding hall, complete with pulsating music and a pop singer belting out her high notes. Daniel offered his best wishes to Jahongir and his son, and then he stepped out into the cool night.

As he called for a ride, Daniel told Rex, "The Wolf's master goes by Misha."

"I have a feeling we will be hunting for him next," Rex said.

22

Washington D.C.
Saturday, September 27, 2002.
Two days later.

"WELL, you nearly set off a major international incident with Russia that could have started yet another war for the United States to fight. But in the end, you caught the legendary Wolf," Officer Carter chided Daniel in her office. For once, Daniel didn't mind sitting in an office opposite his superior. He even looked forward to translating and analyzing in his cubicle for a little bit.

"Actually, we all caught the Wolf," Daniel said with a look to Jenny, Rex, and Muhammad. "And Tina, too, of course. I happened to be there when he slipped up, but all of you were vital to his capture. Any idea how much he's going to be willing to talk once he's medically cleared?"

"You hit him with the rock pretty hard," Officer Carter said. "Perhaps too hard."

"Thanks to the training he received from me," Rex joked.

"I had to make sure he was out cold," Daniel said defensively. "*Sheesh*."

"Even if he doesn't talk," Jenny added, "you won't believe what I've dug up within the last day." For the first time, Daniel noticed the brown grocery sack next to Jenny's chair. He hoped she didn't have cupcakes in it for the team.

"What's that?" Daniel asked.

"Well, I got to thinking," Jenny began to explain. "I knew I couldn't look through every interview the CIA did with people trying to defect or seeking asylum back in the '90s, so—by the way, did you all know that Milli Vanilli was popular way back when the Berlin Wall fell until—"

"Get to the point," Officer Carter cut in.

"Right. So I made some guesses and only looked at those interviewed by CIA personnel already in the mix. I tried to eliminate the easy ones first. Like Edwards."

"Did you find all the evidence necessary to get Edwards without me having to risk my life?" Daniel asked incredulously.

"Sort of, but Edwards could have gotten away," Jenny said. "It turns out that Edwards did some interviews of former Soviets in the '90s, but there was one that he pursued. He signed himself up for it, even though most of the guys hated doing that kind of mind-numbing task. But, it gets even better." Jenny's eyes shone like a child who had just received a pony for her birthday.

"We're all on the edges of our seats," Rex said.

"The man Edwards pursued was killed in a hit-and-run, not much later. It looked so suspicious that the police pursued it until the suspect left the country. We're still hoping to extradite him from Venezuela, all these years later."

"Edwards at least suspected something about this man, interviewed him, probably left stuff out of his report, and then alerted his KGB contacts to eliminate the threat?" Daniel wondered out loud.

"Exactly," Jenny said. "And it gets better. The police still had the man's belongings in evidence from the car crash. Including the coat he was wearing."

Jenny grabbed the brown paper sack and put it on her lap.

"No way!" Muhammad nearly yelled, unable to control himself.

"I totally had to invoke national security to get this out of evidence," Jenny said. Now she looked to Daniel like a child who had received a unicorn for her birthday.

"Michael Devers remembered that Dmitri had freed Vasyli and gave him his coat to keep warm when he left," Daniel recalled.

"Yup again," Jenny agreed. Then she stood up and, after pausing dramatically, pulled from the sack a wool jacket that looked as though it had faced many winters. She placed it on Officer Carter's desk and told the group, "See if you can find the key clue."

Daniel stuck his hands into the pockets, but nobody else had the patience to play along with Jenny's game.

"Just tell us already!" Rex insisted.

With a broad smile, Jenny reached into the fold of a hem inside the jacket and pulled something out. She took it and unfolded it in front of everybody. It was a faded piece of brown paper, folded for so long that it nearly fell into pieces along each crease. The writing was so pale, it was almost impossible to read.

"Dmitri's proof of Edwards' spying, plus the identities of several other codenames," Jenny proudly announced.

"Wow," Rex said. He gave a short whistle.

"The Feebs are cleaning up these guys who are still alive as we speak," Officer Carter said. "Congratulations to all of you. This was good work. Now take it easy and write all your follow-up reports. You can get back to training next week. You all deserve some R and R. But not too much. There's still a war out there. At least one."

"And more brewing," Daniel added.

They got up to leave Carter's office, but she added, "Can I have a private word with you, Daniel?"

Before Daniel could respond, she said, "Never mind. It can wait. But I'll walk out with you."

"Good," Daniel said. "I had something I wanted to mention to you in private as well."

———

DANIEL FOLLOWED Officer Carter out of her office and through the CIA headquarters. Something told him she wasn't interested in small talk along the way.

Others must have caught the same vibe because every CIA employee they passed in the halls and elevator looked away with tight lips. When they approached the lobby on the ground level, Daniel had a good idea of where they were going, but he didn't know why.

Together, Officer Carter and Daniel approached the Memorial Wall. Daniel remembered he had walked by it with Edwards before he began hunting for the Wolf, and he wondered how many of the stars on the Memorial Wall were due to the Wolf.

Officer Carter broke the silence around the hallowed memorial and said to Daniel, "Tell me what you can about Michael. Michael Devers."

"I... I'm not sure what you mean."

"This isn't easy for me," Officer Carter said. "But I don't think I have to prove to you or remind you how tough I am."

"No ma'am," Daniel agreed.

"And I know that you watched Michael Devers die, so it's not easy for you, either."

Daniel watched silently as Officer Carter struggled to maintain her composure. "What was he like? What did you notice about him?"

"He looked worn out," Daniel said, trying to explain, even though he didn't know exactly what Officer Carter wanted from him. "But he was still a solid spy. He tested me. At first, he didn't trust me."

Officer Carter nodded, and Daniel continued.

"Are we here because... Well, I'm sure Michael Devers will get the star he deserves on that wall."

"His star already is there," Officer Carter said. "I know which one it is. I've requested that his name be added to the Book of Honor. His star was added a year after he went missing and was presumed dead, but he had to remain unknown because of the Cold War."

"I can write up a more detailed report about my encounter with Michael Devers if you want me to," Daniel began to say cautiously.

"Okay, promise me that what I say here stays here and never affects our working relationship," Officer Carter said with the same look she gave when she issued an order.

"Of course," Daniel said.

"I knew Michael Devers," Officer Carter said. Daniel noticed she didn't mention that she had also known Billy. "And we had a personal relationship. I had hoped it was really going somewhere and was serious. I dreamed of married life. A home life. That seems nearly impossible in this business."

Daniel nodded in agreement. He thought of his own parents, their separation due in part to his father's service to his country.

"I thought, back then, that Devers was going to propose, and we were going to figure out how to make it work." A tear rolled down Officer Carter's cheek. She quickly wiped it away.

"But then he disappeared," Daniel finished for her. "Devers did mention you. He mentioned Billy and others directly related to his mission, but you were the only person he mentioned who wasn't involved in his mission. But things had to go so fast in those mountains in Uzbekistan, and I was focused on other things—"

"Not worrying about my personal life from over a decade ago, I know," Officer Carter said. Daniel's suspicions about Officer Carter heightened again. Could it be a coincidence she still hadn't mentioned that she knew Billy?

"For what it's worth," Daniel continued, "I think it means something that you were the only non-mission related person he mentioned. And he was still toughing it out after fifteen years in a Soviet-style prison. He died a hero, though tragically he was so close to freedom."

Officer Carter brought her hands up to her face and cried.

Daniel stood by her silently for several moments, uncertain if he should watch or lightly hug her. She took a few deep breaths and said, "And I'll never know what could have happened if he had been freed and was with me now."

"I'm sorry," Daniel said. "I truly am."

"And, for what it's worth, I know you did all that you could to save Devers. Don't feel a burden because of my loss. Watching a good man die is hard enough."

"And he was a good man," Daniel agreed.

Officer Carter took several more moments to wipe away more of her tears and recompose herself for work.

"Remember," Officer Carter said. "Not a word to anybody else about my little emotional episode here."

"Yes, ma'am," Daniel repeated.

"Before I go back to my office, what was it you wanted to say to me?" Officer Carter asked.

"Compared to what we just talked about," Daniel said, "it's not a big deal. I'll mention it later if it still matters then."

Daniel and Officer Carter said goodbye, and Daniel left the CIA headquarters with the final item he had taken from Dmitri's office safe in his pocket. He would have to wait a bit longer to figure out who to return it to. He feared Officer Carter's emotional episode was to dissuade Daniel from suspecting she was compromised and had aided the Wolf.

23

Two days later.
Monday, September 30, 2002.

DANIEL WAITED in the sterile interrogation room for the guards to bring Edwards. Daniel felt terrible going over Officer Carter's head and gaining permission from Peters, but he didn't see another way.

Officer Carter knew Billy, but she still never disclosed that.

Daniel had to chase down every loose end, even if he was confident the Wolf was behind bars.

Buzzes indicating the unlocking of doors and clanking metal preceded the two guards who escorted Edwards into the interrogation room. Daniel noticed that his eyes had the same fire; Edwards gazed at him as the guard sat him down opposite Daniel. Without his suit and slicked-back hair, Edwards appeared less than average.

The guard made a show of handcuffing Edwards to the table, but Daniel waved it off.

"That's not necessary," Daniel said.

"Please," Edwards said with condescension. "Don't think you will win me over by such asinine kindness. What are you doing here, anyway? I'll run circles around you in an interrogation. I trained the people who would train you."

Daniel flashed Edwards a smile.

"The problem for you," Daniel said, "is that we don't need your help. We've acquired all the information we need without you saying a word."

"You wouldn't be here if that were true," Edwards said.

"Honestly, most people think you should rot in prison for about fifteen years to match how long Devers had been held in that secret prison facility in Uzbekistan, and then you should be shot."

"We both know that won't happen," Edwards said.

"Too elaborate and expensive for somebody who was just a pawn in the Cold War," Daniel said.

"A pawn?" Edwards asked indignantly. "You don't know how this works. My lawyer will argue *ad infinitum*, but eventually, the CIA will trade me for something from the Russians. I won't be forgotten in some hole like Uzbekistan."

Daniel leaned forward and said, "And that is exactly why I think you couldn't have been working alone. Somebody else in the CIA was protecting you. You are incredibly overconfident."

"What I told you before was the truth," Edwards nearly spat out. "I was spying effectively against the US when you were learning how to ride a tricycle."

"And because somebody else was protecting and coddling you for the Russians, you don't really know how the game is played."

Edwards threw his hands up in the air. "Did you come here merely to insult me? You got lucky one time, and now you think you're the American Kim Philby? Give me a break."

"I'm here to help you," Daniel said evenly. "Where do you think you are?"

Edwards crossed his arms and looked away.

Daniel continued to turn the screws.

"You aren't on American soil. You're in one of our black sites, designed to detain high-level-targets—"

"While depriving them of their rights," Edwards cut in. "But I'm an American citizen, not a terrorist—"

"Except that I was investigating a terrorist bombing in Uzbekistan."

"You're lying," Edwards shot back.

"I'm not lying. Even I don't even know where we are. I was flown here secretly. And I'll leave here secretly. If you ever want the rights accorded a US citizen, you need to help me, and your transfer to a different facility can be arranged."

Edwards smoldered across the table from Daniel.

"You won't tell me who your handler was because he's still in the game," Daniel asserted. "Am I right? Because I want to know who your handler was."

"My handler died in 1985," Edwards said.

"And then you got a new handler," Daniel said.

"Presumably."

"You were in Berlin then. Then you went to Moscow, and then to Berlin again. Perhaps you had two handlers. One in Berlin, and one in Moscow."

Edwards didn't respond.

"Or, you had lots of handlers," Daniel continued. "You had

many, and you didn't know who they were. That's why you're not telling us who your handlers were. You can't."

"You don't know how the game is played," Edwards said. "I had one handler. Always only one."

Daniel hoped he didn't give away to Edwards that he was making progress. Of course, Edwards was so proud he would think he was an agent who deserved special care from the KGB via one handler.

"Walk me through the Berlin exchange," Daniel said. "When a defector was going to reveal your identity."

"I've already told you about it."

"If you want to be moved out of this black site," Daniel reminded Edwards, "then you need to help me. When you told me about the defector in Berlin, it didn't ring true to me. I suspected something when you told me."

Daniel was lying at this point. He hadn't suspected Edwards until Edwards was pointing his own gun at him. But he knew Edwards couldn't handle the fact that a new officer had seen through his lies.

"I can see why you might be telling yourself that now," Edwards said. "After the mole is captured, all the experts can pontificate about how they all knew who the mole was in the past, but you and I know that's not true. The problem is that my story was entirely truthful. There was no falsehood to detect in it."

Daniel knew it was time to set the trap for the Wolf.

"Here's how I think it went," Daniel said. "You were supposed to meet the defector near the ghost station. You offhandedly mentioned in Tashkent that so much had happened in the Berlin tunnels back then. But your service records don't contain other missions in the subway tunnels. Your story made it sound like you knew how to find your way to the ghost station without trouble."

"Of course I found my way there without trouble. Others researched the route for me, and I simply followed instructions. The records, by design, don't include all of my missions."

"You're not one to rely on others and follow instructions," Daniel countered.

"That was a long time ago, and coming in from the West wasn't difficult. It was a western subway line, I just had to follow instructions."

"No. You set up the meeting with the defector near the ghost station because you were familiar with it. I think that's where you would meet your handler."

Edwards ignored the assertion. "When I got there, the defector was already dead. With his lips cut off. Certainly, I couldn't let the defector reveal who I was. But it wasn't me who killed him."

"Of course you didn't kill him," Daniel said. "The defector was a trained KGB soldier. If you were to attack him, there was a pretty good chance that the defector would end up killing you. You obviously can't handle a weapon."

Daniel's last statement was a low blow. It was intended to infuriate Edwards, even if he remained steadfastly stubborn in concealing his handler's identity.

"When you went to meet the defector, your handler was there to meet with you as well, and he had already killed the defector. But your handler had to be an expert, unlike you. Otherwise, the defector might have killed your handler."

Edwards refused to say anything and sat tensely. Daniel sensed his reconstruction was accurate. He felt Edwards must have been worried about what other things Daniel had been able to figure out.

Now that the trap was set, Daniel decided to drop the bomb and see how Edwards responded.

"Vladimir Putin was your handler," Daniel asserted. "Posted with the KGB in Dresden from 1985 until 1990, and then his personal thugs took over running you as a source for the FSB and Russia."

Edwards flinched. He didn't immediately deny it. He didn't offer another alternative. Daniel had hit a nerve.

"Not Putin," Edwards said calmly. "Like you said, Putin was in Dresden."

Daniel knew he had his chance to completely knock Edwards off balance.

"Don't tell me it was Misha," Daniel said quickly, tightening his trap. "We already know he handled Officer Carter and that you and Billy were coverups for her. Misha was smart to keep her in America. The rest of you were sent to Uzbekistan."

At this, Edwards' rage boiled over, and he shot to his feet. The Marine in the room stepped in to restrain Edwards.

"Officer Carter is an old spinster cow," he yelled as he pointed his finger at Daniel. "She is not the master's spy. I am. I am Misha's Wolf."

Daniel stood up and argued back.

"Billy was a coverup for Carter, not you, and we followed the trail," Daniel continued, giving Edwards more rope from which to hang himself.

"Nonsense," Edwards argued. "The only way Carter was connected to Billy was that Carter received her first promotion because of Billy's help. Not exactly a solid start to her superstar career."

Daniel knew Edwards expected a counterargument, but Daniel relaxed and smiled slightly at the trapped Wolf.

That's all I needed, Daniel thought to himself.

He turned to the guard and said, "We're done." Daniel went

towards the exit, but before he stepped out, he turned and said to Edwards, "I've worked at the CIA for less than one year. I just got the mighty Wolf to tell me all I needed to know in a few minutes."

Daniel left the room, knowing Peters would probably chew him out for the last bit of gloating, but he couldn't stand how smug Edwards was. His pride had been his downfall. Edwards had been so proud, he had confirmed that the master spy behind all the troubles from Russia went by the common nickname of Misha. And Edwards also gave a plausible explanation as to why Officer Carter buried her connection to Billy. In Daniel's mind, Officer Carter was now beyond suspicion.

That meant Daniel could finally give the diamond ring he had found in Dmitri's office safe to her. The gemologist contracted by the CIA was ninety percent certain that the piece of jewelry had been crafted in the Washington D.C. area in the mid to late eighties. Daniel guessed it had been on Michael Devers' person when he was captured, and Dmitri had locked it away in his office safe. If Devers' final mission had been a success, he had planned on proposing to Allison Carter.

Not more than an hour later, a tiny jet was zooming Daniel from one dark corner of the globe back towards America. Daniel wondered if the engagement ring would bring grief, resentment, or a sense of closure to Officer Carter.

Would it be wise to give her the ring?

In the end, he decided to give it to her, and she would have to choose how to respond.

But Daniel had to decide how to respond to Tina. Doctors would soon clear her to leave the hospital.

———

LESS THAN TWENTY-FOUR HOURS LATER, Daniel was back at work.

At practice, really.

Daniel pulled the target towards himself. It was better than he had expected. Under Rex's direction, he was continuing to familiarize himself with a variety of weapons. The current target had been his third round of firing with the standard Swiss rifle, the SG541.

Daniel readied himself for another round before he switched to another rifle, but the door into the shooting range clicked. Daniel knew he was no longer alone.

"Daniel?"

Daniel put the rifle down and ran to the door.

"Your aim still horrible?" Tina joked as Daniel hurried towards her.

Daniel and Tina hugged.

He couldn't remember a time he had felt so happy.

"Don't squeeze so hard," Tina said, pulling away slightly.

"Sorry," Daniel said, "I just—"

But he couldn't stop hugging Tina.

"Jenny told me you were by my bed at the hospital every chance you could get," Tina said. "Thank you."

"What can I say? It was the least I could do. I can't tell you how relieved I was to find you still alive—"

"And why didn't I find you?" Tina said with mock rage. "I was looking for you and nearly got myself killed."

"Sorry. I know. Thank you."

Despite the bruises and bandage on her left arm, Daniel still thought Tina was beautiful, even in a grungy shooting range.

"You want to shoot a few rounds?" Tina finally asked. She nodded towards the targets behind Daniel.

"Of course," Daniel said.

"If I remember correctly, you could still use the practice," Tina joked as she walked past Daniel.

"Hey now," Daniel said defensively. "I shot that Russian mafia who was about to kill you in the courtyard. I even used somebody else's rifle."

Tina returned a blank look.

"I don't remember that," she said. "I must have forgotten it due to my injuries and trauma."

"What? Seriously? I saved your life with that shot."

Tina looked at the guns to choose from and said, "Sorry, I don't remember."

"You're joking."

"No."

Daniel couldn't tell if Tina was serious or not.

She looked at the rifle and said, "Take some shots with that rifle and prove to me you could have saved my life."

"It was a different rifle," Daniel pointed out.

Tina paused and then cracked a smile that made Daniel's knees go weak.

"I'm just joking. I remember somebody shooting from the balcony and saving me. I couldn't see it was you, but Rex told me." Daniel thought he caught a flirty wink.

Daniel hadn't thought it was possible, but he was happier now than when he had hugged Tina just moments earlier.

Tina stepped towards him, hugged him again, and kissed him on the cheek.

Daniel felt like he was heaven, but Tina turned away and said, "Let's shoot."

Daniel emptied several more magazines with the Swiss rifle, and Tina even gave it a try. Daniel was concentrating on his last few shots when Tina stepped away.

Daniel pulled the trigger one last time.

Crack.

"Oh, man," Daniel groaned. He knew Tina was going to make fun of that last shot.

"Where's your famous Glock?" Tina asked. She was standing by Daniel's bag at the back table. "In here? I want to see the famous Glock that was finally responsible for capturing the Wolf."

"It's in there, but maybe we should put it in a trophy case," Daniel joked.

Tina looked through the bag, but instead of pulling out the Glock, she grabbed a small case and held it in her hand.

Daniel realized what was happening just as Tina opened it and nearly dropped it back into the bag. Her hand covered her mouth, and she muffled a shriek. Her hand immediately went to her aching side.

"Daniel?" Tina demanded while giving him a look. "Is that what I think... Is it for me?"

"No," Daniel said quickly. He ran to his bag to put the diamond ring away safely.

"Then who...?" Tina asked, her voice laced with suspicion.

"I'm so sorry," Daniel said, "but it's not for you. It's for, well, it's not my ring. It's a long story, and I can't really explain."

Tina stood frozen to the floor.

"Oh, I didn't think it was for me," Tina said.

"No, of course not," Daniel quickly agreed. "I mean, not of course, but it's—"

"I didn't think our relationship was like that, and I wasn't expecting..." Tina said, finishing Daniel's statement but trailing off.

"Well, I think I've had enough target practice for now," Daniel said. "I need to get home. I promised my mom I would be there."

Daniel was embarrassed to use his mother as an excuse, but it was true, and just as badly as he had wanted to be with Tina moments before, he now wanted to get away.

Daniel grabbed his bag and hurried towards the door.

"I'll put the rifle away for you then," Tina called after Daniel as he left the range.

Daniel realized he had wanted Tina to be disappointed that the ring wasn't for her.

24

THE DOG WAS BARKING AT DANIEL LONG BEFORE DANIEL REACHED his mother's front porch.

"Quiet, Pepper," Daniel said as the dog waited expectantly, wagging its tail. Daniel saw Rex and Jenny walking together from the opposite direction. They held hands, and Daniel had to admit that the changing color of the leaves in the old D.C. neighborhood made for a pleasant stroll. Daniel wasn't sure how he felt about two teammates dating. He never would have guessed that Jenny, the goofy computer nerd, would fall for a SpecOps man like Rex.

How would the others feel if Tina and I...? Daniel began to wonder, but then he saw Tina arrive in a taxi.

Other than a quick hello, Tina ignored Daniel and showered her attention on Pepper, the dog. The awkwardness from the previous night at the shooting range still lingered.

Rex and Jenny arrived and said their hellos to Pepper, and Daniel opened the door to lead them into his mother's house for dinner. Rex and Jenny went in first.

Tina paused before entering. "Your mom said she has a surprise," she said to Daniel.

"You've been talking to my mom?" he asked.

"It's funny how I've bumped into her," Tina responded.

Daniel felt his face turn pink as he imagined his mom trying to win Tina over for him. For once, he couldn't disagree with her choice. He just felt slightly immature relying on his mom to find a girlfriend for him, especially one who could beat him in a fight, with or without her gun. Daniel shut the door behind him and followed Tina and the others towards the kitchen.

Daniel slowed because something seemed… *off*.

After a moment, he realized what was wrong. He noticed the house didn't have the typical aroma of baking. It wasn't like her to order out for dinner with guests.

Daniel's mother stepped into view, welcomed her guests, and invited them to continue into the kitchen.

Daniel's mother spent a little extra time with Tina.

"You decided to get those shoes?" Tina asked, looking down at Daniel's mother's feet.

"Everybody should get a pair," she gushed.

Daniel hadn't noticed new shoes on his mom.

She hugged Tina, who went into the kitchen.

They sure have hit it off well, Daniel thought.

"Thanks for having us all again," Daniel said to his mom.

But she was no longer smiling. Her lips were slightly pursed.

"What's wrong?" Daniel asked in a lowered voice. "Do you need to tell me something?"

Instead of hearing an answer, Daniel saw his father come down the stairs.

Daniel froze, unsure of what to do, let alone feel.

The man was nearly Daniel's twin, except for the age difference.

And your father doesn't have that cute birthmark on your neck like you do, his mother had always said.

"Hi, son," his father said.

"I'm celebrating with friends tonight," Daniel said, before his temper got the best of him. "Leave. Don't ruin things."

"I'm not leaving," his father said. "I need to have a word with you in private."

Daniel's mother silently turned away and shuffled into the kitchen to join the others. Daniel stayed behind with his father, unable to speak.

A million angry questions poured into his mind.

Why is he here now?

How could he treat me and mom the way he has?

And many more.

"You're older now," his father began. "It's not easy to understand, but you don't know my side of the story. I'm sorry my work has hurt my family—you and Diane. You need to understand that, without people like me, it wouldn't be safe for any families."

"Maybe so," Daniel said. "But why mine? Why couldn't I have a normal family with a normal dad?"

"I don't know," his father said. "I was good at getting the bad guy."

Daniel guessed his father was telling the truth about that. So many of the old hands in the intelligence community had told Daniel they knew his father, and they all clearly respected him.

"But I'm not the only one good at catching the bad guy," his father continued. "So are you, my son. You got the Wolf."

"Are you forgetting that I washed out of the military?" Daniel retorted. "What an embarrassment to you. The mighty Mister Knox had his son kicked out before even qualifying."

"I made sure you got kicked out," his father said.

"What?" Daniel stared at his father. "That's ridiculous."

The only reason Daniel wasn't yelling was because of his friends in the kitchen.

"I didn't want you to end up like me. Besides, I knew you were much smarter than me. You have your mother's mind. Diane is intelligent in a way I'm not. I knew you could—"

"And you're the reason I got the grant to study in Central Asia?" Daniel guessed.

His father gave a slight nod.

"I'm here to tell you that I'm done meddling in your life behind the scenes. But you've done a lot of good. You can't deny it. Don't let your relationship with me get in the way. Your MDF team is a good one. We're going to save a lot more American lives and do a lot of good. You wanted into the military because you wanted to do your part to pay the price for our country's freedom. We can do that better on the MDF team."

"What do you mean, 'we?'" Daniel retorted. "The MDF team is my team, and you have nothing to do with it."

Daniel's father continued calmly. "That's part of why I'm here. Peters has assigned me an advisory role to your MDF team."

Daniel's revulsion prevented him from arguing or asking a question.

"Peters said the Wolf you captured was connected to a Russian who goes by Misha. Let's just say that Peters, I, and some others, go way back with Misha."

"Back to the Cold War?"

"Back to 'Nam. Don't throw away your work with the MDF team because of me. It will take time, but we can work together."

Daniel knew his father was right; he didn't want to resign from his MDF team. He hated that his father had worked behind the scenes to manipulate his situation in the past, but refusing to work with his father wouldn't be fair to the rest of the team. But before Daniel could respond, his father continued.

"I've done and seen things I wish I hadn't. I can't undo any of those things. You will probably have to do and see such things as well. A lot of those things you will carry with you to the grave. It's a heavy burden to carry. But you need to know that before this starts. Don't blame me. Don't say I didn't warn you. Americans won't even know they should thank you. Can you live with that?"

"So, you want me to work with my absentee father to acquire a mental illness?" Daniel's voice had an edge to it.

"Always the clever one," his father remarked. "It might feel that way at times, I don't know. But I do know that with you on this team, the bad guys won't know what hit them."

Daniel searched his father's eyes. He detected sincerity. It was the first time Daniel remembered hearing his father say something encouraging to him.

Somehow, it went a long way towards healing his hurts from the past. At least, it was a start.

"But don't get me wrong," his father said, "Misha is a spymaster who has survived in this game for a very long time. There's a reason for that. He's dangerous. We can't afford to underestimate him."

Daniel's anger had lowered from burning to a smolder, and so when his father held out his hand, Daniel slowly accepted it.

"Come on. I'm thirsty."

Daniel followed his father into the kitchen and saw the others joking with his mom.

"Your dad and I are staying in for dinner tonight," Daniel's mom said with a wink, "but you kids should go out and talk about secret spy stuff."

They all took the hint and filed out past Pepper, who desperately wanted to join them but had to remain on the front porch.

The walk to the pub with Rex, Jenny, and Tina was a blur to Daniel because he was too busy thinking about his father. He couldn't believe his father was trying to mend his relationship with his mother.

But it was more than that.

Daniel realized that he was slipping deeper into the world of intelligence.

Will I end up like Officer Carter, with nobody in my life?

Or will I become my father, with broken relationships that spread over the decades?

And what are the odds of Tina and I working out if we're both in intelligence?

Is it better to never know?

Daniel recalled how Officer Carter had responded when he gave her the ring from Dmitri's safe upon his return from interrogating Edwards. He wasn't sure if he could risk such pain in his life.

In the end, Daniel resolved to not be like Officer Carter or his father.

25

Sevastopol, Ukraine.
A few weeks later.

Nigora exited the limousine, leaving her bodyguards in the vehicle. They had strenuously objected, but in the end, only her word mattered. She entered the building and passed the guard beside the private elevator without a glance. The elevator arrived, and she waited for the doors to shut before pressing the button for the top floor.

The meeting had come on short notice.

That wasn't a problem. What made her nervous was that she was unsure of its purpose. She fingered the pearl choker around her neck. One benefit of getting rid of Isaac was that she felt justified in replacing the jewelry he had given her. This choker was the newest addition.

When the private elevator's doors opened, Nigora took in the refined surroundings of the penthouse suite. The marble floors stretched to glass walls that extended from floor to ceiling, and rich wooden furniture adorned the otherwise spartan interior. Animal furs spotted the floors and furniture, adding a unique texture to the interior design. It was simple, yet every detail was an expensive one to the eyes that knew what small things could cost. Nigora wondered if more wealth was contained in this penthouse than in the rest of Sevastopol.

At least Misha's taste for luxury matches mine, Nigora thought to herself.

"Have a seat," a man said in Russian. He was seated on the couch with his back to her. She couldn't tell, but it looked as though he was staring out one of the windows that overlooked the city.

As Nigora walked confidently to sit in the chair perpendicular to Misha, he continued. "The loss of my best-informed agent troubles me."

Nigora sat with her legs crossed, refusing her expression to betray anything. She wondered if he would lay the blame at her feet, though that would be unfair. But she decided he was only trying to unsettle her.

"It troubles me as well," Nigora said, not accepting blame nor blaming another.

"I'm sorry for the loss of your husband," Misha said. "Do you not grieve for him?"

Now he looked her up and down, taking in her ivory-white business suit accented by the pearl piece around her neck.

This is the second most powerful man in Russia, Nigora thought to herself. *He craves luxury, but does he have other appetites?*

She again decided to neither give nor take anything.

"He's more useful to me dead than alive. As with you, I suspect."

Misha held her dark brown eyes for a few moments.

"I don't grieve either," Misha said. "Your predecessor—" Nigora noted he neither referred to him as her husband now or by name — "had grown too unwieldy for my purposes. Besides, I expect you to exceed him."

"I won't disappoint."

Why am I here? Nigora continued to wonder. She had already decided to sleep with him if she had to. What was one more man she would eventually overtake?

"But let me show you this," Misha said as he got up from the couch. Nigora watched him walk to a console cabinet and open a thick book. It was a photo album, and from under it, he removed a photograph. Misha walked back to the couch, now on the end closer to Nigora, and sat down while dangling the photograph before her.

"Do you recognize her?" Misha asked.

Nigora shook her head slightly while studying the black and white photo.

"I thought you might notice the resemblance," he said. "That is your late husband's mother. I've kept a close eye on her. What about your family?"

"They're all dead," Nigora said. "In Afghanistan."

That's why I'm here, Nigora thought. *He wants to make sure he can control me like he did Isaac. If Isaac had ever crossed Misha, his mother would have paid for it.*

Misha studied her face with his gray eyes for a few more seconds. She felt him searching for the truth. If she had relatives tucked away in an obscure corner of the world, she knew that he would find them and use them to his advantage.

But she didn't flinch. It had been the truth.

He believed her.

"No loved ones?" Misha asked.

"Nobody but myself," Nigora stated. For a second, she allowed Daniel to flash through her mind. When she was young, she had nearly thrown herself at him in the way she thought an American desired, but he had scorned her. But that was then. Now, she sensed Misha was searching for leverage on her. If he found none, she feared he would be forced to create some.

Nigora finally decided to give Misha something.

"I love only myself and my business dealings. They're in the bank in Moscow. I can provide you with details."

Both Misha and Nigora understood that he was free to investigate her financial holdings. He could also use them as collateral for her cooperation if he needed.

"Good," Misha said with a thin smile. "I'm confident you can handle my dealings on the ground in Uzbekistan. But I know you lost many of your guards in the last altercation. Allow me to send you some of my best men."

Nigora knew such guards only had one purpose: to keep an eye on her.

"Your generosity, as always," Nigora began, "is unexpected, but..."

"But what?"

Nigora knew she could not refuse. "But all the same, I'm sure your guards would be a most welcome addition in my business dealings."

"Good," Misha said. "And one more thing..."

He rose again and soon returned from the console cabinet with a velvet box in his hands. He opened it before her, revealing a multi-strand diamond necklace. Nigora guessed the largest stone on the pendant weighed several carats.

"Try it on," Misha suggested.

Again, she couldn't refuse. She reluctantly unclasped her new pearl choker and held it in her lap. Misha moved to her and leaned over. He reached behind her neck and fastened the diamond necklace. The massive gemstone rested coolly on her skin.

Nigora remained silent. She knew he would detect falsehood in any show of gratitude.

Misha stood back to take in Nigora wearing his necklace.

If he tries anything, it will be now.

Misha turned around, walked to a nearby wet bar, and said, "Drinks to our future success?"

"Certainly," Nigora replied.

Misha soon returned with two shot glasses of vodka.

"To the new Queen of Tashkent," Misha toasted. They both drank them down in a single gulp and Misha got up.

Nigora knew it was time for her to leave. She rose and walked towards the elevator that would take her back downstairs and to her limousine.

"One of my guards will meet you downstairs to accompany you back home," Misha said. "And, if our business relationship ever turns sour, I will reclaim my necklace from your dead body."

The threat came as casually as his toast to success with vodka.

The elevator doors shut before Nigora could say anything in response. As Nigora descended in the elevator, she replayed the encounter with Misha in her mind.

That was the purpose of our meeting, Nigora thought. *To place his collar around my neck and keep me on his leash. This old spymaster will get more than he bargained for.*

She wondered how soon she could tear off the diamond necklace and replace it with her own pearl choker.

THE END.

W<small>ANT</small> to discover the backstory of Misha, the masterspy?

Join the J.A. Heaton Reader Group and get *The Main Enemy: A Daniel Knox Prequel Short Story* for free.

(Not for sale anywhere. Exclusive for the Reader Group.)

Uncover the backstory of the Russian spymaster pulling all the strings.

Join now:

https://www.flannelandflashlight.com/daniel2

AUTHOR NOTES.

If you liked *The Missing Spy*, please leave a review. I can't tell you how thankful I would be because it truly helps new readers discover the Daniel Knox series.

I wrote The Missing Spy because the hunt for a mole is a staple of spy novels (think: *Tinker, Tailor, Soldier, Spy*). Additionally, the theme of amateurism vs. professionalism is prevalent in spy novels. For that theme, I had *Funeral in Berlin* in mind, but also Bernard in Len Deighton's first trilogy (*Berlin Game, Mexico Set, London Match*). I haven't written a book to match those excellent works, but I am indebted to them for the themes which I played with in *The Missing Spy*.

One last note on historical accuracy in The Missing Spy: I have seen old maps of the mountains near Shahrisabz which had large, blank areas. The locals seemed to know better than to go snooping. Is there a secret Soviet facility there? Probably not. But maybe. ;)

Thanks again for reading, and please leave a review. Lastly, if you haven't already, join the J.A. Heaton Reader Group and get the exclusive prequel short story at:

www.flannelandflashlight.com/Daniel2.

J.A. Heaton
john@flannelandflashlight.com
April 2019.

Made in the USA
Middletown, DE
11 March 2021